HOTEL OBSCURE

A Collection of Short Stories

LISETTE BRODEY

SABERLEE BOOKS

Published by:

SABERLEE BOOKS
Los Angeles, CA
United States of America

Copyright @2018, Lisette Brodey
Published: October 2018

All rights reserved, which includes the right to
reproduce this book or portions thereof
in any form whatsoever except as
provided by U.S. Copyright Law.

Copy Editing: Chryse Wymer
Cover design: Charles M. Roth

ISBN-13: 978-0-9909606-7-6 (paperback)
ISBN-13: 978-0-9909606-8-3 (e-book)

To Charles Roth

Thank you for being there for me all of these years, and for always believing in me.

There is a crack, a crack in everything
That's how the light gets in.

Leonard Cohen (Anthem)

ACKNOWLEDGMENTS

To Chryse Wymer, for being such a positive and insightful editor

To Charles Roth, for his brilliant cover design

To Deborah Nam Krane, for being a superb beta reader

To Lisa Wentworth, for helping me with every aspect of this novel

To James E. Tobin and Billy C. Camble, for their invaluable contribution

To Talatha Allen, Shykia Bell, Kenneth Brodey, Dody Cox, PattiAnn Cutter, Laura Daly, Jennifer Nelson, D.L. Savvides, and Sheri A. Wilkinson, for their ongoing support and kindness

There are so many more people who have supported me in so many ways. I wish it were possible for me to thank each and every one of you. I hope you all know who you are. And last, but not least, thank you to my fellow authors for your support, advice, inspiration, and friendship. You all mean so much to me.

SABERLEE BOOKS BY LISETTE BRODEY

Crooked Moon
Squalor, New Mexico
Molly Hacker Is Too Picky!
Mystical High (Book 1, The Desert Series)
Desert Star (Book 2, The Desert Series)
Drawn Apart (Book 3, The Desert Series)
Barrie Hill Reunion
Hotel Obscure

HOTEL OBSCURE

Dollar Hot Dog Man

Every day at lunch hour, Cassidy left her office to walk her dog, Barnaby, around the old neighborhood. This was the time when she became the most contemplative, the most introspective, and the most at peace with her life. Sometimes, she'd laugh at herself … for going through the same cycle of self-doubt, logic, and reasoning. Without fail, she never deviated from reaching the same conclusion: she was content with the decisions she had made.

The neighborhood she called home was way past its glory days when Cassidy first decided to move into it twenty-three years ago. Some friends had tried to talk her out of the move, but those who understood her the best, knew her mind was made up and nothing would change it.

She'd had the choice between a spacious two-bedroom apartment with historic bay windows and vintage black-and-white tiling in the kitchen and bathroom, versus a small, cheerless one-bedroom apartment in a better area. Even her acute awareness that the neighborhood would continue on its downtrodden path never altered her decision. She related far more to "quaint and quirky" than she ever had to "dull and suburban." And, she thought, one day the neighborhood might become hip again, and hopefully, she'd live long enough to see it.

Cassidy chose her apartment not only for its square footage and personality, but also because it was three blocks from her job, which not only meant a five-minute commute, but she could also go home at lunch to see her cats, Saber and Saki.

For years, she had handled graphic design and writing for a small vegetarian specialty magazine. When technology nearly killed the business, Cassidy, along with a co-worker, revived it, transforming the magazine to digital and narrowly holding onto the low-paying jobs they so dearly loved—and needed. At fifty-two, Cassidy knew it wasn't just love that kept her there — few were hiring, and working women over fifty were permanent residents on the endangered species list. And so she stayed put ... in the neighborhood known for two things: the "Hotel Obscure" and the once-regal Blue Palace Cinema. Outside the old theater, sitting inside the recess of a wall by the side emergency exit, he made his regular plea to the passersby: "Can you help a homeless man with a dollar for a hot dog?"

The nameless man whose life had deteriorated into alcoholism and panhandling was symbiotic with the once-elegant theater that had been considered a crowned jewel among theaters in its day.

Cassidy didn't know how many afternoons he had been claiming that spot, but she'd been aware of him for three years, ever since she got Barnaby and began taking longer walks.

Every day that weather permitted, and even on some days when it didn't, she saw him. There were shelters somewhere in the city, but she had no idea where they were. It wouldn't matter if she knew; it would change nothing. Over the years, she'd heard that most homeless people preferred to tough it out alone. Shelters were scary places with drugs, theft, bed bugs, scabies, overcrowding, violence, sickness, and mental illness. To many, staying in a shelter posed a greater risk than tucking oneself away outdoors. And there were few who didn't mind the restrictions imposed upon them.

Cassidy felt pangs of guilt for the years she avoided him. She would either walk on the opposite side of the street, hold her cell phone to her ear and talk with urgency, or do what many did: walk by and pretend not to notice. It was never that she didn't care; she just didn't know what to do. To stand on the street and take money out of her purse wasn't the best idea, either, so she kept moving.

Although he was always sitting when she saw him, she could see he was a tall man. He had to be at least six foot three. His face was deeply tanned from so much time in the sun and etched with lines that likely made him look years older than he was. He had piercing light-blue eyes, but sadly, they had the unmistakable gloss of an alcoholic. She could see that he must have once been a striking man before alcohol intervened.

Pondering his alcoholism led to the other reason that always stopped her from giving: the I-don't-want-to-pay-for-cigarettes-or-alcohol rationale. Cassidy had heard others say that they were happy to buy food for a homeless person, but they refused to give money that would go to booze or cigarettes. For a long time, that reasoning justified her decision not to give.

Occasionally, she would see an abandoned hot dog (or more) wrapped in aluminum foil sitting in his spot long after he'd left for the day. She knew he couldn't bear to eat them anymore—homeless or not. *Why didn't those people just give him a dollar? Why didn't he give the unwanted hot dogs to other homeless people who were hungry?*

One day, before walking Barnaby on her lunch hour, Cassidy found herself taking a dollar from her purse and slipping it into her side pants pocket. She purposely walked down the street where he regularly stationed himself. She no longer cared what he did with the money. If she were in his worn-out shoes, would she want someone deciding or speculating on what she should do with the money? No, she wouldn't. She would hate it. Living on the streets was demoralizing enough.

That day, Cassidy smiled and gave him the first dollar. It felt good to hear, "Thank you, dear."

After that day, she never walked on the opposite side of the street. She never walked by him without a dollar in her pocket. He always thanked her and told her that she did too much for him, and she felt sick to her stomach because she didn't think she did anything that really mattered. But she also knew he was the only one with the power to fix himself.

One day, she handed him a dollar, and he called after her, "Thank you! It's my birthday!" Cassidy turned around with a half smile, realizing that the usual response to such a statement was far from appropriate. "Oh, gee. I hope things get better. This can't be a happy birthday for you." That was the day she found out he was four months younger than she was.

Cassidy wished she had known it was his birthday. She would have done something. The next time she saw him, she handed him a five-dollar bill and told him it was a belated birthday gift. He thanked her, but he had been drinking more than usual, and could barely meet her eyes or express his usual gratitude. Embarrassed, she admitted to herself that she felt cheated.

Despite the bits and pieces of conversation the two began to exchange, Cassidy never asked his name. She thought it better that the relationship didn't move beyond what it was. Besides, she'd thought of him as "Dollar Hot Dog Man" for so long that any name sounded bizarre. She could get used to thinking of him as John, maybe because it reminded her of "John Doe," or maybe even Ed, but names like Dave, Steve, Ernie, Henry, Carl, Michael, or Aaron seemed as ill fitting as dressing a frog in a suit and tie.

One day, while chastising herself for overthinking the name thing, she wondered if the knowing of her name was even a blip on *his* radar screen. Am I "Dollar Lady" to him? Would the sound of my name be jarring to his ears? Will he ask my name?

He didn't ask her name. Something in her gut told her that he felt no right to know it. She hoped she was wrong. Several times, however, he asked Barnaby's name. One day, he gave Barnaby several bites from his cookie that sat beside him on the dirty pavement. She couldn't help but be touched, though she inwardly winced. That was the day that he told her he had five years of college and was an educated man. He pointed to an office building across the street. "See that building? I can fix pretty much anything that goes wrong in there. But nobody will give me a job. They don't want to pay me what I'm worth. I've even offered to work for much less."

He then pointed down the street to the old six-story hotel known as Hotel Obscure. "That place needs a whole lot of fixin', but hell, I doubt they care much. I'll work for less, but not for the minimum wage they'd pay—if that."

Cassidy was fascinated to learn more about him. She knew that showered, cleanly dressed, and sober, he would qualify for many jobs. But there was a long road between what could be and what would be, and with only public transportation, his options were limited. She wasn't writing him off, though.

She thought about her life and the job she had managed to save—for the time being, anyway. His skills were more in demand than hers, but his work experience wasn't why he was turned away. He had to know that, but she had no idea how living on the street could change one's thinking or shape one's conception of denial. And, she considered that *not* living on the street altered her perceptions as well. In a world with so many realities, was anyone right? Did anyone really see the world as it was?

The day he told her that he hoped to get disability soon, and that she wouldn't see him out on the street any longer, she was thrilled. She told him she hoped she'd still see him around town, only in a better situation.

"Well, I'll have enough to live at the Obscure. And if they give me a room with maintenance problems, I'll fix them myself and they can deduct my pay from the rent."

But over a year went by and his situation never changed. She'd long forgotten the real name of the "Hotel Obscure," which she often thought of as the "Last Resort Inn." And now, she was feeling disappointment for a man who couldn't even get enough money together to make the shabby old residence his home.

Cassidy often mused about the eclectic miscellany of people who came and went through the doors of the gloomy establishment. To the casual observer, they would be a homogenous group, but aside from the usual suspects, she'd seen representations of more groups than most people would believe. Once in a while, she'd sketch the people she saw—when she was home watching TV and felt restless.

She surprised herself the time she realized she'd drawn Dollar Hot Dog Man at least ten times, but then she realized why. She had ceased to know him anonymously, and now, though she didn't know his name, his presence, his being, and his plight were a part of her world, if only on the periphery of it.

While she felt no responsibility for him, it nagged at her that she should do more, but that was not possible. As the days wore on, she offered dollar bills every day she saw him, and it wasn't long before he told her that she didn't have to help him every time. He knew she didn't have a lot and didn't feel right taking too much from her. She assured him it was okay, but he stood resolute in his pride and concern for her well-being. Often, he would tell her, "It's all coming back to you one day."

Most days, Cassidy ate lunch before walking Barnaby. But after a call from Helen, a childhood friend who was in the neighborhood, Cassidy met her at a local antique shop she often did business with, and the two walked to the closest eatery, the diner on Fourth Street. On the way, they passed Dollar Hot Dog Man, in his usual spot, making his plea. Cassidy smiled and handed him the usual dollar. The moment she did so, she intuitively felt her friend's discomfort. She tried to ignore it. But halfway through lunch, it was still there, gnawing at her, clawing at her. It did not want to go away.

Cassidy knew herself well: matters disregarded will inevitably fester. That's when she made the choice to confide in Helen about Dollar Hot Dog Man.

"... so, since that first time, I give him a dollar every time I see him. I make it a point to get singles when I cash my check. He told me he's been homeless for seven years. I hope he's able to have a home in this lifetime. He and all of the other people deserve better."

Helen sighed. "Well, you know, Cassidy, hard work didn't put these people on the streets. And to be honest, when people are so low and down on themselves, it's hard for them to imagine life being any better. Most of them give up. Addiction doesn't cure itself. I think most of them cease to care about chasing creature comforts. I mean, really, when do you think the man last had a good shower and spent the night in a bed?"

"I don't know, Helen. But I think about it. A lot. I want to do something, but I'm powerless to change his situation or anyone else's."

"Why not offer him a night at the Hotel Obscure? Isn't that what people call that godforsaken place across the street?"

"Yes, they do." Cassidy pondered the suggestion. "The man has a lot of pride. He'd never accept such a gift, for one. I'm sure of that."

Helen shivered as she looked out the window at a disheveled old woman pushing a large cart stuffed with possessions. "Well then, tell him a friend of yours paid for three nights and left after two, giving you the third night to offer to someone who might need it. He might accept it under those conditions. And really, he'd look so much better after a shower. He might even remember what it feels like to be human and find some motivation to get off the street. And that would be a positive for everyone … an improvement to the neighborhood. Call it 'shower power.' Listen, I'll pony up the money. It's pocket change for me."

Cassidy fixated on her veggie wrap to avoid Helen's intense stare. "I don't think a shower will change anyone's life. As for offering him a room for the night, I don't know. That's kind of major."

"No it's not." Helen leaned forward across the table. "Look at me. I want to do this. Truth time, Cass: wouldn't it be great to see that guy looking better?"

"This is about how *he* would feel, Helen. Not about what would be pleasing to my eyes, my psyche, or my survivor guilt, for lack of a better term. Or yours."

Lost in her own thoughts, Helen continued. "The thing is, though, you'd have to check the weather report first. It would really suck if he took you up on the offer, only to have it rain the next day."

Cassidy choked on her drink and threw her wrap onto the foil. "Jesus Christ, Helen. He's a man, not a sedan that's just come through the car wash on a cloudy day!"

Helen shrugged while simultaneously expelling air through her Botox-enhanced lips. "You've always been such a semanticist, Cassidy. You're so fucking intense. Lighten up. Let me give you the money. Helping this guy will raise you up. Make you feel more like a benefactor than an equal, and trust me, that's just what you need. You've lived in this neighborhood way too long to see clearly anymore."

Her right hand balled into a fist, Cassidy pounded her forehead, then paused. "I am his equal. And I hate to break it to you, but you are too, Helen."

Vehemently, with both hands, Helen waved her off. "Oh, no. Nuh-uh. Nah-ah. No way! That filthy, chain-smoking alcoholic is *not* my equal. If you want to lower yourself to his status, that's your bailiwick, darlin', but count me out."

"If you think he's so worthless, why did you offer to pay for him to stay at the Obscure for a few nights?"

"Because I'm a kind person," Helen said, taking a dainty bite of her sandwich, then putting it back on the plate.

"Kind people don't label others as being less than their equal."

"Really, Cassidy, do you expect me to believe that you see that man as your equal? Because I'm not buying that. Not for a minute." Helen smirked. "But then again, you *have* lowered the bar on your own life. Even the best limbo dancer would have trouble getting under it."

Cassidy's eyes darkened. "Oh, that's rich. Literally." She took a few bites from her veggie wrap before speaking again. "First, to answer your question, no, I don't believe I'm superior to anyone. Second, I happen to love my apartment and my job. I'm not going to exchange either one just to have an acceptable zip code so that people like you won't snub their snobby noses at it."

"Oh, please. The pot calls the kettle judgmental. I'm not the snob you think I am. For starters, a snob would hire someone to come here and handle business for her."

"Not in your case, though. You're too much of a control freak to let anyone else handle your precious antiques."

Helen shook off the rebuff. "Well, a snob wouldn't have lunch with someone who lives in this godforsaken part of the city, much less be friends with her."

"Say what?" Cassidy said, sitting up straight. "So, you're not a snob because you have lunch with the likes of me?"

Helen sighed. "Again, stop being so fucking intense and 'read between the linesy,' will you? And stop looking to be offended. I'm only trying to say that there *are* people I know who wouldn't think of socializing with anyone outside their small circle. And I'm not one of them." She smiled insincerely. "Again, I'm a kind person."

Cassidy groaned. "You know, Helen, I don't get together with friends out of kindness. I get together with people because I care about them. And I don't have friends that are even a part of any circle, square, or rectangle. And I certainly don't see sharing a meal or going to a movie together as an act of charity."

"Charity is your word, darlin'. Not mine."

"Let me ask you this," Cassidy said, putting her veggie wrap down. "Do you have to go back to the dealer after our lunch?"

"Yes, he's just polishing something for me today. Why?"

"Because every time we have lunch, you always have to go back to the dealer afterward."

"What is your fucking point, Cassidy? You're trying my patience."

"There are also times when you leave things with him and come back another day, right?"

"Wow, you've unearthed a bombshell." Helen sighed in exasperation. "The food journalist uncovers actual news!"

Cassidy glowered at her but stayed on message. "Well, on those days, when you don't need to wait for anything, you never have lunch with me. Ever. So, maybe the only reason you deign to see me, on the days when it is necessary for you to hang around, is so you won't be seen by your lonesome in this neighborhood. In other words, you're using me."

"That's ridiculous."

"But it's true, isn't it? I save you from looking less than respectable."

"Look at me. Look at my designer clothing! My hair. My makeup. I'm as respectable as a person can get! I exude class and you know it. Now, do you think I give a damn about what people down here think of me? Because I'm here to tell you I don't."

Cassidy smiled. "In one sense, no, you don't." She paused. "However, you definitely don't want them to think you belong here. Even the thought makes your stomach churn. Not that *they* give a damn." She picked up a slice of avocado on her plate that had dropped out of the wrap and ate it. "But you do. And wanting to pay for my homeless friend to take a shower is your way of making sure you're situated well above him."

Helen shivered again. "Ugh! The word 'homeless' and the word 'friend' should never be used together like that. Way too oxymoron-ish for my taste. I don't have friends who consider homeless people to be their … ugh!"

"Friend? Equal?" Cassidy snarled. "Ugh is right!" Her appetite gone, she threw her napkin on top of her veggie wrap just as a server was approaching.

"Looks like you're done here."

Cassidy picked up her plate and handed it to the woman. "More than you know. I'll take the check, please."

Affronted, Helen looked at Cassidy. "You don't pay for me. I always pay for you."

"I've got this one, Helen."

"I'd prefer to pay."

"No, it's my turn to treat you. It's my distinct pleasure. I insist."

Helen stood. "How dare you lower me to that man's stature by paying for my lunch in this ramshackle neighborhood. Just how dare you!"

Cassidy sat expressionless except for a pleasant nod to the server who handed her a check. "You're welcome, Helen. Any time. It's great to have a hearty lunch and feel human again, isn't it? This 'food journalist' is happy to treat the fallen aristocracy to some sustenance. Perhaps you'd like to check in across the street and have a shower too."

Seething, Helen glared at her. "I take it you'll understand when you never hear from me again."

Cassidy reached into her purse for money, not even bothering to watch Helen's swift and dramatic departure through the diner doors.

After work that day, as Cassidy walked Barnaby toward Dollar Hot Dog Man, he seemed exceptionally eager to speak to her.

"Hey, I think I upset your friend ... that lady you were with earlier."

Stunned, Cassidy stopped while Barnaby greeted Dollar Hot Dog Man.

"Hey, buddy!" Dollar Hot Dog Man lovingly rubbed Barnaby on both sides of his neck, then looked up at Cassidy. "She gave me forty dollars. That was very generous, but I told her I couldn't take that kind of money. Not right."

Cassidy was fuming. Helen's transparent ploy to rise above the hoi polloi was anything but generous. But the spirit in which the money was given didn't matter. Her homeless friend could use the money; Helen's twisted rationale was irrelevant. "Well, consider it a one-time gift. I don't think you'll ever see her again. The only reason she even steps foot in this area is because there's a top-notch antique restoration specialist she comes to see once every few months." She smiled warmly. "I just hope the money she gave you will help."

"Oh yeah, it would have. But I gave it right back to her."

Cassidy moved from the center of the sidewalk to the wall as several moviegoers hurried by her. She looped Barnaby's leash twice around her wrist and pulled him to her side. "You did?"

Dollar Hot Dog Man shook his head. "Didn't make her happy. She told me to take a damn shower and go eff myself." He looked up to address a young family walking by. "Can you help a homeless man with a dollar for a hot dog?"

REQUIESCAT IN PACE

Evan Drake could feel the eyes on him before he entered the building. Men in Brioni suits carrying Italian leather duffel bags rarely, if ever, ventured into the Hotel Obscure. (At least that's what people called it. The real name eluded him.) And that was good. It was far better that he didn't know the name of the dwelling that was to become the final resting place for a meaningless life.

Two old men sat side by side in the small lobby to the left of the door. He saw them slowly turn to share a look when he entered. But to his surprise, his bright and shining incongruity was of little interest to them. One man stared blankly into space, while the other repeated the process of pulling every blade and tool from a Swiss Army knife, then returning them all back to their original positions in the iconic red handle.

In the center of the room, two other men sat. One wore earbuds and gently tapped his foot to whatever sounds floated into his ears. Evan envied the peace that seemed to embrace this man who likely had little in his life. Sitting across from the music lover, an older man briefly stopped flipping through a sports magazine to look him up and down.

Evan was surprised that despite looking so different from everyone else, he inspired, at best, a mere once-over. Surely a Brioni suit and an expensive haircut deserved a "twice-over," but then again, he imagined many dapper men with overpriced barbers probably visited the derelict establishment as well, only for very different reasons. The eyes he'd imagined watching him were apparently nearly closed.

For the mere whimsy of it, Evan had a long list of things he wanted to say to the hotel clerk. Being a man who'd had little to laugh about, the idea of doing something for no purpose other than sheer amusement delighted him. His mind raced with possibilities: I trust my reservation is in order. Is there a bellhop about? Is room service open all night? Do you have any rooms left with a view? Has the mini-bar been freshly stocked? Can you direct me to your gift shop? Pardon me, have you any Grey Poupon?

Why shouldn't he say whatever he wanted to the clerk? Sometimes you have to force a lucid dream if you're not lucky enough to have one naturally.

Before he could indulge his whim, behind the counter, a sixty-something-year-old woman with jet-black hair sized him up. "You can't be serious. You … want to stay *here*. Your suit costs more than this building."

The clerk obviously saw Evan as nothing more than a walking cliché of a wealthy man, so he might as well play along. "And your point, Madam? Do you or do you not have a room for me?"

She searched the lobby as if she were expecting to find a hidden camera. "Yeah, I got a room for you … Oh, wait. I get it. You're expecting company. Slumming for some—"

"Indeed *not*, Madam. As a matter of fact, I'd like strict privacy. Absolutely no visitors for any reason."

"Really? I was so sure that … all right, then. And by the way, name's Josephine. Use it or lose it. Just eighty-six the 'Madam' thing, will you? I'm just fillin' in for my guy Henry. Pulled his back out last night. Now, what's your name?"

"Jude. Jude Fawley."

Evan was thankful that the Hotel Obscure did not require identification, but even if it did, some extra cash in the clerk's hands would take care of that sort of nuisance.

Josephine shoved a clipboard at him. "Put your John

Hancock here, Mr. Fawley. Now, you can give me thirty-five dollars for the standard room or fifty bucks for a deluxe. What'll it be?"

"You've certainly sparked my curiosity," Evan said as he scribbled on the clipboard. "Exactly what does the deluxe offer?"

Josephine tipped her head to one side and rolled her eyes. "A working television, a clock radio, curtains instead of blinds, a queen-size bed, and the best toilet in the house. And all rooms come with Wi-Fi. Surprise, surprise, huh? Can't beat that with a stick, can you? Right now, there's only one short-term deluxe available. We have lower rates and other options available for our long-term guests, but my psychic powers tell me this will be a short stay."

"Hmm. As tempting as that deluxe room sounds, I don't think I'll need anything that fancy. And your powers have not betrayed you; this will be a very short stay. I'll be gone in no time. But under different circumstances, that treasure trove of amenities you rattled off would certainly tickle my fancy."

"You're a real funny one, mister. Cash up-front. With tax.'"

Evan reached into his pocket and put forty-five dollars on the counter. "This ought to cover it. May I have my key, please?"

Josephine turned around, pulled a key from the pegboard on the wall, then handed him the key. "Room 14, third floor. Right up those stairs."

"Thank you."

Evan smiled and turned to walk away, but felt Josephine's suspicious gaze shadowing him.

Ah, what the hell, he told himself. Straightening his face, then his tie, Evan turned around to address Josephine just as he set foot on the first step. "Pardon me, but what hours does your valet keep?"

Josephine met his eyes dead on. "He works the graveyard shift. Sews suits for corpses. Makes sure they get buried with a good fit. Then he downs a couple shots of bourbon and goes zombie hunting for an hour or two … you know, just to wind down before hittin' the sack. All the usual stuff. Anything else you wanna know?"

Evan nodded. "Nope. But I do appreciate you fielding that one. Hit it right out of the park, you did. That will be all."

Fucking lunatic, Josephine thought. But damn cute.

☠☠☠

Evan threw the duffel bag on the bed and watched what was left of the mattress sag in the middle like a pot of soup that had just been dipped into with an oversized ladle.

He spotted a ratty floral print armchair, which kept company with a battered old table, and collapsed into it. Laying his head back, he looked at the nicotine stains on the textured ceiling. Hmm … the ceiling appeared to have a dandruff problem. The plaster flakes on the bed were akin to a snowfall for the damned. Beautiful. He couldn't imagine a more perfect hell.

At forty-seven years of age, Evan barely remembered a happy day. He was only five, staying with his Aunt Edna, while his father lingered on life support after a fatal accident at the manufacturing plant where he worked.

While eating breakfast in the kitchen one morning, Edna received a visitor in the living room. From his seat at the table, he could see and hear the woman with a pink suit and matching pillbox hat softly asking Edna if he was the nephew from the wrong side of the tracks that she was so concerned about.

"Indeed he is. I refuse to play Auntie to the son of a rapist. It's genetic, you know. And I'm not going to explain to others why I have family at my dinner table who don't know what fork to use first or what a *clafouti* is. Honestly, Patricia, people will think I've gone batty. And what if the child has his father's rapist genes? I'm certainly not subjecting my loved ones to that kind of danger."

When he was eleven, Evan learned that he came into the

world as a product of date rape and that the man who he called Daddy was not his biological father, but the longtime boyfriend his mother never married because he was crushed by machinery three months before the intended nuptials. He also learned that having a less-than-complete knowledge about cutlery etiquette coupled with a shocking ignorance of French desserts was apparently as damning as potentially having "rapist genes."

His mother, Audrey, was six years younger than her sister, Edna. By the time Edna was old enough to understand how different life was for those of privilege, she was determined to marry the first man of fortune who would have her. Evan's grandmother, Harriet, barely recognized Edna as the humble and gracious daughter she had tried to rear. Instead, she watched her eldest devolve into a coldhearted, pretentious, and uncharitable socialite. As time passed, Edna put more and more distance between herself and her family. But Harriet, forever optimistic, never stopped hoping that by some miracle, her daughters would someday be close.

When Evan was seven, his grandmother, who lived three-hundred miles away and was unable to travel, was invited to Thanksgiving dinner by her eldest daughter, only because Edna was confident that she would never be able to make the trip. Desperate to bring her daughters together, Harriet told Edna that she indeed would attend, escorted by a close friend.

Edna was unhappy, not knowing who in God's name might accompany her mother to *her* home, but for the sake of civility, agreed. Harriet, knowing there would be two extra seats at the table, then told Audrey that she and Evan had been invited.

Audrey wasn't happy that the first invitation to Thanksgiving dinner had been indirectly extended through her mother, but desperate to provide Evan with some sense of family, holiday, and tradition, she didn't hesitate to go.

"This is your 'little man shirt,'" Audrey told Evan as she

dressed him in a button-down cotton shirt with thin blue pinstripes. "You're going to make a glorious debut into this family."

Evan remembered raising his little arms up as his proud mother slid a V-necked navy-blue sweater over his head. "My goodness, you're a handsome boy. I'm so proud of you, Son."

Unsettled by the memory, Evan looked toward the window and watched as two stinkbugs made their way inside and climbed the wall. One stopped to rest on a broken blind while the other continued to ascend.

He remembered how proud his mother had been that Thanksgiving Day. All the way into the city, as they sat on the train, she told him that he would melt the hearts of everyone in the family. When Evan's face expressed alarm, she laughed, then explained to him that the melting of hearts was just an expression, nothing like the melting of marshmallows over fire or the melting of ice cream down the side of a cone on a hot summer's day.

Edna's eyes went black with fury when she saw them at the door. Fear: it was the one thing Evan and his aunt had in common that day. They both took a step back upon seeing one another while Audrey's mouth dropped open as she realized her mother, with only the best of intentions, had done a really stupid thing by trying to get her rich daughter to accept her poor one and her son.

"Heavens, Audrey. Surely our mother taught you better manners than to show up anywhere uninvited."

"She told me you had invited us. I never would have ...."

Edna, now making the same realization as her sister, sighed and shook her head. "What a foolhardy thing for her to do! Well, clearly this means that Mother and her presumably nonexistent mystery companion will not be joining us."

"No," Audrey said. "That's pretty obvious."

The two sisters looked at each other across the threshold. Evan was only seven, but from what he'd learned about manners, you invite someone inside, if you know them, if they're outside your door. And that was what he was sure the woman with the angry eyes would do.

"Well, Audrey, I'm sorry Mother's recklessness brought you all of this way with the boy, but I'm not prepared for children." Just as she spoke, a young girl in a green holiday dress dashed gaily through the living room, giggling, as a boy about Evan's age chased her. Edna appeared only mildly embarrassed.

Audrey looked at the longing in her son's eyes and pleaded silently with her sister to invite them in, for Evan's sake. Edna wasn't budging. "I'm sorry, Audrey. It would be simply inappropriate to foist strangers upon my company. And, considering the circumstances of the child's conception, well, I really can't know who I'd be allowing into my home."

Locking the fingers on each hand together was the only way Audrey knew to avoid putting them around her sister's neck. She tried to calm herself down. "My son is your flesh-and-blood nephew. That's who he is."

Pursing her lips, Edna moved closer to her sister and spoke in a whisper. "He has a rapist for a father."

"He is an innocent child. He is a joy and I am privileged to be his mother."

"Wait here," Edna said as she walked away, leaving the front door open.

Evan could still remember the gaiety that filled the living room. The laughter and high spirits of strangers taunted him as he soaked in what was not meant to be his.

Within a minute, Edna rushed back to the door and shoved a fistful of bills into her sister's hand. "This is enough to not only buy you Thanksgiving dinner, but also to have a merry Christmas as well. There's a diner around here somewhere. It never closes; I know that much. Although I wish it would."

"We walked here from the train station, Edna. It's freezing outside, and I don't have a car."

"Oh. That figures. Well, I've given you more than enough for a cab. Wait on the sidewalk and I'll call one to come fetch you. Happy Thanksgiving, Audrey. *Carpe diem!*"

Edna closed the door so hard that it made both Evan and his mother jump. As they walked down the stone path with fallen leaves on either side of it, his mother's tears tortured him. He expected her to wait on the sidewalk, as instructed, but she grabbed his hand and walked hurriedly down the street. It was about a mile and a half back to the train station. Upon arriving, they learned that because it was a holiday, there would be a two-hour wait for the next train home.

And so they sat on the bench and cuddled as a light snow began to fall. Audrey put her arm around Evan, and he buried his head into her chest and cried for her as she cried for him.

Two hours and ten minutes later, the train arrived. By the time they got back to the station near their home, it was nearly ten o'clock. The only place open to get any kind of food was a convenience store at the gas station.

Even now, at forty-seven, Evan could not forget how hard his mother fought back the tears when she bought two turkey sandwiches, a pumpkin pie with an orange "reduced" sticker on the lid, and a pint of vanilla ice cream. As they were leaving the convenience store, a group of older teens, clearly inebriated, crashed into his mother as they came barreling into the store, and she and the bag fell to the ground.

"Mommy!"

Tears slid down Audrey's cheeks as she looked at the smashed pie before her. The two sandwiches and the ice cream lay on the curb by the parking lot. Evan scrambled to pick up the mess, but his mother stopped him. "Don't touch anything, sweetheart. I'll pick it all up. Stand back from the parking lot. Too many people are driving who have been drinking. Parking lots are dangerous places. Even when people are sober."

Evan didn't really understand much about drinking, but he knew to obey his mother.

As Audrey got up, Evan noticed her knees were scratched and bleeding, as were the palms of her hands. Inside, the young men were buying cigarettes and snacks and didn't care that they had knocked a woman down in their haste to get them.

"I have to clean this up, Evan. I'm a good citizen; it's the right thing to do."

As Audrey bent down to reach the pie, a young man with a large store bag came outside. "I'm so sorry, ma'am. I'm Joe Ribaldi. I'm the manager. I saw everything that happened. Don't worry about this mess. I'll clean it up. Here's a fresh bag. I've replaced everything you purchased and added in a few extras."

Audrey managed a weak smile and took the bag. "I know you. You're Linda and Joseph's son. I used to babysit for you some years ago."

The manager took a long look at Audrey. "Ms. Drake. Oh, wow. I certainly do remember you. You used to draw for me. As a matter of fact, I still have a picture you drew that was inspired by my train set. It's beautiful. My wife got it framed for my birthday last year. We hung it in our baby son's room."

"Oh, Joe. I remember that now. You loved those trains, and you asked me to draw them pulling into a station where there was lots of snow and people waiting. And you were specific in requesting that the conductor wore a blue suit and had red cheeks."

"Yes, that's right. My grandfather was a conductor and that's exactly as I remembered him." He took a good look at her. "Oh no, you're bleeding, Ms. Drake. Let me get you something for those scratches. The asphalt and concrete did a number on you."

"I'll clean up at home, Joe. You get back to your store."

"Well, then, let me walk you to your car."

Audrey could barely make eye contact, but Joe understood.

"Oh, you're on foot tonight. It's too late and too cold for you to be walking. Would you please let me drive you home? It's the very least I can do. I've got two great employees inside who can handle everything while I'm gone. You won't be putting me out at all. And on the way, I'll tell you about my boy."

Audrey started to protest, but thought better of it. "Thank you, Joe."

It was nearly eleven when they got home. They had both been starving, but they'd moved past hunger, and splitting a turkey sandwich was more than enough for both of them. And that was the first Thanksgiving Evan remembered.

And now here he was in the Hotel Obscure … a final stop on the pathetic road of life. He looked at the water stain on the front wall by the window. When he tilted his head to the left, the way the light fell on the stain made it look like Australia, and one of the stinkbugs, who was now crawling on it, had landed somewhere around Queensland.

He felt angry all over again when he remembered his mother's conversation with the store manager. He had never known that she had any artistic talent at all. Yet, she had drawn a beautiful picture for a boy she once babysat for, but never for him. When he asked her why that was so, Audrey explained that she had lost her interest in art but would happily draw something for her favorite person in the world. When she asked Evan what he would like her to draw, he had simply said, "Daddy."

When he was twelve, his mother told him the truth. Her artistic life ended when she painted a watercolor for a cousin with a newborn baby and had presented the gift at a baby shower.

When her cousin pulled the framed picture out of the box, before she could thank Audrey, Edna broadcast to everyone that her sister had apparently forgotten that she wasn't in the third grade anymore and didn't know that one *buys* gifts; one does not create them with a school girl's paint box and stick them into a cheap frame.

Audrey, devastated, embarrassed, and humiliated, never painted or drew again until she did so for Evan.

How ironic, he mused, that had it not been for that horrible Thanksgiving night, standing in front of the convenience store, he may never have learned that his mother had artistic talent nor would he have known where his own talent came from. The talent that he never had time to nurture and always wished that he could do so.

At his grandmother's funeral, when he was nearly seventeen, Evan and Audrey saw Edna again for the first time. He met Edna's only child, Anna, two years his senior, a cousin he didn't even know he had.

Anna was everything her mother was not: warm, engaging, accepting, generous, and wild about Evan. At first, she tried to hide the fact that she barely remembered he existed, but as she and Evan spoke, he could see Anna shooting daggers at her mother. After a half hour of conversation, Anna became open about her feelings.

"We have so much to make up for, Cousin," she told him. "I've made a thousand stupid excuses over the years for my mother, but I'm fresh out of them, Evan. I know that Mother took care of you once, after your father died tragically, but she sent me away during the two days you were at our home. I'm so sorry."

"Oh," Evan said. "I remember asking her if she had any children I could play with. And she said no. I never understood why she was so angered by my question."

"Mother went to great lengths to keep us apart. While I always knew you existed, I was told you and your mom moved far away, wanting nothing to do with us. When I was old enough to know differently, she threatened me. You see, I had two wonderful grandmothers. My father's mother, Annalise, for whom I was named, loved me very much, as I did her. When she died, she bequeathed a small fortune to me, along with a letter asking that I do something good and important with the money … something I believed would make the world a better place.

"It was then that I decided that I wanted to start a charity for boys and girls who did not have the funds for a good education. From the time I was small, I thought it so unfair that I had so much that was denied to other children. Anyway, as I was only fourteen, I didn't have legal control over my foundation. When I told Mother one day that I wanted to find you and Aunt Audrey, she told me that if I did, she would shut down my foundation and made a loathsome remark about the poor children in need that I won't repeat.

"So, Evan, as much as I wanted to know you, I couldn't. Now that I am of age, and in control of my foundation, I can communicate with anyone I wish."

"I'm so sad that Grandma died," Evan said. "But I'm so happy to know you." He looked embarrassed. "Everything you said sounds just like the woman I remember."

"She has a way of making indelible impressions on people of every age." Anna glanced in her mother's direction. "Look at her. Staring at us. Seeing us meet is hell for her. No doubt she forced our grandmother, God rest her soul, to keep one another's existence quiet."

Evan nodded. "Yeah. She must have. I remember visiting Grandma once, and I caught her caregiver hurrying out of the room with some framed photos when I arrived. I thought it was weird, but Grandma said she was just doing some last-minute cleaning."

"Ah, hiding my photos, no doubt!"

"Yeah, probably. Except she missed one. Now I know it was you and your mother. I remember thinking the little girl in the photo was the same one in the green dress I'd seen that Thanksgiving when we were turned away. I asked Grandma who was in the picture, and she said you were the child of one of your mother's friends. I remember she looked away from me when she said it. It was weird. I wondered why she would feel sad about something like that."

"Grams hated lying. I think she'd still be alive if Mother hadn't broken her heart so many times. It finally gave out on her."

At that moment, Audrey came over to the two, introduced herself to Anna, who responded by giving her a big hug.

"Evan, will you forgive me for not telling you that you had a cousin?"

Anna tried to stop her from continuing. "Please don't blame yourself, Aunt Audrey. Mother is the grand puppeteer. She pulls everybody's strings. She wore my poor father out. You probably wouldn't even know this, but when I was twelve, he divorced her and took a job at his company's Berlin headquarters. We've remained very close, though, and I visit Germany twice a year and he comes to see me as well. And he's remarried as well, to a lovely woman.

"Mother tells everyone he's just away on business a lot, which is a joke because everybody knows exactly what happened and everybody understands exactly why it did. She's a horror! I don't want to even think of the friends I've lost over the years because Mommie Dearest didn't approve of their lineage, their parents' jobs, the street they lived on, the car they drove, their inability to understand Latin, or a million other meaningless and stupid things. And you know what? She didn't even want me to come to my own grandmother's funeral today because she knew we'd meet. Look at her over there. Did you ever see anyone give a side eye like my mother?"

"I know it well." Audrey lowered her eyes in shame and looked at Evan. "Again, I am so sorry, Son. I really should have told you that you have a cousin. But under the circumstances, I thought it would hurt you too much to learn Anna existed when you couldn't know one another."

Anna put her arm around Evan. "Well, we're sure as heck acquainted now! And we're going to stay in touch. Real touch. Not cards-at-Christmas in touch, but like real family. Mother is never going to hurt any of us anymore."

Evan stuck his index finger into a cigarette burn on the arm of the old floral chair. The day he met Anna was a happy one, but the rage still burned. Unaware of what he was doing, he began twisting his finger like a drill that was boring a hole into the head of his aunt.

Anna had kept her promise and had been a faithful friend and cousin to Evan for all these years.

It was after meeting Anna and learning the depth of her mother's evil that Evan lost himself as he fought his soul-crushing obsession with his mother's hateful sister. It was a burden that had ruined his life. And one he kept secret because he knew the women who loved him most, his mother and his cousin, would have wrested him from it until it became their shared burden.

Edna was a malignancy that drove him to abandon his dreams and forge a path in life for the sole purpose of showing her up, of becoming well respected in her circles, of making friends with her friends, of winning honors just to make her seethe, and of making her sorely regret she had ever branded him as the "son of a rapist from the wrong side of the tracks."

Instead of accepting a scholarship to art school, he studied tirelessly to get into law school and graduated with the highest honors in his class. Before graduation, he was recruited by a top firm and had a starting six-figure salary and a signing bonus. He was able to subsidize his mother's life and give her everything that had fallen out of her grasp.

But to his greatest chagrin, Edna refused to acknowledge Evan or his accomplishments. And his wrath toward her became even greater when she treated her only daughter with such disdain and cruelty.

After college, Anna joined the Peace Corps. While in the service, she met a German man named Otto, and the two of them continued to live and work overseas to help feed and educate the hungry.

Ashamed of her daughter, angry that she was now geographically and emotionally closer to her father, and disgusted that she'd married a German man with a long ugly name ending in Schmidt, Edna openly referred to Anna and Otto as "The Palindromes." Her daughter and her son-in-law were nothing more than do-gooders whose first names were the same spelled forward as they were in reverse.

Edna's mocking of her daughter only fueled Evan's obsession. He married the granddaughter of her close friend, just to shove himself and his success in her face. He did care about his wife, but over time, she became more like the aunt he detested and less like the young woman he'd married. His children were chauffeured to and from a myriad of activities, and they became virtual strangers to him.

Enough. He was tired of suffering. Tired of living a life that belonged to a faceless stranger. He had lived his life like an actor in a play that never ended. There was no curtain call, no applause. Just a theater long gone dark … a place where nobody cared. But there he was on the stage: still acting, still pretending, still trying to prove himself for no valid reason.

His obsession with his aunt had destroyed the man he longed to be. He was putting an end to that. Yes, he was putting an end to a miserable life here in the Hotel Obscure. Here in a room where hookers plied their trade, where junkies overdosed, where the down-and-out drank themselves into oblivion, and the tired and lonely took refuge from the stink of the streets.

Everything he needed was in his Italian leather duffel bag, still resting in the center of the sagging bed. In five or ten minutes, the job would be done.

Evan pulled the large urn out of the duffel bag and laid it on the bed. He pulled out an envelope with a letter sent to him by his cousin. Carefully, he took the letter out and unfolded it. He needed to read it one last time.

Dear Evan,

In the end, Mother had no one but me, and even that was an illusion. She has left me her vast fortune, acquired from her never-ending greed and parsimony, the entirety of which I will use to help the poor and hungry both in the United States and abroad. As you know, Mother always used her knowledge of Latin to prove herself worthy. She insisted that I learn it, too. That's one of the only good things she's ever done for me. Because at such a time like this, the phrase inopiae multa, avaritiae omnia *comes to mind: to poverty, many things are lacking; to avarice, everything.*

Every cent will go to those less fortunate. Every cent made from the liquidation of her estate will do the same. Isn't it glorious?

Mother did not wish to be buried. Her final wish was to have her ashes spread among her favorite places in Europe. You know, Versailles and other such hot spots popular with the aristocracy. I'm afraid I'm too busy with my work in Africa to see to Mother's final wishes. I know you will dispose of her ashes in a way that you feel most befitting. And then, dear cousin, you will finally be free.

All my love, Anna

She did know of his obsession after all.

Evan grabbed the urn from the bed and rested it on the nightstand. He grabbed the end of the old mattress and pulled it from the bed. Opening the urn, he sprinkled some ashes, like powder onto the top of a fancy cake, onto the box spring. Then, with his right knee, he shoved the mattress back to its original spot. He couldn't help but praise himself for his attention to detail; how wise he had been to remove all of the bone fragments before performing this long-awaited, much-deserved, and macabre ceremony.

Pulling the bedding off until the bare, weathered mattress gave him the courage to go ahead. He poured ashes on semen and bloodstains. He then stood on the bed and ground with his feet, as if crushing grapes for fine wine, as hard as he could ….

He reached into the duffel bag and pulled out a pair of rubber gloves, carefully putting them on each hand. Spilling more of his aunt onto the floral chair he'd been sitting on, he rubbed and rubbed until every last bit of her dissolved, the greatest amount going under the seat cushion.

With more to go, he sprinkled ashes around the old carpet as if it were a cleaning powder one used prior to vacuuming. Again, he ground the ashes into the floor as best he could. What remained, he resolved, could easily be sucked up by an old Hoover. Or not.

His job still not done, Evan grabbed a handful of ashes and smeared them all over the wall until they were no longer obviously discernable.

He looked in the urn. His job was not finished. He walked into the bathroom, lifted the toilet seat, and poured the remainder of his aunt in the john. Flushing, he enthusiastically exclaimed, "Bon Voyage."

He walked back over to the bed and put the urn back into the bag. Pulling five twenty-dollar bills from his pocket, he lay them on the nightstand as a tip to whomever cleaned the place.

Holding his head high, feeling true joy for the first time in his life, Evan put the bag over his shoulder, said good-bye to Room 14, then set forth to live in a world he'd never known as the person he had never before allowed himself to be.

"You now have the honorable home you so deserved. Only those who will share it with you, surpass you in every way. My apologies to each and every one of them. Rest in peace, Edna. Or, as you may prefer, '*requiescat in pace.*'"

I'M A FUCKING CLICHÉ

I've lived in this dive for over three years now. The only thing I brought with me, aside from the petrified relics of my emotional past, is this big-ass desk in whose company I spend damn near most of my waking hours … and even some of my sleeping ones, too.

When I first moved into this imposing erection (yeah, I'm a big dick who moved into one), I had every intention of living on the top floor where there is no better vantage point than a sixth-floor penthouse to survey a suffering metropolis with its downtrodden proletariat and distressed homeless. But some lady already had the prime space. Turns out that didn't matter. There was a room on the fifth floor, but I couldn't even take that. Nobody would carry my mahogany monster more than two flights of stairs. Not even for an extra twenty. Somewhere out there are big strapping he-men who could easily lug a desk up five flights, but they're not coming here for chicken feed. And that's about all I've got. Except the supplements I take to keep me sane … or insane … depending on your perspective.

Yeah, I could have left my desk behind and gotten some of that Swedish do-it-yourself crap, but I can't follow visual instructions to save my life. And if I have to pick up a tool, which is never a preference, at the very least I want to use a manly screwdriver, not some little gadget that looks like an S with squared edges that slips through my fingers and hides until I no longer need it. The couple of times I went that route, I ended up breaking every piece of that particleboard and veneer crap in my line of sight … creating even more useless pieces of crap.

Thing is, I love this damn desk. It was once a brand-new and proud fixture in my great-grandfather's accounting office in the

1930s. It's been through my family and has the marks to show it. It's got history while that Swedish put-it-together-yourself stuff is history before it can *have* any real history.

The left side of this baby kisses the wall. But I still see it in my mind's eye. There are long claw marks, courtesy of Bonzo. Had that cat for nineteen years. Man, I miss him … a whole lot more than I miss my ex-wife. The first time my boy met her, he hissed at her. And he didn't stop. He had her number before I did. And when we left, I swear "The Bonz" was every bit as happy as I was … if not more.

Right now, I'm seething as I stare down these little specks of color in various shades of red and pink on my desk, trying to will them to disappear. I must have asked her a million times to stop using my sacred workplace as her manicure table, but she was one relentless bitch. I never did any writing at her makeup table, but maybe I should have. Maybe that would have gotten my point across, had I stubbed out some cigarettes in her eye-shadow palette or used her whore-red lipstick to make notes.

The surface also has rings from coffee cups and whiskey glasses going back three generations. My ex-mother-in-law—a pearl-clutching, holy-rolling know-it-all—told me that mayonnaise gets rid of rings on furniture. I told her my desk wasn't a goddamn BLT sandwich and that rings give it character.

To the occasional observer, this desk is good for nothing more than firewood. To me, it is command central. My whole life takes place here. The great American fucking novel will be written from this desk. I want people to know that. Someday, they're gonna want to write about me. That's why, every so often, I record shit about myself … to give the biographers some red meat for their scholarly research. This is how I'm making my voice heard from the grave. Don't want anyone speaking to my ex. She's got nothing to say … unless commentary from a shallow, overly made up, and born-with-a-silver-shovel-in-her-hand-so-that-she-can-always-dig-for-gold bitch is a sought-after source. There's no more to her. She's a half-inch deep at best. And I don't say that out of bitterness. Only truth.

My reasons for marrying her were as shallow as she is. I was barely twenty-one, and my romantic illusions were already decimated when the real love of my life left me for her married philosophy professor. In a retaliatory mindset, I thought a babe who serviced my every whim (as a protest to her mother's professed religiosity) was sweet revenge and proof that I could withstand any hurt. I outgrew her faster than my beloved Batman shirt that welcomed me to age six. If I'm grateful for anything, it's that we never had kids. That's all I've got to say about my marriage.

I really do wish someone could have carried my desk up three more flights. So, hell. I live on the third floor. It's a good thing, though, that I don't get so winded coming home.

The only real view from this window is the entrance to the diner across the street. I get tired of seeing the same people come and go. Rarely is there a new face. Sometimes, on a good day, a fight will break out, but that's usually frustrating because I can only hear voices. That would be fine, had I been born in the golden age of radio, but I'm only thirty-six. I grew up decades later ... watching TV ... color TV. So, when something's going down, I want visuals, despite my rather vivid imagination.

A lot of stuff happens in this godforsaken structure. I hear about some of it, but I don't see much when I'm cooped up in this room. Some days I go to the park. It's about four blocks from here. I can't say it's a thing of beauty, but it's got benches, trees, lampposts, grass, and the usual kind of fixtures you see at parks. Oh, and it's also where I can usually find my pharmacist.

I made such a visit yesterday. After transacting business and taking what I needed to reach my preferred "heightened state of mellow," I sat on a bench across from Sleeping Bee. Most homeless people go to bed on the earlier side because they have to be gone from their crash site by morning. But Bee (damned if I know her actual name) is a night owl who sleeps on a park bench throughout a good deal of the morning and early afternoon. And nobody bothers her.

So, I'm watching her, wondering if she's dreaming, and I see a murder of crows fly in and surround her. Two of them are pecking on the big shiny buttons on her coat that lies on top of her cart, and about ten of them are walking around the bench and nearby grass, eating the crumbs from her breakfast. She's so fucking sound asleep that she doesn't even know that three crows are walking on top of her. I think they're trying to wake her up. See, crows recognize people, especially ones who give them food, and Bee regularly gives them unsalted peanuts courtesy of the grocer on the corner. These birds are the only family she seems to have. They leave calling cards as thank-you gifts on top of her sleeping form, and I don't think she even notices. Or cares. Who knows?—they may even please her.

Crows are afraid of owls, for good reason, but they love their human night owl.

That day, I got so absorbed in watching the crows … and maybe distracted by the change in my body chemistry … that I barely noticed the sobbing woman who sat down on the same bench. I'm sure she would have preferred to be alone, but my bench had the only empty seat left in the park.

I felt compelled, after only a minute, to ask her if something was wrong. She put up her hand, as if to push me away, so I watched as more crows joined the party. That's when she told me that three days ago, she had given her boyfriend the news she was pregnant; two days ago, he had walked out on her, and that morning, she had suffered a miscarriage. Her grief was like a fucking tsunami encroaching on my artificially induced safe zone of contentment. I wanted to run. But damn, if her pain wasn't so palpable that it reached inside of me and triggered my own grief, which had been in semi-hibernation, and borne out of the same type of fucking abandonment. Every bloody detail that I had so carefully medicated into semi-permanent hibernation was once again raw and exposed. But somehow, that day, comforting her was as if my emotions had morphed into the mirage of a distraught twenty-six-year-old woman, allowing me to comfort myself, to feel every nuance of my years-long desolation, and to cry my shredded heart out.

    That was the day, two months ago, when I met the first friend I've had in years. In the beginning, we'd go for walks, talk on the phone, and sometimes even take in a movie at the second-run theater in the neighborhood. Then, just three days ago, I introduced her to the only other friend I have in the world … yeah … my desk. She said it was beautiful. Told me her uncle is an antiques dealer in the southwest somewhere. Right away, she takes a photo and texts it to him. Two minutes later, we learn it's a Victorian Mahogany Kneehole desk.

    Man, that felt good. Yeah, it's not in the best of shape, but my long-ridiculed companion is a damn *something,* and at that moment, I felt like maybe I could be a damn some*one* who sat at it. When I looked at her, I saw that she felt my happiness … my vindication … in the same overpowering way I felt her grief on the day that we met.

    She reached over and kissed me. I kissed back. I wanted to fuck her so bad but not as the person I am now. I asked her to give me time to get it together. I could see how disappointed she was because she was more than fine with the as-is version of me, but she deserves better. Way better. For the first time, an actual living, breathing person was a part of my vision for the future … one that didn't include the abandonment of my writing dreams … only limitations to my daily self-medication rituals. *Only*—that word kills me. It's deceptive as fuck. Yeah, it has *only* four letters in it, but it's the longest damn word I know. It tricks the mind with its brevity while being stuffed with implausibility and hellish odds at every turn. Fucking word.

She's called me every day since the kiss. We talk, but I haven't seen her again. I promised we'd get together soon. She's still grieving for her lost baby, but not for its father. I think maybe she's falling in love with me. So I need a little distance to decide how I feel about that.

I quit smoking a few years ago, but I still like to have a couple when I drink. Right now, I'm keeping company with Jack. Mr. Daniels has been my companion since I stopped stocking the proverbial medicine cabinet so full. But he doesn't get along so well with my other personality enhancements. No, they don't like one another so much, and I'm not in the best shape to break up any fights. That's not so good because right now, I need them both to become a better man. I'm likely in denial, but I continue to tell myself that I'm doing this the *only* way it can be done. One day at a time. I buoy myself up with the knowledge that I'm popping fewer of those babies than before. That's got to mean I'm making some kind of progress. Slow and steady and all that.

Opening the center drawer, I pull out a CD player, plug it into a speaker on the desk, and turn it on. Smoking has hoarsened my voice, and I'm smooth as I sing "Hallelujah" like I'm Leonard Cohen and the Obscure is the fucking Chelsea Hotel. And yeah, my dick is just cooling off after fucking a rock star for three hours. Yeah, I'm good. She's fast asleep on the bed. I smile as I look at her ass.

I reach under my desk and pull out my old manual typewriter. I'm not going to use a computer anymore. I like this image better. I just need to type on and crumple up a dozen or so sheets of paper and toss them over my shoulder. I don't have the paper to waste, so I just imagine that part. I envision old black-and-white photos of myself pounding away at the keys, creating a masterpiece … a naked woman, fuzzy, but visible in the background.

I stop daydreaming enough to write three pages. A sixty-something-year-old man is at the Port Authority Bus Terminal in New York. He's reading a three-day-old newspaper and doesn't know the difference. His mind is somewhere else. He's waiting for a bus to Maryland, but after waiting for four hours, lets it leave without him. His estranged daughter has asked him to come live with her and her daughter at their home outside of Baltimore. Her husband has died after a long illness, and she needs help. She's drained and bereft. He tells her he'll be there … wants to make up for not having been there when she was a child. Misses her and can't even remember what it's like to have a family. But he just couldn't quite bring himself to board that bus … to seal that commitment … not yet.

Three days before, his past had come knocking. The drummer from the jazz quintet he used to sing with is arranging a worldwide comeback tour. Music is this man's life; it is also what estranged him from his daughter in the first place—being all over the goddamned world, often for years at a time.

He knows he'll love the granddaughter he's never met and that it will feel damn good to be loved in return. But he has no doubt that idling in someone else's house every day, playing grandpa, will slowly kill him, especially with his real life screaming for him. From the jump, he'll be jonesing to be with the quintet and cursing the vocalist who will replace him. In a fit of despair, he will probably leave his daughter and hurt her all over again … devastate the fuck out of her and the kid. He can't bear to do that … to go back on his word. So, he sits on a bench in Port Authority. The quintet is still assuming he's on board, and he hasn't told them otherwise. Couldn't bring himself—just yet —to say no. Being conflicted is a bitch.

I don't know what he's going to do yet. I'm the writer … I can twist the plot anyway I want so that he somehow gets to do both, live happily fucking every after, and die without regrets. But that would be bullshit. Nobody lives or dies without regrets … not anyone that I know.

What am I gonna do? Have the daughter lose her job, then get hired as the manager for the group? Everyone's happy, and the little girl gets to see the world with her long-lost grandpa? That's not going to happen in my story.

Life is about hard choices. Not the easy ones. No matter what he does, he's going to sacrifice his happiness. If he goes to Maryland, he'll be miserable. If he joins the tour, he'll be riddled with guilt, but he'll probably live better in his own world. My plot won't be simple. Just as readers think they see where I'm going, something else is going to happen to gut this bitch. It will be something real. No high-concept shit.

But I haven't gotten that far. He looks through the hordes of hurrying people, searching for some kind of sign: maybe a messiah in a business suit or maybe one in rags. He only knows that if the messiah comes, he'll recognize him … or her. Or not. I've spent the last two hours detailing this man's agony as he grapples with every nuance of his existence. Now, it's time to pour a drink and grapple with every nuance of my own.

I light up a cigarette, and a clap of thunder startles me so bad that the cig flies into the air and lands on the bed behind me, burning a hole in the blanket. Just as I pick it up, the phone rings, and the damn thing flies in the air again … landing back on my desk. And yeah, now my desk has even more character. I'm thinking how I'd never write this scene in one of my stories because it would sound too contrived. So often, the fucking truth sounds implausible, and made-up shit sounds real. Most of the time anyway.

Now the rain is coming down hard. I get up to shut the window because the water gets in and runs down the wall, but I hate that doing so muffles the sound. I think about how if I were in the penthouse, I'd hear the raindrops banging the roof. It's gonna rain all night; I heard that earlier. Rain helps me to write, so I'm happy.

I put a Coltrane CD on, lean back in my chair, and think about how my character is still sitting at Port Authority, waiting for me to write his next move.

For one thing, he was right about the messiah coming. Some dude sitting nearby has a boom box and it's playing jazz. The music is the messiah, not the dude.

My man listens, and as he pictures the electric megalopolis that is New York City, he thinks about going to a bar to cogitate on his predicament and down a few malt whiskeys. But he knows that once he steps outside of Port Authority, he'll have already made his decision. So he stays on the bench and imagines he's in a club, somewhere in the Village, and closes his eyes while the music plays.

When the next song comes on, he reaches into his tattered canvas bag and pulls out the notebook he never goes anywhere without. Yeah, the song needs lyrics, and they come to him as fast as he can write them.

> In the night
> The day seems villainous
> Uncle Sam is really
> killin' us …
>
> Have a drink,
> Forget what matters,
> Seems once again,
> Your life's in tatters.
>
> Baby, you got to — sneak away
> Somehow got to lose today
> Need to — elude the masses

Slow down, like sweet molasses and …

Avoid the angered world out there,
Breathe the — cool night air, I swear
You got to go somewhere

In the night, our pain is easier,
Though in fact, the world is sleazier,
Mad-brained schemes become exciting,
Blind to troubles they're inviting, and

What's the difference if we stay t'long,
Can feeling good be so wrong?
In the night, the girls are prettier,
Cliché come-ons so much wittier,

(There is no more pain here,
Washed away like rain here,
      So much less disdain, dear …
In the night ….)

Oh, fuck! The fact that those lyrics spilled out so quickly, that he can't wait to put music to them, to sing them … oh, yeah, as much as it pains him … he's still the same man. Getting older hasn't changed his priorities. He lied to himself because he was depressed … thought music had abandoned him. He wanted to teach it a lesson. Let it know he had something better.

    His phone rings. He's been expecting his drummer pal to call. He's going to say yes. Only it's his granddaughter and she's saying, "Grandpa, where are you? Mommy is freaking out because you didn't get off the bus." And this is the first time he's ever heard her voice. "She thinks you're dead or not coming."

The fact that he's never heard her voice also means she's never heard his. He doesn't know what to do—and I need another drink to help him make up his mind.

Now my own phone is ringing. My young lady wants to come over. She wants to spend the night with me. But I know that if I let her in, I'll be saying good-bye to *my* music ... my word music. I know it. She needs me too much, and she needs too much *of* me. I realize it's that last part that's pushing me away.

I tell her I'm not feeling well. Then I say good-bye and hear her fighting back sobs. Fuck, I don't want to hurt her, but I'll hurt her more by letting her come over. I know it. I think about how the universe has its own plan and how not everyone we meet is destined to stay together forever. The answers aren't always in the stars like people think. Maybe when the stars aren't sure who is supposed to go where, they just scribble notes on the moon while they go somewhere to think shit over. Maybe they have a star-studded gala, get plastered, and forget everything. I'm not up there, so I don't know.

I'm down here. Down and out on planet-fucking Earth living the low life in the Hotel Obscure.

I mute my phone while my man at Port Authority does the same. At least I was able to say good-bye. He just ended the call and let his grand-flesh-and-blood think the call dropped. He looks up and sees a crazy man waving a gun and running through the terminal shouting some indecipherable lunacy. Maybe the stars went back to the moon and reviewed their notes. They know what is supposed to happen now. But I don't. Is this man going to live or die? And if he lives, will he truly be living? And if he dies, will he be dead? I don't fucking know. I just think that if you're alive, you should really be living. Unless misery fuels your soul and pathos drives your creativity.

I look at my beat-up old manual typewriter. I don't like to use names a lot, but I call him Manuel. I bought him in a secondhand shop where he was languishing under a cover of dust. I was eighteen. By the time I was born, people in this part of the world had stopped using typewriters. Eventually, I gave in to technology and stopped too. But I'm not proud of that. I know I hurt Manuel's feelings, but I think he might forgive me now that he's out again. Before I start using him, maybe I ought to give his carriage return a lube job and unstick the F key. I gotta hit that bastard like twenty times to get an F out of it. Maybe it would be easier to re-create an alphabet with twenty-five letters. But something about "uck you!" just doesn't throw much of a punch.

I pop and then I pour. I see myself in the cracked mirror inside the drawer. It belonged to my ex, and I left it here as a reminder of how I suffered through that farce of a marriage. Yeah, now I'm free and I've got stories to tell. Oh yeah; I really do think that playing the starving writer who thrives in the inn of dilapidation and fills his body with toxic shit is going to give me a Hemingway or Faulkner–like legacy.

I take a sheet of paper out of a left drawer, stick it in Manuel, and roll the knob on the right. And then I type: I'm an 'ucking cliché. I stare at my words for a long time before I come to the conclusion: there are worse things to be. And what if there weren't. What if I lived some pristine-ass life? What would I have to say?

Two weeks have passed, and my man is still waiting at Port Authority. He survived the lunatic-with-the-gun incident, although it was a close call and not without casualties. Everything in his orbit is frozen until I decide what happens next. I think about how I can't freeze my own orbit; then I realize that if I could, I'd never grow old. Nothing new would ever happen. I wouldn't be able to take Dylan Thomas's advice and "rage against the dying of the light." Then I remember: he died at thirty-nine and didn't take his own advice either. He soaked in the whole of his dysfunction and drowned in drink.

    I think maybe I'd be okay with that, but I've yet to produce work that will survive without my living form. Hell, what I've written can barely breathe along with me. Maybe I should think about getting sober so I can accomplish something. So I can be loved. The more I think about it, maybe it's not such a bad idea. I'm actually liking it. The fewer brain cells I kill, the more that are left to soak up life in other ways.

    My guy in Port Authority isn't waiting for me. He's hungry and heads for the diner inside the terminal. It's a big room. Every table is full. He sees an overweight suit get up. He can't wait for the dishes to be cleared, or someone else will take the seat. He grabs the still-warm red leather stool at the counter. In no time at all, the dirty dishes are gone, and someone is wiping down the counter. Holy fuck. That someone is my guy's first love … the one that got away when he was twenty-something … now here she is, working at a Port Authority diner. She's not looking too bad, either. Sure, she's put on a few pounds, but she's well-groomed with just the right amount of voluptuous. Her blond hair is pulled back, but even so, he envisions it long and flowing over her big breasts. He still has a vivid memory of what they look like in the flesh.

    Soon as she sees him, her eyes light up and twinkle—like little miniature hearts are gonna float out of them and circle her head. There's some bitchin' chemistry going down. They're crazy happy to see one another, and people around them are noticing. So now, I'm trying to figure out how I want to pull her into the story. Do I want to give him a third option? I'm not sure. Maybe I'll just let him get laid a couple of times … to this married woman he's loved and hasn't seen for nearly forty years. I put everything in my mental pot and stir. I turn up the heat so my thoughts boil over and make a mess on the stove. Then, the trick is whether I want to clean up the slop or let it transmute into something else.

Thing is, no matter how much I think about him and everything his brain is wrassling with, I know he's going to choose that tour in Europe. Tortured as fuck, back in love, and riddled with guilt, but he'll go. I know this because when it comes down to it, whether it's a person's weakness or just the nature of any given beast, people most always go back to what they know the best. They just do. Good or bad. It's fucked, but that's a human being for you.

And hell, I need a drink.

SPARKLE

Aiden checked his image in the mirror that hung over the sink. His dark-blond hair was neatly combed to one side, and his navy-and-white-striped shirt was carefully tucked into his jeans. He stared defiantly at himself. *Does it really matter what you look like?*

Answering his own question, feeling a rush of self-loathing, he looked down and walked out into the room that was as threadbare as his optimism. As if it were a daily ritual, he sat on the edge of the bed, checked his watch, then glanced at the door. He held out his hands to inspect the nails he had just cut. They hadn't grown back in the fifteen minutes since his manicure. And they were still clean.

Even though he had been expecting a visitor, he jumped when a soft knock at the door broke the silence. Standing, he took a breath, then walked over to the door.

Aiden opened it and let the young blond woman in the short black skirt inside. *She can't be a day over eighteen, if that.* "Hello, I'm John …." *Holy fuck, why did I use that name?* "Why don't you take a seat?"

"Where do you want me to sit?" She looked around the room. "On the bed?"

"Uh … oh … no." Aiden pointed to an old upholstered chair on the opposite side of the small room. "How about there? It's shabby chic, in keeping with the hotel décor."

A faint smile appeared on her lips, then vanished as she sat. Self-conscious about what she was wearing, Aiden watched as she struggled to cross her legs appropriately. He hurried into the bathroom, grabbed a thin white towel, then rushed out to hand it to her. "Here. Uh, maybe you want to put this on your lap; I think you'll feel more comfortable." *It will make me feel more comfortable, too.*

"Do you always call for whores and then cover them up? Don't you want to see what's between my legs? Don't you want to ogle me and stare while your tongue wags or something?" She stuck her tongue out of the side of her mouth and moved it back and forth as crudely as she could.

"I just—"

"Wanna fuck without the foreplay? What? Say it, dude, because the time you're wasting is your own. You got that?"

"I'm fine with this arrangement."

"Seriously?"

"Yeah. Uh … I'm a kinky bastard. I get off on seeing a towel across a girl's lap. You know, so I can imagine what's under it."

She sighed in exasperation. "I can fucking show you, dude."

"No," Aiden said, his voice louder. "Please, just cover yourself with the towel."

Trying to hide her relief, she complied as Aiden sat on the edge of the bed. "Yeah, okay."

"What's your name?"

"Sparkle."

"Spar … oh, that's the name you use for—"

She thought for a moment. "It does sound like a whore name, doesn't it? But it's actually my real name. My mom said my eyes sparkled the first time she looked into them. She never considered what people would think … maybe she just knew that she'd be a whore someday, and I would too." She stared at him. "Don't you get all warm and fuzzy from that story?"

Aiden tried to hide his discomfiture. "I think it's a charming name, actually. You can't have been doing this for long."

"Actually … this is my first time." Sparkle fidgeted with the large rings that sat awkwardly on her fingers. "I know that sounds like bullshit, but it's true. I have no reason to lie."

"I believe you. And you know what will really sound like a lie?"

"What?"

"This is my first time … you know … calling for someone … ever." Aiden reached into his pocket and pulled out the cash he had ready. Standing, he walked over and handed it to her. "Here you go. Can we just talk? Would that be okay?"

She pulled the towel away to gauge his reaction. "You sure you don't want any of this? Tight and juicy."

"No, I really don't," Aiden said, averting his gaze. "Can you please put the towel back on your lap? I just want to talk to you. Is that okay?"

She looked at the money, then at him. "Yeah, I guess."

"I thought you'd be happy about that."

"I am. But … if I have to do this … if there has to be a first time, I thought it would be better with a clean-cut guy like yourself."

"You don't have to do this with *anyone*," Aiden said, sitting down again.

Sparkle said nothing and looked down at the towel protecting her modesty.

"I mean it. You don't."

"Yeah, whatever." She looked around the room. "So, what do you wanna talk about? Or do you just want me to listen? I'm a cheap whore, not a mind reader."

"Don't call yourself that!"

"Why not? Isn't that exactly what you ordered?"

"Yes … no … um … not really. I don't know."

"You always so wishy-washy, dude?"

"No, but we've just met."

"You know," Sparkle said, leaning forward. "Let me school you. When you come into a strange neighborhood and call for a whore, you're gonna get someone you 'just met.' What part of that is too fucking deep for you?"

"I know. I sound a bit strange," he said, resisting the temptation to get up and walk over to her.

"Hey, if that's your thing, say as much weird shit as you want."

Aiden steeled himself. "What I'd really like to say to you is this: I can help you if you let me."

"Oh, please! Who are you? Some ghetto superhero? No. You can't help me," Sparkle said, looking suspiciously at him. "And how come you don't want to be with me? Just curious is all."

Aiden felt his face redden. "You're way too young. And you remind me of someone … it doesn't matter. I'm really not game to be with anyone."

"But you called for a hooker!" Sparkle looked around the room. "Do you go out to dinner when you're not hungry, too? Take your car to the gas station when your tank is full?"

"You're right. That sounded pretty stupid. I'm recently divorced, and I haven't been with anyone in a long time. My head isn't in a place to get involved, but—"

"Your dick is."

Embarrassed, Aiden looked down, then met her eyes. "No, not really. I had a momentary lapse of clarity. Even if you were older, I would have changed my mind. The best part of sex is intimacy; you can't have that with a stranger."

"I thought that's what most men try to avoid."

Aiden attempted to laugh. "You're wise. May I ask how old you are?"

"Nineteen on my next birthday." Sparkle removed a large ring from her index finger that was bothering her and stuck it in the small purse she was holding. "So what made you come down this way … to the armpit of humanity? Didn't wanna run into anyone you know?"

Aiden stood, walked to the window, and looked outside. "A couple of decades ago, I lived down here. It was a pretty happening place then. Still run-down, but kind of artsy. I have some very special memories from that time."

Making a face, Sparkle looked defiantly at him. "Oh … how special … and so you wanted to re-create them by paying for—"

"No, no!" Aiden leaned against the wall. "I could never re-create those times. They're gone. Down the drain of life. But I suppose I never stop thinking about them … that's why I'm here. I'm just empty right now. Searching. Don't you think it is human nature to go back to what you know?"

"Fuck no!" Sparkle said. "I'd like to get away from pretty near everything and everyone I know and go far away. You may have gravitated back to this hellhole, but not me. Not if I had my way."

Aiden began to walk toward her, but seeing her instinctively lean back, he sat on the bed again. "Can you tell me something about yourself, Sparkle?" He looked at the torment in her eyes. "I can't believe there are no options for you."

"Not if I don't care about seeing my mom and my baby sister killed."

Agitated, Aiden ran his fingers through his hair. "You said earlier that your mother … um … that she did this kind of work."

"You can say it. She's a whore, too. And her pimp of a boyfriend beats the shit out of her. He's hit me, too. Hasn't hit my little sis yet, and I'm trying to make sure he never does. That's why I'm here. If I don't do this, he said he'll kill both of them. Not to mention anyone he thinks I care about."

Aiden sighed. "I don't mean to sound like I'm reaching into the plot of some feel-good movie, but couldn't you put your heads together and plan an escape? Move to another area? Another state? There must be times when he's not around, right?"

"Yeah, there are. What of it?"

"So have you thought about doing that? Planning an escape when he's gone?"

Sparkle shook her head in despair. "You try dragging an addict away from her drugs and see how far you get."

"Oh, I see." Aiden pressed the palm of his hand to his forehead, as if doing so would give him answers. "I hate to ask this, but where's your father?"

"Dead. That's where."

"I'm sorry. Was he a good man?"

"You'll have to ask someone who knew him. But I guess. He wasn't a coward; I know that. Back when she was pregnant with me, he and my mom were out walking one night when someone tried to rob them. This guy lunged right at my mom for her purse, calling her all kinds of ugly names. My dad got so scared that he would hurt my mom—and me—that he fought back hard, trying to keep the guy off her. That's when the guy's scumbag friend came along, and the two of them beat my dad to death. Right in front of my mom's eyes. She freaked her shit right into drug addiction. When I was seven, I went into the system. I was in foster care for five years, but then she got clean, and this judge made me go me back when I was twelve. I had a nice foster family, unlike some other kids. I really wanted to stay. Anyway, my mom got pregnant again. She started using again after my sis was born, said that taking care of a baby was too *stressful* for her. So, I couldn't go back to foster care because I didn't want to be separated from my sister. I had to protect her. She needs me, John, or whatever the fuck your real name is."

"It's Aiden. Really. Aiden. And I'm so sorry to hear this. Do you have any other family?"

"Nope. My mom's parents are dead. I only have a grandmother."

"Where does she live?"

"In a frame."

"Like an A-frame house?"

"No, like in a picture frame that sits on the table by my bed. She's my dad's mother. She's only like thirty-eight in the photo, so if I saw her on the street, I'd never recognize her. But my mom said she lives far away."

"Do you know your dad's name?"

Sparkle blew air threw her lips in frustration. "My mom told me it was John. Man, you liars aren't very clever."

"I didn't mean to lie, Sparkle. I just panicked in the moment."

"Yeah … well, my mom hasn't changed her story."

"John is a popular name. Maybe that really was his name."

Rolling her eyes, Sparkle glared at him. "No way. When I first asked, she said it real fast, just like you did, and it was obvious that was the first name she could think of."

"Did she tell you your grandmother's name?"

"Yeah. Mary. Like I said, not a clever liar."

"What's your mom's name?"

Sparkle tensed. "Seriously, who are you? A freakin' cop? You're asking me too many damn questions. If you wanna talk away your fuck time, that's fine with me. But I don't have to answer any more questions."

"I'm not a cop," Aiden told her. "And I certainly am not going to arrest you and read your Miranda rights to you."

"Who's Miranda Wright? The last whore you called and didn't wanna fuck, either?"

"No … Miranda means … never mind. Really, I'm not a cop."

"And I'm just supposed to take your word for it?"

Pulling his wallet out of his pocket, Aiden held it out to her. "You are welcome to inspect my wallet. You'll see that my name is Aiden Welsh and that I have no connection to the police or any other authority. I work in real estate. You can check out my card. I like to paint watercolors and I rescue dogs. But I have no written proof of that."

Sparkle dismissed him with the wave of her hand. "Put that thing back in your pants … I mean, put your wallet away … whatever … wherever you want it. Shit."

Aiden stood and put his wallet back in his pocket. "S-sorry. I just wanted you to know I'm on the level."

"Jade," Sparkle blurted out.

"What? What about jade?"

Irritated, she took the rest of the rings off her fingers and threw them into the purse. "My mom's name. It's Jade."

"Oh, okay."

"Sparkle, is there anyone out there that you can talk to? Anyone at all?"

She looked away, as if to hide her emotion.

"Well?"

Straightening in the chair, she looked at him. "Just my grandmother. I talk to her photo all the time and pretend that she's with me in real life. My mom said she was more like a mom to her than her own parents. That's why she gave me her picture. It was like she thought a photo could give me what she couldn't. But you know … in a weird kind of way, it has. I can tell her anything at all, and I never have to worry about him hurting her. I even got a copy of the photo made and put the real photo somewhere he'll never find it. That's in case he ever tries to destroy the photo … knowing what it means to me and all."

"That's very clever."

"I guess. What's that people say about when you need to do stuff—it's a mother?"

Aiden wrinkled his brow. "Oh, right. 'Necessity is the mother of invention.'"

"Yeah, that!"

"It's true. I first really became aware of that when I learned about all of the clever ways people escaped East Berlin."

"You mean when they had that wall up?"

"Exactly."

"Give me an example."

"Well, people would take all of the stuffing out of a car seat, then insert themselves where the stuffing used to be. Clearly, only the smaller, thinner people could do this, but it was pretty ingenious. When a car would pass through the border, it would look like it was just the driver and an empty seat."

Sparkle looked amazed. "Wow, I would have never thought a person could hide under an empty seat."

"But they did. When you're desperate, you become all the more clever."

"I'm pretty desperate," Sparkle said sullenly. "So how come I'm here. How come I haven't been able to figure out more than how to hide a photo?"

Aiden fought his urge to get up and comfort her. "Because you've been threatened ... you've been hit .... I *hate* that he's hurt you. You're worried about the people you love. Sometimes, that kind of fear is so stuck in your brain that you can't get past it .... I used to have friends in this neighborhood. They're all gone now. There was one guy in particular, the brother of a close friend. I'll bet he could stop this guy. Somebody has to stop him and help your mother. I just met you, Sparkle, but I can't let you leave to become a prostitute and live in the home of a man who beats your mother ... and you. Or who threatens your little sister."

Sparkle bit her lip to stop herself from crying. "What are you going to do? You're a nice guy and everything, but this stuff happens everywhere ... all the time. People know about it, and what the hell can they do?"

"I don't know what the hell they do; I've never been in a position to think about it before. But I'm determined to find out."

Pulling off the bangle bracelets she had on, Sparkle stuffed them in the bag with her rings. "This is my mother's whore jewelry. I hate it." Crossing her legs in a lotus position, the towel still covering her, she looked at Aiden. "So, I guess this would be a good time for the mother of invention to show herself. You know, my mom is real skinny. Maybe I could knock her out with pills and make car-seat stuffing out of her. Just long enough to get her far away from here."

Aiden smiled. "Doesn't your mom have any friends who are upset by what is going on?"

"Get real. Any friends she has are as fucked up and scared as she is. When I was young, she used to talk about people she knew, but she said they're all in another solar system now."

"I'm sure."

"Why do you have that weird look on your face?"

"Do I?" Aiden asked. "I guess that's my thinking-hard look. I know a lot of people: lawyers, cops, doctors … I'm trying to figure out who I can call that might have an idea. I can't let you get into this life. Or your sister."

"I don't believe in good guys."

"I can understand that. I'm far from perfect, but I like to think of myself as a good guy. Can you just try to trust me? Just a little?"

Sparkle stared curiously at him. "You do seem like you really care … but so do pimps when you first meet them. This better not be some bullshit act."

"It's not, Sparkle. I promise you. I hate the idea of *any* woman selling herself. I don't even know how they do it. I guess like anything, one becomes desensitized, but no human being should be for sale. It's horrible. It's barbaric. Demoralizing."

Sparkle's eyes narrowed as she considered his words. "I pretty much suck at math, but it doesn't take a genius to know that something isn't adding up here."

"What do you mean?"

"I've got really good bullshit radar. It's how I survive. And my gut tells me you're really a decent guy. I wouldn't have told you jack if I didn't feel that way."

"So what's the problem?"

"The problem is why you're here in the first place. If you hate that women have to work as whores, why would you come down here to hire one? You said that even if I was older, you would've probably changed your mind. See, here's the thing … Aiden. A guy who feels like you do wouldn't have even come *this close* to being with one." Sparkle held her index finger and thumb together until they nearly touched to illustrate her point.

Aiden looked at her as he considered her words.

"What? Nothing? Seems even the mother of invention can't come up with a quick answer?"

"Guess not."

"That's it? That's all you've got to say."

Aiden stood and walked over to a bag on the side of the bed he'd brought with him. "I need a drink of water. I've got an extra bottle here. Would you like it?"

Sparkle looked suspiciously at him. "It's not laced with anything, is it? It better not be."

Picking up the two bottles of water, Aiden walked over to her. "You can choose either bottle you want, and I'll drink from the other one first. How's that?"

Taking a bottle from him, Sparkle cracked the cap. "Not necessary. I believe you, but there's something you're not telling me, and I really want to know what it is."

Aiden returned to the edge of the bed and took a long drink of water. "I needed that."

"So," Sparkle said, "who do I remind you of?"

"What?"

"You said you didn't want to be with me because I was too young, and I reminded you of someone. Like an ex-girlfriend?"

Aiden looked embarrassed. "No, actually. Like someone in my family."

"Oh, that's gross. But that still doesn't explain why you hauled your ass down here in the first place."

"I had a reason. I did. But it seems insignificant after meeting you and knowing the situation you're in. Right now, nothing is as important to me as helping you get out of this. Nothing. And I mean that."

Sparkle took a drink of water, then put the cap back on the bottle. "See, Aiden, here's the thing …." Clutching her throat, Sparkle groaned as her eyes went crazy and her body appeared to convulse. "Ahhhhhhh!"

"Jesus!" Aiden said, jumping up and running over to her. "What the hell? Are you choking? Having a seizure?"

Flailing her arms, her groans got louder as Aiden gripped her shoulders. "Sparkle! Holy shit! I'm calling 911. What happened? Just stay with me, okay?"

Sparkle groaned again and then abruptly stopped. Taking hold of his hands, she removed them from her shoulders. "I'm fine. Go back to the edge of the bed."

Expelling a long breath, Aiden stood and stared at her. "Did you just fake that?"

"Yeah … maybe."

Baffled, Aiden walked over to the bed and sat down. "Why in the hell would you do something like that?"

"I wanted to see if you would be surprised or not. If you had poisoned me, you wouldn't have panicked."

"Oh for Chrissake!" Aiden said. "That's ridiculous. If I had, it would be too late to even see my reaction. Besides, what made you assume I used a fast-acting poison? Maybe I laced the water with something that will put you to sleep an hour from now. Did you think about that?"

"Nah. I won't be here in an hour. You would have done it this way."

"Okay, you win. Can you pick it up from where you were … if you can even remember after that performance you just gave. I don't suppose you care that you nearly gave me a heart attack."

"You're young. I wasn't worried." Sparkle smirked. "I was just messing with you. This is heavy shit. I needed a break. Anyway, I was saying … in order for me to trust you with my life, I can't have any unanswered questions because they stick in my side like red-hot pokers. And until I get the fuckers out, I can't focus on squat. And that's how it is for me. So, if you really want to help me like you say you do, you'll be straight up with me … like right now. And if you can't be, then I can't trust you and I need to haul *my* ass outta here."

Aiden stared at her. "You really are smart."

Sparkle cocked her head to one side and stared at him for a moment. "Don't try to suck up to me saying shit like that. Of course I'm smart. Like there was any doubt."

"No, never any doubt. Just stating the obvious, I guess."

"Talk, dude."

Aiden took another sip of water. "Okay, so everything I said about being divorced; that's true. And what I said about not being ready for a new relationship, true as well. But see, after I split with my wife, I started thinking about the real love of my life. Her name was Joanna, and I met her in this neighborhood, back when it was more of an arts community than anything else. She had an amazing voice, maybe could have sang opera professionally, but she never got the training. Tough childhood. And I was going to be some great artist. We were really in love and then she started changing."

"Like how."

"Oh, like disappearing on me. Lying. Acting strange."

"So you took off?"

"No, actually, I didn't. I did everything I could to find out what was happening and one day she told me to go away and never come near her again. I told her I wasn't leaving, and she said she didn't love me anymore, had someone else, and after a week of hearing her say that, I finally believed her. And I left."

"So you're back here now for what?" Sparkle twisted the cap off the bottle and took another drink. "You said everyone you knew from here moved away."

"I thought she had. Maybe she did. I don't know. But about a week ago, a friend of mine, who works in commercial real estate, came down this way to look at a space. He used to live in this neighborhood back when I did. He said that he stopped into a bar before heading home and saw this woman … you know … in the life … and he caught her staring at him … but she turned away fast when he saw her. And he is very sure she was Joanna."

Sparkle stared incredulously at him. "That doesn't make sense."

"What? What doesn't make sense?"

"Nothing," she said, looking away, as if she were in a trance.

"No, something's tweaked you," Aiden insisted. "What is it? You look absolutely spooked. Like the color left your face and took a walk."

"That's just stupid. I'm not tweaked, spooked, or anything else." Sparkle recovered, turning to face him again. "Just when you said that about your friend thinking he saw your ex, well, that reminded me how sometimes I think I see my foster sister, Megan. But it's never her. I just want it to be. Even though people are alive, I think they still have ghosts, and those ghosts follow us sometimes. So I guess what I said earlier wasn't completely true. I would like to go back to my past. At least a part of it."

"You continue to impress me," Aiden told her.

"And you continue to change the subject," Sparkle said. "And that kind of shit makes me nervous."

Aiden leaned forward. "I'm not trying to do that. Honestly. What I just said, about my friend seeing Joanna—that's why I'm here."

"You want to save her like you want to save me."

"Yes, I do. Do you know her?"

"No. And if I looked confused, that's why. I know pretty much everyone in this neighborhood, and I don't know one single person who goes by that name."

"Maybe she's changed it."

"I'm not the name police. So I wouldn't know."

"Would you mind looking at a photo?" Aiden asked.

Sparkle stiffened. "You don't want to help me. You want to use me to help *her*, don't you? This nice-guy routine has all been bullshit to get me to trust you."

"No," Aiden said. "I promise, it has not been. There's no limit on how many people I can help. I'd help every last person here if I had the wherewithal. Would you mind ... will you just look at a photo for me?"

"Yeah, okay ... whatever."

Aiden took his wallet out, carefully pulling an old color photo out. He stood and walked over to Sparkle. "This is the two of us. Taken at a friend's twenty-first birthday party. I think we were at our happiest here. But she broke up with me six months later."

Sparkle stared at the photo for a long time, her eyes glazed over, as if she had returned to her earlier trance-like state. After a long minute, a slight tremble in her voice, she handed the photo back to him. "You're freaking me out, dude."

"Sorry! That's the last thing I want to do." Seeing her distress,

Aiden walked back to the bed and sat down.

Sparkle stared at him for several moments before speaking again. "Remember I told you about the photo I have of my grandmother?"

"Of course. You can't possibly have it with you."

"No. Like I said. It's by my bed."

Confused, Aiden looked at her. "Okay ...."

"But I have a picture of it on my phone. That way, I never go anywhere without my grandma to talk to." She laughed. "Not your typical whore, am I?"

"Please don't call yourself ... that's beautiful," Aiden said. "What a wonderful thing to do. Of course you would do that."

"I want to show it to you." For the first time, Sparkle took the towel off her lap, got up from the chair, and walked over to Aiden, feeling even more self-conscious about her attire than before. Reaching into her purse, she pulled out her phone. She swiped the screen and quickly found the photo. Enlarging it, so that the woman's face filled the screen, she handed it to Aiden. "This is my grandmother."

Sparkle studied Aiden's face as shock washed over it. She watched his hands as he tried to steady them, but instead, dropped the phone, then looked up at her in disbelief.

"You know," she said, watching his reaction closely. "I just remembered— like a second ago. A couple times, when I was young, I was out with my mom, and people called out to her. They didn't call her Jade. They called her Joanna. And both times, my mom grabbed me and left wherever we were. I asked her who Joanna was, and she told me she was someone she used to know. She said that person didn't exist anymore. I thought that meant she had a friend who had died. I swear, I just remembered. Man, the brain is a really weird thing ... the way it hides shit away from us and makes us think we've forgotten it. And then bam!"

Aiden didn't try to fight the tears that welled in his eyes as he watched the tears well up in Sparkle's. "That beautiful lady in the photo you just showed me ... your grandmother. She's my mother. Her name is Amaryllis, like the flower. She's in her sixties now, but still youthful and every bit as beautiful. And you know what—my father used to call her Mary."

"Oh ..."

Reaching into his wallet, Aiden pulled out another photo. This was taken just three years ago, on her sixtieth birthday. See, there's the two of us."

Sparkle took the photo from him and cradled it in her hand. "Oh ... that's her! I thought I wouldn't recognize her so many years later, but I do. I would have known her anywhere. I would have. This means ... that maybe I don't have a father who was killed on the street. I hope my mom made the whole thing up. I hope nobody got murdered like that." She was determined not to let her emotions best her facade. "I don't know what the fuck to believe. At least she cared enough to make him a good guy." She stared at Aiden, examining his features. "You and I have the same nose. Totally. This is some surreal shit. I don't understand any of it."

Aiden looked at her. "We do have the same nose ... Sparkle, when I tell you I had no idea Joanna was pregnant ... I mean that. She always used to tell me she would never do anything to ruin my life. I guess she thought being a father was something that would ... but it wouldn't have. It definitely wouldn't have. I swear to you. Her own father was such a monster; I thought maybe everything was just jumbled up in her brain."

Sparkle stared past him, lost in thought. After a moment, her eyes focused on him. "This is freaking me out."

"Please ... don't let it."

"I believe you. But if my mother dumped you like you say, it wasn't because she didn't wanna ruin your life. Not exactly. It was the drugs. She started doing them when she was pregnant with me." She paused. "Where does your mother live?"

"Out west … in California. Would you like to meet her?"

"Of course I would," Sparkle said. "But that's only gonna happen in some fairy tale. I can't leave—"

"We'll figure something out. We will. And I think you'll find she's every bit as easy to talk to as the photo is. She's rock solid, as they say."

"Not too judgmental?"

"Not at all," Aiden said. I hope you don't mind me asking … but can I have a hug?"

"I guess." She looked uneasy. "I'm not feeling all huggly wuggly and shit like you are. But since you paid for it."

Aiden put up his palm. "If you're only going to hug me for that reason, then let's not. I mean that. Absolutely not!"

"No. It's okay." Sparkle softened. "We can hug."

Aiden smiled, then threw his arms around her and held her for a very long time. When they pulled apart, they just looked at each other.

"My mom really loved your mom. I'll bet she still does."

"That's true," Aiden said. "She did. And speaking of mothers, I think that now, the mother of invention is going to come up with a really great plan for all of us."

"I have to go soon," Sparkle said. "He'll come looking for me if I don't come back in time. I doubt if the mother of invention works that fast."

"Have a seat, honey," Aiden said, indicating the edge of the bed. "She works as fast as she has to. I know what to do now. I just need to make some phone calls. Hang tight."

Sparkle sat down. "You know, I didn't say this before because I really thought I was losing my smarts … my streets smarts … my bullshit radar. I never trusted any man in my entire life. Never. And I kept trying not to trust you but something in me just did. I'm even smarter than I thought. Or dumber. I hope not."

Aiden laughed heartily. "Your grandmother is going to love you, Sparkle. And your dad already does."

As if she had been conked on the head by a baseball bat and was merely watching little stars dance around her in confusion, she stopped, struggling to maintain her breath. "And they all lived happily ever after. And the delusional king thought he could save the princess, but the palace pimp killed them all."

"No," Aiden said, swiping his phone as he got ready to make a call. "I will find a way. I have friends."

Sparkle shifted to face him. "You really think you can round up these guys, and they'll come up with a master plan in the next half hour? No. They won't! Put the phone down."

Aiden clutched the phone tightly as Sparkle stood. "Put the fucking phone down. Don't give me this, 'your-dad-already-does' shit. Man, hearing you say that totally blew my mind. Right back to reality! Sorry, but people's lives don't go from being a whore with training wheels to being some fucking suburban daddy's girl like that." Sparkle snapped her fingers. "No way. Good shit doesn't happen to me or to many other people. Not like this. I don't know who you are or how you set me up like this, but I'm not buying any of it."

"I'm not setting anything up," Aiden said, his eyes pleading with her to believe him. "And I think you know that. You're just afraid to let your guard down. Look, you're the one who brought your grandmother into the conversation. I showed you a photo of your mom and me. Then you showed me your grandmother's photo. And only then did I show you a recent photo of my mother. I couldn't set something like this up if my life were at stake. This is real. You're smart; you know that. Why doesn't this make sense to you? I came down to this neighborhood to find your mother. And I found you instead. It was meant to be. I'm sure of it. Please, if you could just find a way to let Joanna see me … you'd believe me. Even if she denies ever knowing me, you'll see the truth in her reaction … in her eyes. I know you will."

Sparkle covered her ears with both hands. "Stop! Just stop! And what kind of man carries his mom's photo in his wallet?"

"Oh, just a guy who has a great mother who he wishes lived closer. A sap. A loving son. Take your pick. But not a liar. And certainly not a con artist."

"I'm leaving," Sparkle said. "Something's out of whack, and I don't have time to figure out what it is."

"What's out of whack is that you've been deprived of the good life you deserve. And you're not used to things going well. Optimism is as rare for you as a life without fear. That's what you're feeling," Aiden said, standing. "I can't let you walk out of here. What can I do to convince you to let me get help? How about if I set up a video call with your grandmother? You can talk to her. She'll tell you everything."

"Stop! And sit the fuck down. I can't think when you talk shit."

Reluctantly, Aiden sat down. "Don't throw—"

"Don't throw it all away! Don't throw *us* away. We've only just met. We've already lost over eighteen years. We can't lose a minute more!" Sparkle resumed pacing. "Is that the touchy-feely bullshit you were going to spew all over me? Well, there, I said it for you so there's no need." She walked over to the window and looked down. "I'm sure you're familiar with that hellhole of a diner below. Well, he's probably waiting there for me. He's probably got my little sister at home watching my mom for him. And if you're thinking they'd make a run for it while he's gone, you're delusional. My sister wouldn't think of doing anything because he tells her he's gonna kill me and her mom if she even thinks about it. Poor kid doesn't deserve this."

"Neither do you!"

"No, I don't, but I can't stay here and let you try to pull me into some fantasy world while we all get killed by your bogus-ass hope. If I don't get down there, he'll come looking for me."

"Let him!" Aiden said.

"Oh my God," Sparkle cried. "Are you a special kind of stupid or what? Do you really think you can go up against an angry pimp with a gun and live to tell about it? And even if you got someone else to do it, do you really think he wouldn't retaliate by killing me, my mom, or my sister? You have no clue. Those friends you want to call …." Sparkle nodded in the direction of his phone. "They're probably bigger clowns than you. Just stay the fuck away. You'll get us all killed. Go rescue some dogs. They don't have gun-toting pimps!"

"L-look," Aiden stammered. "Maybe things have changed down here, and I've got some learning to do. But my friends, trust me—they know their way around. I have every faith in them."

Sparkled glared at him. "Stay. The. Fuck. Away. Have all the faith you want. Just don't expect me to."

"No, please! Don't you think that it's a miracle that we found one another? What are the chances that my friend saw your mother, told me about it, and that I came down here only to meet you? I don't see that as a coincidence. Like I said a minute ago. It was meant to be. I see that as a miracle. You should, too."

Sparkle folded her arms and scowled at him. "Let me clue you in. First, tell me how you hired me. And don't leave anything out."

"Okay … um … after I checked in here, I went to the bar where my friend said he saw Joanna. I asked the bartender how I might hire a … um … you know. He didn't give me a number or anything. Just said he'd arrange things and where did I want to meet her. I gave him this room number, and he made a call. Came back, gave me a price, and told me someone would be here in an hour. And in just that amount of time, you came to the door."

"Yeah, well, my mom and her friend were the only whores you could have hired from that dump. Except my mom's friend—well, she fucking OD'd two weeks ago—dead on the fucking street, her head in the gutter with bugs crawling in her hair and outta her mouth and nose. And that freaked my mom so bad she started getting too messed up to work. Right now, she's passed out in bed. Otherwise, you would have seen her for yourself. Isn't that what you were hoping? Isn't that why you got a room first? Because you thought you might have to hire her to even talk to her?"

"Yes, exactly. And when I didn't see her, after hanging around for an hour, that's when I spoke with the bartender." Aiden put his hand to his throat as if to dislodge the words that were stuck there.

Sparkle frowned. "So, I guess the real miracle—praise be!—is that my own biological daddy jump-started my whore career. See, I don't know if Fuckface ever planned to make me work in the life. But today, when he had a john and no whores available, that's when he had to do some quick thinking and came to the quick conclusion that today I would 'pop my whore cherry.' See, John, necessity is the mother of invention."

"No, no, no, no, no!" Aiden swallowed. "That makes me so sick!"

"Yeah, well, it doesn't do much for me. Ya know."

"Sparkle, I didn't mean—"

"Just let me finish!"

"Sorry, please go on."

"See, it's not like there are fifty fillies in his stable. He only has six women, and the other four work in a different neighborhood … maybe thirty-five minutes away. People who live here are dirt poor … most of them. A porn magazine and a free hand is all they need. As for the johns who come to this hotel, they're mostly men who are too chickenshit to play nasty in their own backyards. So they slither on down here, hoping nobody will recognize their asses."

"And your … this man, this pimp, this goddamned bastard … the pig you call 'Fuckface—' has no control over the women who work out of this building?"

"Nope. There are only three of them, and their friends would snuff his ass out in a nanosecond if he even tried to *think* about doing that. The one who works most often is this tall black lady with bright red hair. She's just the nicest person ever; I don't even know why she does this. People say she never touches drugs. And that she's got three little grandchildren." Sparkle paused to think. "I might have heard that her daughter is kind of a mess and so she does this to help the kids. I sure hope not. I guess she's just used to making a living this way. Pays more than any other job around here. She and a couple of friends of hers pretty much get all the business. So, Fuckface only has a tiny piece of the whore pie. But years ago, before that big warehouse was abandoned, this neighborhood was a gold mine for him. No more, though. So you see, it's no miracle that you ended up with me when you hired a whore from the bar. A sick cosmic joke, maybe, but not any damn miracle. Got that?"

Aiden, self-conscious that he was fiddling with his hands, locked his fingers together and rested them on his lap. "Oh, Jesus. Well, um … maybe it was just a miracle that my friend just happened to go into the bar when Joanna was there."

Sparkle walked over to the window again, looked down, then strode back over to Aiden. "Not even close. She practically lives in that place because he manages it. And let me tell you, a clueless suburban dude on an imaginary white horse isn't any kind of miracle. The kind of miracle I need, my mom, my sister, and I all need, doesn't just show up in this kind of neighborhood. Just like Santa Claus doesn't come here either—or the fucking Easter Bunny."

"But—"

"But nothing. The fact that we share DNA doesn't change squat. Don't try to help me. You'll only fuck it up and get us all killed. Celebrate your cluelessness. Go back to the suburbs and have a glass of champagne. Life will be easier. Just forget about me. And my mom."

Aiden felt nauseated as sweat dripped from his brow. "I can't do that, and I certainly don't want to be clueless. Just let me help. I don't want you to do this, and I don't want your mother to OD like her friend did."

"Fuckface told me he's taking care of that, and she's gonna be okay. Which is why I have to take her place. Didn't you hear what I said?"

Aiden balled his left hand and pounded the bed. "Let me help! Please! I promise, I won't do anything stupid."

"You already have." She paused to look at him. "I'm going now."

He stood and called after her as she headed for the door and turned the knob. "Please! I'm begging you. Don't go. Please, Sparkle!"

She turned and gave him one last look. "You didn't really buy that bullshit about Sparkle being my name, did you? I just made that shit up on the spot, John. Like father, like daughter." Opening the door, she walked out and slammed it behind her.

Aiden stared at the door. Every crack in the wood seemed to speak to him, to remind him out that life is fragile, and hope is elusive … nonexistent for some. He put his hand on the doorknob, held it there for a moment, then took it away. Sullen and defeated, he walked over to the window. He looked out over the tops of buildings. In the distance, he could make out a woman hanging laundry. Another woman came onto the rooftop and said something to her. She dropped the clothes she was holding and ran toward the exit door. Aiden wondered what the emergency was and hoped nobody was in danger. He let his mind disengage as he stared at the abandoned laundry.

A few minutes later, he looked down. She was leaning against the brick wall next to the diner. Her defenses were gone. Tears streamed down her face.

"Sparkle," he cried softly. "Sparkle …"

THURSDAY, WRAPPED IN SADNESS

Today I found out that my mother died … two years ago.

We were estranged for the worst of reasons. Ten years ago, at age twenty-nine, I summoned up the courage to tell her the awful secret I had carried with me throughout my childhood: my father had routinely and brutally abused me. Because he was a serial philanderer with a wicked temper, I was confident she would believe me. I was certain that the moment I uncaged the truth, the disparate pieces would fit together. Repressed memories, confusing fragments of words and time—everything that once perplexed or possibly frightened her would become clear. My mother would hold me tight, tell me how sorry she was, and never let me go.

After making the agonizing decision to unfurl the past, I carefully chose what I hoped would be the right time. She had just celebrated her sixty-second birthday three weeks before. I waited, what I considered to be a respectable amount of time, so that my long-anticipated disclosure would not be associated with the anniversary of her birth. I was living with my boyfriend, about forty-five minutes from my parents' house, and I called to ask if I could come over and speak to her. Just before we hung up, she told me my tone sounded ominous. I wondered if she already knew. But I still had great optimism that everything would go as planned. My father, a restaurant manager, was "out of town on business." I wouldn't be telling her that my boyfriend's brother had seen him that morning, coming out of this very hotel where I live today. It was nicer then, but not by much.

I think it's rather common knowledge that restaurant managers don't routinely go out of town, if at all. I know she never questioned him because she didn't want any accusation to be the catalyst that ended her marriage. She always said she didn't know how to be alone, which just slayed me because she was alone in every sense.

She looked rather glum when I arrived. "Glumly suspicious" is what I told my boyfriend that night. The usual offering of something to eat or drink was nonexistent. She told me to sit down, even pointing to a specific chair, which she had never done, and told me to come out with it. It was as if she had been expecting the day for years.

With no hesitation, I divulged everything. The words came pouring out of me like a broken dam. In detail, I described how he began coming into my bedroom when I was only ten, late at night, reeking of alcohol … savagely raping me. He would tell me that being the proper orifice for "Mr. Hungry" would be my greatest accomplishment in life. I saw her suppress a gasp when I said that, but she was trying hard to hide her emotions. I explained that I had been diagnosed with PTSD years ago and that unexpected events often triggered my suffering. I gave her specific examples in hopes that doing so would lessen anything that sounded remotely hyperbolic. Perspiration took form on my brow as I spoke, and at times, I trembled. Not only were these actions not intentional, but I tried to suppress them. Everything about me spoke the truth.

She allowed me to speak my piece in its entirety. When I had finished, about fifty minutes later, without so much as a question, a pause, or a look of uncertainty, she branded me a liar. So in love with him, despite who he was and all he had done to her, I was nothing more than a vengeful ingrate plotting to ruin my parents' marriage. Stunned, I asked her why I would want to do such a thing. "Unhappy people want to see other people unhappy." Unable to wrap myself in the warmth of her blanket statement, I plunged into a depressive state. And that was before the rest of my family shunned me.

My younger sister believed I was trying to punish my father for his infidelities at my mother's expense, and hers, especially as she had not suffered any abuse. Suddenly, being a cheater didn't seem so bad; my father was positively virtuous compared to what I was accusing him of having done. My older sister had died in a war-torn country … helping refugees. But she had never suffered any abuse either. Well, not from our father.

My mother told me I was dead to her … to the family. Stone-faced, she asked me to leave immediately and never come back. I really believed that she was tormented by the shock of it all and would change her mind. For four years, I tried to contact her, but the response, or lack thereof, was always the same.

My boyfriend left me about four months after that last meeting with my mother. As he went off into the mist, searching for a drama-free relationship, I wished him well in Utopia and then cried for two weeks straight. As news of his subsequent three failed relationships reached me a year later, I was too numb to rejoice, too over him to care, but nonetheless, a smidge of vindication brightened my spirit … then left me.

Eventually, after taking several odd jobs, I decided to go to night school to get a degree in social work. For years, during the day, I drove senior citizens and disabled people to doctors' appointments, supermarkets, friends' homes, or wherever they needed to go. Before long, people liked me so much that I had become the community cab driver. I made decent money, but I was physically and emotionally spent. Going to school and studying after a long day of driving was tough.

Some days, chatty passengers helped me to forget my family. Other days, human voices could not drown out the pain and the ugly words that played in my head. My discontent was always there, frittering away at my soul, obscuring my identity, and annihilating my sense of self-worth. Maintaining my busy schedule was a struggle. I barely saw my new boyfriend, though somehow we managed to stay together … for a couple of years. Now I know that it was *because* we had so little time together that it lasted as long as it did; I hid my dysfunction well.

In my last year of school, I found a bag of cocaine in the back seat of my car. It must have dropped out of someone's pocket. I put it in *my* pocket … and shortly thereafter … in my nose. It made driving easier and helped me to get through the long nights. Proudly, I graduated after having convinced myself that it was unlikely to happen. I was idiotic and delusional to believe the answer to all of my problems had been left in the back of my car. I thought I was pretty slick. With every snort, I had figured out how to stay awake and better manage my demons. Bloody genius. Yeah right.

My genius, soon demoted to regretful idiocy, informed me that money I'd put away for a much-needed master's degree had been snorted away. Having few choices left, I took an entry-level job at a rehab home for senior citizens, despondent that without additional education, I would never get far in my chosen field. I met lots of wonderful people who became like real parents to me. And then they all died. And every single time, a piece of me died with them. Eventually, I was fired. My employer was kind enough not to mention my drug habit, just the fact that I was unable to handle death in a professional manner. Those weren't her exact words, but they're pretty close. I do not strive to be able to handle death well. It was because of my compassion for others that I chose this field; it is for the same reason I cannot work in it.

When I got fired, six years had elapsed since that day I last saw my mother. I tried again … and failed. Even attempts to contact other family members were rebuffed. I had rained pain on my mother's already miserable existence, and nobody wanted to hear about me or entertain the telling of what they perceived as egregious lies. Some days I believed that a few of them accepted the truth, but that none of them wanted to hurt my mother by admitting that. The end result for me was the same: I had no family.

I was dead inside. At least my older sister had died helping people. I doubted that she had witnessed the ravages of war and terror "professionally."

About a week after I lost my job, a former co-worker got in touch with me and offered his assistance to get me into rehab for my cocaine addiction. I accepted his help, grateful that he had pushed me into something I was too weak to do on my own. My treatment was successful, but I had been too altered to realize that he wanted more from me as repayment for his caring and guidance. When I rejected him, he turned on me. His castigation was ugly enough to push most addicts into using again, but I preferred depression as my drug of choice.

I moved into a room in a house owned by the daughter of one of my former clients. Grateful that I had been there for her mother at the end, this lovely woman allowed me to live in her multimillion-dollar home for a sinfully low rent. She didn't need the money I paid her, but I'm sure she wanted me to feel good about paying my own way. She introduced me to a friend of hers who owned an upscale grocery store, and I soon learned everything I'd always wanted to know about produce. With confident expertise, I was advising people on the best way to cook an artichoke, explaining how to cook dishes such as braised fennel with oil and garlic, and touting the diversity of cauliflower. With a little bit of coaxing from interested ears, I could modestly boast of my abilities to explain the virtues of Braeburns, Fujis, Granny Smiths and the rest.

One day, due to floods elsewhere, the store's selection of apples was dismal. Shipments had not made it to our little store. Late that afternoon, a man came in and asked me why we had so few apples. After explaining as best as I could, I told him we were experiencing an apple-ocalypse.

He laughed heartily as I stumbled on my newly created tongue-twisting word. As I unpacked onions and arranged them for display, he stood in the produce section and talked to me. The next night, he took me to dinner.

I was happy. Never did I believe that a year and three quarters spent in a grocery store would be the best time of my life. But it was. This striking man with the crooked smile didn't care what I did for a living. I didn't feel intimidated that he was so successful, and I was not. He didn't seem to care. I had never connected to another human being with such intensity and passion. All of my misery had served a purpose: it led me to him.

Had he worn another cologne on our third date, I believe our relationship might still be alive today. But it died a premature and brutal death, akin to a car crash on a bucolic country road.

We had been out for a romantic dinner and come back to his place for what was certain to be our first sexual experience. I was basking in the unfamiliar glow of happiness when he poured me another glass of cider and himself another glass of scotch. He came out from the bathroom in a white terrycloth robe. He looked divine. But when he sat on the couch and leaned in to kiss me, our relationship ended in a split second. He had doused himself with the same designer cologne my father wore, and that, combined with the smell of alcohol on his breath, triggered not only my PTSD, but also the first full-blown psychotic episode I ever had.

I only know what I was told when I woke up in the psych ward two days later. He had called an ambulance to take me away, as I was in such a state that he could not drive me. He gave the hospital ten thousand dollars toward my care and left me an apologetic note saying that my demons only resuscitated his, and with great regret, he would have to find me in another life.

Despite his generous donation toward my care, it was not enough to keep me in the hospital for long at all, and I was released, with orders to continue outpatient treatment on a regular basis.

Losing what I thought I would never find was devastating. Not being able to continue working was an even greater blow. I not only lost my salary, but the many customers who were the center of my world … my friends … my family. But the part that really slayed me: the smell of my father's cologne had triggered the nuanced return of every monstrous memory.

I ceased to function. Cradled in the fetal position, I lay on my bed most days, trying not to feel his hot noxious breath on my neck, his large sticky hands jostling me into whatever position was desirable to him at the moment, and trying not to hear the guttural sounds he made as he thrust himself into me. One day, my psychosis cranked up full blast, and I believed he was raping me again. My dear landlady had no choice but to send me to the psych ward again.

This time, I stayed there for a month until they were convinced that with the right cocktail of medications, I was free to exist on my own. My landlady told me, with great sorrow, that I could not stay with her anymore. Once again, while being dismissed, I was met with another generous contribution to my upkeep. This time, she could do nothing to help me maintain my dignity. There was little of it left.

With the money she gave me, I could have moved into nicer digs than this one. But here, where I have been for well over two years, I can stay indefinitely while government bureaucrats debate my ability to thrive. Here, I don't stand out among the lost souls. I can look out the window at a broken diner sign that flashes "DIE" every night and during the day imagine working in the now-abandoned warehouse—clocking in and clocking out as I wonder how technology will do us all in.

Until today, I had been fine with my dull existence. I felt a sense of peaceful diminishment, but I was happy with it. Then, the night clerk called me and said that a letter had been left for me.

I hurried down two flights of stairs. He said an attractive young woman claiming to be my younger sister had left me the note. My former landlady and friend had told her where to find me. There is a note scribbled on the back of the envelope saying that she didn't want to see me because she is ashamed that she waited two years to deliver this letter from our mother.

I held onto the letter overnight. I could not read it.

I am going to read it now. I am holding it in my trembling hands. It is written on pale pink stationery with embossed roses on the bottom. I remember this paper. It was a birthday gift from her sister. She liked it so much she never used it. I never understood that, but she told me it was only for special occasions. I suppose this qualifies.

My dearest son,

Today is Thursday, wrapped in sadness. Your father has left me ... for a man. I am mortified, ashamed, and utterly alone. My shame is not in being left, nor is it in being left for a man. My shame is in the despicable way that I treated you and anyone else who told me the truth.

I am trying to be elegant as I leave these words on paper, but there is nothing elegant or redeemable about me. Even now, in my own sick way, I'm trying to dress up the atrocious with just the right words. I cannot learn ... I've had so many chances. I just keep failing. Why am I so horrible!! So contemptible!

It was just over a decade ago that you told me about the abuse I had long suspected had been done to you. My inexcusable fear kept me from doing the right thing. I told you that you were dead to me, but that was a lie. You have never been dead to me. I have never stopped thinking of you, pitifully apologizing to you in whispers you could never hear. But the wretched crime of disowning you is not the only one that I have committed.

Three years before, your older sister came to me with a similar revelation of abuse. God help me, Son, I was jealous that he preferred her to me. I told her to get out. After a year or so, I found out that your father's actions, coupled with my cruel dismissal, led her down a terrible and destructive road. I was unable to handle the pain, nor did I have the personal resources to fix her. As much as I wanted her to get help, I certainly couldn't explain it to friends or family. I was not able to expose everything to the world, not even to help my own daughter. So, coward that I was, I told everyone she died in a foreign country ... helping people. That was my pathetic way of giving her the dignity she so deserved. I should have tried to find her and help her. I didn't have the strength to help myself. Despicable. Am I not the most horrible person you have ever been so closely connected to? Of course I am. Say it without guilt; maybe it will help you.

Your sister, I heard, had long disassociated herself with family. I know that she was no longer using her given name. I heard that she had named herself after some kind of stone ... amethyst ... no, I believe it was jade. I have no doubt she wanted nothing from me. Not even the name I lovingly chose.

Your younger sister, while being spared the abuse of your father, has been drowning in my dysfunction for years. Despite my wishes for a horrid disease to take me, I am in excellent health for a neurotic, contemptible woman of seventy-three. But when I finish this letter, I will swallow a bottle of pills as my last contemptible act, leaving your sister to find me when she returns from an overnight trip tomorrow. I will then have destroyed all three of my children, leaving the earth with the dim hope that somehow you will find one another again. I don't expect any of you to forgive me, but I do want you all to know that I have never stopped loving any of you. I am deeply sorry. I am a worthless human being and a horrible mother.

Thank you for all of the times you attempted to reconnect with me. I am sorry I was so brutal. I couldn't take the pain, and I needed you to stop trying ... for both of our sakes. Every time I put a knife through your heart, I put a sword through my own. That doesn't matter now but there ... I have put it on record.

With all of my love and deepest regret,

Mom

P.S. I tried to locate an address for your older sister but failed. If you ever find her, please share this letter with her.

I am stunned. I want to react, but I don't know how to do so. I note the irony that today is Thursday, and that I, like my mother, am also wrapped in sadness. But there are many more emotions coming at me. I don't have the wherewithal to deal with any more of them. Not now. I need to distract myself from this letter and pretend that it hasn't crushed me.

I get up from the bed I'm sitting on and walk to the window.

I look down at the diner and notice a teenage girl. I saw her for the first time yesterday. Just like she is doing now … she is standing against the wall … crying. I'm going to go downstairs and talk to her. I have been trained how to do so, after all.

    I just want to help someone.

TINY SILVER BALL

Emery sat cross-legged on the bed as she guided the plastic-coated wire through the last blue glass bead. Smiling, she was just about to congratulate herself for perfectly calculating the number of beads needed for the necklace, when a knock at the door sent everything flying out of her hands and onto the floor.

"Fuck my life," she moaned as she watched the beads scatter on the floor like ants under a refrigerator that had just been moved. She glanced at the door. Someone was still knocking on it. Loudly.

"You have the wrong room," she said defiantly. Nobody ever came to her room for any reason. "Knock it off."

She heard a familiar laugh outside the door.

"Oh, fuck, no!"

Emery walked over to the door and opened it. "What the ever-lovin' fuck are you even doing here? How did you find me?"

The tall man with the long hair and the scarf around his neck laughed. "I love that: 'knock it off.' You're funny when you're pissed. Even more so when it's unintentional."

"How about if I unintentionally knee your balls, Wes? Let's see how funny that will be."

Wes grimaced. "Don't talk like that. You know I have synesthesia. And you know even saying that hurts."

"Oh, gosh. I must have forgotten all about your weird neurological phenomenon. If I had, I never would have mention *kneeing you in the balls.*"

"Ouch!" Wes said, putting his hands over his crotch. "Stop that!"

Emery looked down and picked up a few of the beads she

could see. "Who told you where to find me? And please don't tell me it was my mother."

"Do you mind if I sit down? I'll tell you everything."

"You totally fucked up my necklace. I had just enough beads left to make it, and a customer is waiting for it."

"You'll find them, Em. They didn't go anywhere." He looked around the room. "But you should. I can't believe you're living here. Your mom said … uh …."

"I knew it! She promised me she wouldn't tell anyone where I was."

"It's not her fault. I really pressed her. You know how convincing I can be."

"Sit down," Emery said, nodding toward the bed. "Tell me what you want and be gone with you."

Wes laughed. "Be gone with me? Is that from Shakespeare or something? Whilst thou sit with me?"

Emery glared at him, her lips pressed tightly together.

"You're trying so hard not to laugh," Wes said, taking a seat on the bed. "That's what you do. You fuse your lips like they're glued shut … trying to keep that smile from getting loose. Such a beautiful smile, too."

"Fuck you," Emery said. "What do you want?"

Wes smiled. "Please … just sit."

Reluctantly, Emery sat on the bed, taking care not to sit too close. "I'm sitting. Spill."

"Okay. No long drawn-out speech: I want you back; that's all." He winked. "See how simple that is."

"Simple? Are you serious? What's simple about it? And why do you even want to get back together? Why now?"

"Because there's nobody else in the world that can give me what you can. Nobody."

"Unreal, Wes. Listen to yourself. It's all about what I can give *you.* There's nothing in your head about what you want to do for me. Just what I can do for you."

"Give me a break, Emery. That's not all I have to say. That was just an opening line. There's *a lot* I want to give to you."

"Really? Like what?"

"Like the opportunity to be with someone who loves you." His eyes scanned the room. "Why did you move here? I don't get why you'd leave a nice neighborhood to live in this janky-assed place. It looks like the end of the world. I don't know … like the last stop on the humanity train. You're only thirty-two and you've totally given up."

"Is that what my mother told you? That I'd totally given up?"

"I don't need an opinion from your mother to form my own. I know you. This isn't you. Maybe you in a parallel dystopian universe."

Emery shifted on the bed. "Does that mean that you think it's me living in an apartment with some loud bitch meddling in my business, parading her friends in and out, eating my food, blaring her music, and bringing home and having loud sex with every piece of walking sediment she meets in a bar?"

"You know I don't. But this isn't any better. I just saw a hooker walk through the lobby just before I did," Wes protested. "A tall woman with wicked red hair, right out of the box. A guy sitting in the lobby and the desk clerk called her Margaret. They all seem kinda chummy. Guess she does business here on a regular basis. In fact, they started singing to her: Hi, ho, hi, ho, it's off to work you go."

"That is so not funny, Wes."

"Then why are your eyes smiling?"

Emery started to respond, then thought better of it.

"Seriously, Em, do you consider this an improved living situation?"

"Yeah, actually. I do. I don't cross paths with anyone here. Not in my living space."

"This is dying space," Wes said, looking around.

Emery stood, her eyes searching the floor for her beads. "You call it what you want, Wes. Besides, I'm going to fix it up. I just haven't gotten around to it yet."

Anxious, Wes looked at her. "Will you stop staring at this filthy floor and talk to me? Just sit, please."

Picking up a few blue beads and putting them in her jeans pocket, Emery sat back on the bed. "I moved here because I didn't want to pay all of that rent and have to tolerate a roommate. It was hell."

Wes took a breath. "Okay, I get that. But there had to be other options."

"You mean like moving in with you?" Emery said. "Done being an idiot. I'd rather wait for Godot; he'd come through for me before you ever would. Stupid me: I just kept waiting for *something* to happen with us. But of course it never did. But that didn't stop me from changing my whole life around for you while you just kept selling dreams at Guitar City, living in that tiny one-bedroom apartment, going nowhere on your own, telling me to just 'hang in there.'"

"I'm sorry for that, Em. I really am." Wes tried to take her hand, but she pulled it away. "I was just offered a promotion with a good raise," he told her. "To manager."

"Good for you. But, really, do you expect me to congratulate you for that? Do you think being made manager is bringing you closer to your dreams? Because it's not. They're sucking you in and you'll be there forever. At Guitar fucking City."

"Emery—"

"What?"

"I turned it down. Everything you just said is right. I don't want to work in retail. I don't want to get sucked in. I don't want to sell dreams; I want to live them."

"So what are you going to do instead? No, wait. I don't care. I *really* don't care."

"Yes you do," Wes said with pained eyes. "I know you care."

"No I don't."

"I'm going to look into driving a cab," Wes said. "I'll get a deal where I can make my own hours. That means I can still play gigs."

"Madison Square Garden will be happy to know you won't have to cancel next week's sell-out event," Emery said, on her knees as she searched the floor for beads. "And when your concert's over, you can go outside and pick up a fare. Hey, remind me, when are you playing the Staples Center?"

Wes rolled his eyes. "Would you stop crawling like a damn baby?"

Emery looked up at him. "The beads from the necklace I just sold are on this floor. I need to find every last one of them. Thanks to you, I'm still missing eleven."

"It's between ten and twelve."

"Hilarious," Emery said, peeking under the bed and grabbing a bead.

"You're laughing on the inside. I always make you laugh. Even when your face is scowling."

Emery's eyes squinted as she shot him a nasty look.

"Nothing says you love me more than that scrunched-up face. Especially when you throw in the evil stare. Icing on the Emery cake."

She looked away so he couldn't see the light dancing in her eyes. "I really need to find these beads. Like right now."

"Sheesh, Em, they're not going to grow legs and walk out of here. But then again, your arthropod roommates might carry them out of here."

"What?"

"Insects. Those things with lots of legs that like to show up without an invitation."

"Oh, like you just did?" Emery said. "Well, they're preferable to the cockroach who has spent years hurting me. A brooding, self-absorbed cockroach that I waited years to live with and to be loved by. Every time I ever came to you with a problem, I don't think I was able to talk for more than thirty seconds before you'd steer the conversation back to yourself. To your music. To your problems. Your fucking everything. And you know what's really sad? I don't even think you know that you do that. Because it's just who you are: a self-absorbed cockroach."

"Please don't call me a cockroach. And I'm not self-absorbed," Wes protested. "I'm focused. You can't make it if you're not focused. Nobody ever became a superstar by just sitting under a tree and strumming a guitar."

Emery stopped crawling and sat up, clasping her hands behind her back to stretch it. "I never wanted you to sit and strum. But being focused doesn't mean that you tune everyone out … and that the world turns for you alone."

"I understand why you feel that way, but really, that's not me." Wes reached out a hand to her. "Can you sit up here on the bed so I can argue with you at eye level?"

Emery grunted. "You're used to looking down on me. You should be in your wheelhouse."

Wes stood, grabbed Emery by the arm, then pulled her up. "You can outwit me any day of the week. This isn't a contest."

"I'm not trying to outwit you or win a contest," she said, sitting on the bed and looking at him. "I don't even know why you're here or what you want. You've just burst—without any apology whatsoever—into my solitude."

"You call this—"

"If you insult this place one more time, you're out of here. I know this is a hellhole. But it's my hellhole. I'm at peace here. I have no expectations of anyone, and nobody disappoints me."

Wes grabbed her hand. "And that's enough for you?"

Taking her hand back, Emery just looked at him. "Yes."

"I don't believe you for a second."

Emery exhaled in frustration. "It doesn't matter to me, Wes. You're not my judge and jury. I don't have to answer to you or deal with your bullshit or your selfishness anymore. That's one of the perks of my life here."

"Some perk." Wes waved her off. "Yeah, yeah. I know. But it's your perk."

"Exactly. So why are you here?"

"I told you. I want you back in my life. I want us to be forever. You're my soul mate and we both know that."

Looking down, Emery felt a rush of emotion land in her throat. She put the palm of her hand to her forehead and let her head fall against it.

"You're thinking about how much you love me. And that I'm right."

Emery looked up at him. "No. I'm thinking about how much I used to love you. I'll admit, that love isn't completely gone, but there's only a little piece left. It's like eating a cake because you love the tiny silver ball in the center of the flower, but nothing else. Not the cake, not the icing, or even the flowers. Just the silver ball."

"Are you so perfect, Emery? Because there were so many times when I felt like the spare battery in your vibrator. Like you kept me around just in case of an emergency."

"That's ridiculous, especially since I was the one who waited around for you. And if you'd showed up more often, I wouldn't have even owned one. But fine. I'm a spare battery and you're a tiny silver ball."

"Em, I don't want us to call each other names. Not those names anyway."

Emery clicked her tongue, then looked at him. "You know how it is when you chew a piece of gum forever and then you get to that point where you can't stand to chew it even one more time? But there's absolutely nowhere to throw it and so you have to wait until you find a place to dispose of it."

Wes crinkled his brow. "Now I'm a wad of flavorless gum?"

"Yeah, maybe. I kept you way too long. All you did was hurt me. I can't even count the number of times I went so out of my way to dress up for you because we were going out ... and then you would just cancel on me ... like it was nothing. It didn't matter that I'd spent all day cooking dinner or trying to look pretty. You just fucking bailed on me ... so many times."

"Because I was on the verge of creating something brilliant! Artists can't just stop when they're in the zone."

"And jewelry designing isn't art?"

"I didn't mean it that way. I was just talking about my situation."

"Of course," Emery told him. "You're always talking about *your* situation."

"That's not fair. And composing music isn't the same thing as designing jewelry."

"No, it's not. So what are you saying—I'm clueless about the creative zone that you're BFFs with?"

"It's not ... I can't say anything that's gonna come out right."

"No, you can't. Because what you really want to say is that your creativity far surpasses mine. I mean, most anyone can ramble off famous composers: Beethoven, Brahms, Bach, Wagner, Mozart, Vivaldi, Verdi, and all of those classical geniuses, then Berlin, Porter, Gershwin ... Lennon and McCartney ... and on and on. But seriously, ask the average person to name one famous jewelry designer. They probably can't. And even if someone can, it's not going to be a name that rolls trippingly off the tongue. Isn't that kind of what you wanted to say, Wes? That your field of endeavor is more important than mine? Your kind of artistry is immortalized and mine isn't. And because of that, your needs, by all rights, have and always will come first?"

Wes looked around the room as if there was something in the air that would help him respond. "You're putting words in my mouth."

"Am I? Okay, then take them out. Give me your own spin on all of this."

"I hate the way you always try to box me in with eloquence."

Emery jumped off the bed and stood in front of him. "Box you in with eloquence? This coming from the guy who points out how often I say 'fuck?'"

"You did and you do. And I don't care. It was just an observation. But the two things aren't mutually exclusive, Em."

Emery sat down again as defeat overwhelmed her. "I don't know why I even let you in. I don't know why I'm engaging you in conversation. All we do is go 'round and 'round. We go over the same things, and we get nowhere. And that is precisely why I am here. I wanted to leave the fucking neighborhood so I would never run into you. But you followed me here. At least when you leave, I won't have to worry about seeing you again. We can finally go our separate ways."

"No," Wes said. "I'm not giving up on us. Can't we just have a conversation about everything we have in common and not about all of the ways I've let you down. It's not like you've never hurt me, you know."

"Yes, I'm well aware of your grievances. You called me a spare battery. So lame." She sighed. "Have you had some kind of epiphany? I'm not being sarcastic, either. Have you? Is there something that happened to change your basic nature? Full disclosure: I ask that, knowing that a person's basic nature almost never changes."

"Do you want me to say that I'm not a flawed human being? Because we're all flawed."

"I agree. But there are some flaws a person can live with … or wait around to live with … and some flaws that are just too toxic."

"I meet a lot of women," Wes said, playing with the fringe on his scarf. "And I could have my pick. But I don't. I'm not a player, and I don't want someone who doesn't have the capacity to get me. And you know exactly what I mean because you totally get me. You get me more than I get me."

"Yeah, I know, Wes. I do. But what does that mean? How is that good for *me*?"

"Because I see a lot more clearly now and can give you the love you deserve. I finally understand that I can't go on the way I have been. I know that the same conversations and the same excuses just aren't going to cut it anymore. I see the light. It took me long enough, but I do."

"Do you have any proof of concept? Again, not trying to be sarcastic, but what does saying that really mean? I'm not even sure what you're offering me."

Wes took Emery's hands in his, surprised that she allowed him to do so, and looked into his eyes as he did. "I'm offering *me*. And all the love I have for you."

Exasperated, Emery pulled her hands away. "And that means *what?*"

"It means that if we commit to being together, we'll figure that part out. You're not some prospective business deal, Em. It's not like I wrote out a plan or anything."

"But you had to have something in mind? When are you

starting your new job?"

"Um ...."

"What does 'um' mean?"

"I never said I had a new job. I said I was going to look into driving a cab."

Emery moaned. "So, you not only turned down the promotion but you quit your job to 'look into' another one? Nowhere to go, just somewhere to look."

"I had to quit, Em. I don't want to be a manager. And I couldn't stay on as a salesperson. I wasn't going to let them put me through training just to quit. I've worked there for years. I couldn't just fuck them over."

"I wish you'd been that considerate with me." Emery stood, walked over to the wall, and lightly banged her head against it. Turning around, she looked at Wes. "So you came to me to profess undying love, ask for a new life together, but you've quit your job and have no income. Am I getting that right?"

"I'm doing semiregular gigs. I'm getting some income from that."

"You know what 'some income from that' will get you?"

Wes frowned and looked around the room. "This place?"

"Right," Emery said, her voice louder. "This 'janky-assed' place."

"Well, it's got more square footage than my apartment."

"Yeah ... that sprawling living space you live in. Just love how they took a studio apartment, built a wall in the middle of it, and called it a one-bedroom. One larger room like this is far less claustrophobic."

"You have a point," Wes said. "And this place has windows, too."

"It does. I always know the weather. And who's coming and going from the bodega below. Windows are so convenient that way.

Whoever invented them was very clever."

Wes smiled at her, got up, then walked over to the window and looked out. "Lots of inspiration for songs here. The streets, rife with suffering, are crying out to end their misery, yet rejecting gentrification at any cost." He paused to think. "Melancholy has to exist as long as there are human beings. It's the sister of happiness. And not the evil twin, either ... just the sister. Part of the yin and yang of life, you know? It's the balance ... separate and distinct forces. One not better than the other, just integral parts of life's fabric."

"Yeah, that," Emery said. "It's hard to know great joy if that's all you've ever experienced. How can one truly be euphoric about anything?" She walked over to join Wes at the window. "Not sure Utopia is all it's cracked up to be."

"Nope."

Emery looked out the window at an old woman pushing a cart filled with two bags of groceries. As the front wheel came off, the cart lurched forward, and two oranges fell out and rolled down the street. Helpless, the woman stood there, tears rolling down her face. Only seconds passed when a homeless man, carrying the wheel and two oranges, walked over to her. Putting the oranges back into her bag, he knelt down and began reattaching the wheel. When he had finished, he stood, and turned to go. With a smile, the woman called to him, and handed him the two oranges as he turned around. Giving one orange back to her and putting the other in his pocket, he walked away as she resumed pushing her cart.

"That's humanity," Wes said.

"It is." She swallowed the lump in her throat. "And I've got to find those beads."

"Em ... come on."

She looked into his eyes. "I promised myself."

"What?"

"That I would not be sucked into your ability to distract me from the pain you cause me."

"I'm trying to get you to understand that I'm more self-aware than I've ever been. I'm not trying to say I'm not flawed, fucked-up Wes anymore. But when I look back on things, on our life together, I can see how I unintentionally abandoned you … emotionally and physically. I still have my dreams and I'm not wavering from them, but they're not enough, even if they all come true. Without you by my side, they won't mean as much. Not even close. I've done a lot of thinking, and I really do think I can finally give part of me away and remain a whole man. There's so much I just didn't get. I'm not there yet, either. But I'm on my way."

"I don't know, Wes."

He held up his wrist. "Look, I still wear the hammered silver cuff bracelet you made for me. I get compliments on it all the time. People ask me to see it close up, but I never take it off. And when they ask me where I got it, I tell them the love of my life is a brilliant jewelry designer, and the bracelet is one of a kind—just like she is."

"Sweet," she said, sitting on the bed again, as sadness overwhelmed her. "But I'm not getting back together with because you still wear the bracelet I made for you."

Wes continued. "Sometimes, people are really sorry they even noticed my bracelet and complimented me on it. Know why? Because I go on and on about how talented you are and why I love you so much. For starters, I tell them you're scrappy, snarky, smart, and sexy."

Stone-faced, Emery looked at him. "Maybe you should leaf through your dictionary and see what other letters of the alphabet have to offer."

Wes burst out laughing and sat down next to her. "See, that's how I know. It's how I've always known."

"Known what?"

"That you love me. You know your sarcasm turns me on. And you wouldn't keep zinging me if you wanted to turn me off. And you sure as hell wouldn't laugh at the things I say, either. You can tell me that I'm no more than a tiny silver ball to you, but I know I'm way more, Em. I know you're as much in love with me as I am with you."

"Yeah okay. Whatever. I'm not going to argue with you. You're right. Happy now?"

Wes beamed.

"But before you light up like the fucking Christmas tree at Rockefeller Center, I'll just add two words to that: so what. No, make that three words: so *fucking* what."

Wes was determined to push past her dissent. "Em, remember that night when we got caught in the rain and came home soaking wet? We both ripped off our clothes to take a hot shower, and ended up in bed for three hours, exploring every inch of one another, being more intimate than we ever had before. The things you did with your tongue. Damn!" He took a moment to go back in time. "I get hard every time I think about it." He reached over and gently caressed the side of her face. "When we were lying there afterward, knowing we were going to do it all over again for the fifth time, you told me that your greatest highs and your rock-bottom lows came when we were together." He paused to reflect. "I'm trying really hard to fix that last part. More than you know." He brightened. "But I'll never forget the part when you said the worst thing you could ever imagine was to just flatline it through life. And then you made me promise that if you ever slipped into monotony, I should remind you of what you'd just said until you came to your senses." He smiled. "I say this knowing that a person's basic nature almost never changes."

"Touché and fuck you."

Wes put his arms on Emery's shoulders and looked into her

eyes. When she didn't object, he pulled her closer, kissing her deeply as the world went on outside. After a few minutes, they stopped and looked at each other.

"I feel that tiny silver ball getting bigger," Emery said.

"Oh, yeah. It is."

"Damn you." Emery looked at him, the hunger in her eyes reminding him of his favorite aphrodisiac: her undeniable want. "I hate you."

Pulling off his scarf, then his shirt, Wes stood and pulled Emery up with him. After they had both removed their clothing, they crashed back onto the bed and fell into passion … explosive, sensual, death-defying, and boundless passion.

Two hours later, Emery lay with her head on his chest. "Fuck you for making me feel again."

"Didn't you just do that?"

"I was speaking metaphorically."

"You loved every minute of that. And so did I. We are so connected, Em. There are a million invisible threads between us. Yeah, they get tangled up sometimes and communication really sucks, but they're there and always will be. I could never come close to loving anyone the way I love you. And you can tell me to go fuck myself as many times as you want, because you say it with such passion. You don't even need to say the L word."

"I'm not afraid of the L word," Emery told him.

"Then tell me that you love me. You just showed me. So tell me."

"I-I—"

"Shit, is that my phone?" Wes said, as the sound of his ringtone interrupted them.

"Ignore it," Emery said.

"I can't. Could be business." Wes jumped out of the bed and grabbed his jeans on the floor, quickly taking his cell out of the pocket. "Hello? ... Yeah. Um ... not really .... Are you kidding? Just tonight? Okay, dude. I'll be there."

Guilt dripped down his face like a melting candle. "I know what you're thinking, but it's not what you're thinking."

"I can't fucking believe you just told someone you'll 'be there.' You just fucked me for two hours, and now you're going to leave. Where could you possibly have to be?"

"This cat I've been gigging with ... he's doing a solo tonight at this coffeehouse and this dude who I've been trying to connect with for years ... is coming to see him. We're going to do a few numbers together." Wes stood and started dressing. "This could be really big, Em. This could be the biggest fucking break ever. The one I've waited for. I can't pass it up."

"Know what I can't pass up? Messing with your synesthesia. Do you know what a red-hot poker up the ass feels like?"

"Ouch!" Wes said, jumping. "That hurt. Don't say that again."

"HOT POKER UP THE ASS!" Emery said loudly. "Turning like a fucking rotisserie."

"Em, seriously! Stop it! I'm in pain! Are you trying to blow this opportunity for me?"

"Not at all, poker butt."

Wes stood and looked at her. "Look, I know how pissed you must be. But you were in the middle of making a necklace. While I'm gone, you can find the missing beads and finish it. And I'll be back. I promise."

Emery got out of bed and put a long shirt on. "You know what promise I want from you?"

Wes walked over to her. "What, honey? Anything."

"Never fucking come near me again. Ever. Go back to being the fucking tiny silver ball and let me move on."

"You don't mean that," Wes said as he slipped the scarf

around his neck. "There's absolutely nothing you can say to make me believe you mean that."

"How about your dick in a vise?"

Wes grabbed his crotch. "Damn! Stop it!"

Angry, Emery looked at him with seething satisfaction.

"You can set off my synesthesia all you want," Wes said. "It kind of actually turns me on once I get past the pain."

"Fuck you."

"Don't you want me to be successful?" Wes asked her. "Why would you want me to pass up this opportunity?"

Defeated, Emery sat on the bed. "It's not *this* opportunity. It's just you. You always have a reason to run off and leave me … or not show up at all. You always have a good reason to go, but I'm never enough of a reason to stay."

"Come on, baby, be fair. This is what I've got to do."

"You know, I'm hard pressed to even remember a time together when your mind wasn't on something else. You are constantly distracted. I'm never enough. So no, it's not this *thing* tonight; it's just that it's never any different. And I should have never even let you in the door. But I won't make that mistake again. So don't come back here. Go to your stupid studio apartment with the wall in the middle that calls itself a one-bedroom. Bang your head against it and think of me."

Wes smiled. "I forgot to tell you something. I moved out of there. This morning."

"Good. It's reassuring to know that if I ever have another moment of reckless stupidity, I won't know where to find you."

"Oh yeah you will," Wes said.

"How's that?" Emery said. "Do you think I have a GPS in my brain that navigates only for you?"

Wes walked over and kissed the top of her head, then hurried to the door. As he opened it, he turned to her before leaving. "I live here now. In the janky-assed room next door."

VIA DOLOROSA

I woke up one day to find I was old. The magnificence of my youth, which I had vastly over-appreciated, had been swept away from me. I had not been able to hold onto my beauty, or my fortune, and had little to sustain me. But I had myself—the whole of my tired being was intact. Though weary, my mind remained strong. Even during the worst of times, decades earlier, I had resisted myriad attempts to addle it by those who had tried to take the little I had and declare me incompetent.

Even before my teens, the world insisted that it was mine for the asking. It wasn't because it knew of my talents nor because destiny had whispered in its ear. It was simply because my features were arranged just perfectly. My large brown eyes, my slightly upturned nose, and my full and shapely lips, all set with precision on my oval visage, were guarantors of a successful future. As I segued into adulthood, those with less-fortunate faces insisted that had they been blessed with my gifts, their options in life would be vastly different.

I knew there was great truth in their words, but I hated to admit it … even to myself. I surveyed the people in my life. Did I like the prettiest or the handsomest ones the best? Love and carnal desire aside, was I seduced only by those possessing society's notion of beauty? No. I was not. I was drawn to the witty, the compassionate, the wise, the sentient, the quirky, and the daring. But when I learned that my face and my slender body could open doors more rapidly, I smiled gracefully and walked through them. Every day, I checked my mirror to make sure that my passport to good living was groomed, buffed, painted, colored, and tended to in every way. But I was blind to terms like "trophy wife" and "arm candy." Even as I became the very definition of them, I trudged through the swamp of ignorance, never noticing that my life was nothing like I perceived it to be.

I was nearly three years into marriage and eight months pregnant with my daughter when a call from a local jeweler changed my life. A family emergency had put the poor man in the unfortunate position of closing his store for two weeks. He wanted to assure me that the diamond necklace my husband had brought in for repair (on my behalf) would be a priority upon his return. While he politely offered me the option of taking it elsewhere, my naiveté lost its virginity for evermore.

I had no diamond necklace fitting the description, but the jeweler's account of my husband and my mind's instant replay of his insane reasons for being elsewhere of late rained hard on me.

Being human, my instinct was to confide in someone. But my mother was ill, my father would have swung first and thought about the prudent thing to do later (if at all), and I had no siblings. My baby sister had died at birth, ending my mother's childbearing days forever. Friends: a sticky wicket that was.

There wasn't one among them who I believe had genuine feelings for me nor one who I could rule out as being the "other woman." If I had been born into another kind of life, I imagine I would have had a garden of friends in all different colors, shapes, and sizes.

Refusing to be bamboozled again, I did what a smart woman with money can easily do: I hired a private detective. It took him little time to supply the loosely concealed evidence. Dare I admit I was insulted that attempts to hide the sordid dalliance were pathetic at best. Why go out of one's way to hide one's misdeeds from someone too ignorant to even be suspicious. In my own defense, the initial call from the jeweler only confirmed what I had been denying. I'd like to believe that I would have figured it all out. No, to be fair, I did figure it out. In retrospect, denial is a greater sin than ignorance, though I punished myself unduly for both.

I divorced with a settlement large enough to sustain me for years, but nowhere near enough to return me to the lavish lifestyle I once maintained and no longer craved. However, my ex-husband, with more connections than a master circuit board, was able to obtain sole custody of my daughter despite my herculean attempts to stop him. Laying aside despair and grief, I carried on. Even with the lowly status of being a mere visitor in my child's life, for years, I took advantage of every opportunity to help her grow into a woman of fine stature. I worked part-time at a vintage clothing store to supplement my income yet still have time to be there for my child.

I blinked and she was a grown woman. Despite my most diligent efforts, she fell prey to the ambient sycophants and socialites who comprised her world. Her appetite to see and be seen, and to have all that she saw, became ravenous. The humanity and humility I had tried to instill in her got lost in a lump of Beluga caviar and swallowed whole. She may even have choked on it.

Unlike my daughter, who had been permanently kidnapped by illusions and delusions, my ever-dwindling desires led me to live in an ordinary apartment in a less-than-prestigious neighborhood. It was shortly afterward that my embarrassed daughter, spurred on by her new husband, decided to declare me incompetent and take control over my money. By simply entering my apartment when I was gone and rearranging furniture and other items, it was hoped that my confusion would prove my inability to make rational decisions on my own behalf. I allowed a court date to be set. The judge, upon hearing the absurd case, admonished my child and her spouse (and their attorney) with a reprimand, suggesting that perhaps I should take control of *their* funds, and warned them that any more frivolous lawsuits (or attempts to gaslight) would be justly rewarded. Upon my request, he forbade them to communicate with me. It was at that time that I quietly slipped into the city and into the "penthouse apartment" at the Hotel Obscure. It was, however, a pyrrhic victory for me. But a victory nonetheless.

I've been here too many years to count. I'm the only permanent resident who resides on the sixth floor. The seventh floor is the rooftop, and the eighth floor—well, that's where we'll all end up, provided we haven't done anything to become eternal residents of the sub-basement. I have the nicest room because I've made it so. By special arrangement, I had it painted a few times. I've always been happy to give a poor man a day's work. I brought in my own furniture too. Not much of it, as it's only a room, but a Persian rug of red and dark blue, a love seat, a recliner, a mahogany coffee table, a mahogany dresser with fading gold trim, several framed pieces of art, and a mattress, purchased by me and never slept on by another soul. My bed linens and sheets belong to me, too. I don't think I'd be bragging to say that the curtains are mine as well.

Oh, and I have a black-and-white cat. I named him Obscurity but I call him Obbie. He is my best friend. From his carpeted perch attached to the window, he watches the tiny speck of the world that he can see. He is content. He has many toys and is almost never alone.

In the corner of the room, I have a small refrigerator and a microwave. It bears no resemblance to the elegant kitchen I used to have, nor does it even match the functionality of the kitchen in my former apartment. But I do not match the functionality of my former self. On some days, I believe I surpass it. On other days, I try not to think at all.

The view out of my window boasts a flickering diner sign. It used to say NER but after two years, the owner replaced the DI and stopped the flickering. The neon red letters, then all in working order, were almost incongruous with the neighborhood. After about six months, the N and R burnt out and the flickering resumed. As if planned by a dystopian decorator, the sign now flickers DI E! And I am reminded of what I came here to do. Not today or tomorrow. But eventually.

Across the street, there is a warehouse that has been boarded up for years. I am fearful of what will go in its place. I hear vague rumors about what may replace it. Rumors make me anxious. Construction is always noisy and change is scary.

I have enough money to live out my days here. I could have managed a nicer place, but here among the downtrodden, I wear a cloak of invisibility. I do not have to exchange glances with judgmental eyes or hear their whispers through the walls at night. I do not like the proximity of long-term neighbors or the perceived entitlements that go with it. I prefer ephemeral relationships, although I do maintain a friendship with the night clerk.

Under a pen name, I write stories for magazines. I have for years. Nobody but Obbie knows I do this. Each story I write is based on someone I used to know. Living here, I witness varying degrees of morality, sobriety, sanity, wealth, and poverty on any given day. But these are not the stories I tell. My stories rip the salon-tanned skins off the social-climbing frauds as they climb decaying ladders. My words tear the designer accoutrements from the gold diggers as they chafe their manicured hands with rusted shovels, never knowing they have gouged out their final resting places.

I kill a fair number of my characters, but not in a traditional manner. In my last story, the character, whom I shall refer to only as Narcissa, was at the height of her narcissistic apex when she happened into an antiques store, owned by an old man who was nearly blind. In a dusty corner, she spotted a vintage floor mirror with a solid gold frame and immediately recognized its rare historical origins and extraordinary value. Excited by the find, she asked the old man how much he would take for it.

He walked over to the mirror that reflected an image of

himself he could barely see. As he caressed the edges, he admitted it had been a long time since he had seen the mirror and asked her to describe it to him.

Just as she was going to do so, she spotted three nearby mirrors of far lesser value, but with a similar oval shape. With no hesitation, she began to describe the one she had mentally appraised to have the least value, and as she described it, she embellished her narrative by attributing flaws to it that she knew would further diminish its value.

The old man gave her the low price she had hoped to get. Ecstatic, she made a call and had the mirror picked up and delivered to her stately manor. She had no idea that the nearly sightless man could see more than she ever would.

I killed her slowly.

From the first day she admired herself in the stolen mirror, she saw something she had not noticed before. Although a mere scratch on her forearm, it bothered her that anything imperfect should reflect back. Day by day, in tiny increments, the mirror began to reflect the ugliness of her soul by taking the form of physical decay. Her thick shiny locks appeared to dull and thin. Her nearly flawless complexion began to show signs of untreatable eczema. Tiny lines of age appeared before their time, deepening with fury as she cursed them. Her neck began to sag like an overfilled sack of finger potatoes. Her eyelids drooped and creased while crow's feet spread out from the corner of each eye like fireworks exploding into a night sky. And her white teeth, once the centerpiece of her ersatz smile, began to yellow and degrade.

While others still saw outward beauty, she was doomed to see herself only as she truly was. Even when she stood in front of mirrors not possessed by the ghost of moral integrity, mirrors that reflected what was outwardly visible, she could no longer see the image of herself that she so loved. Her reason for pretense no longer existed.

And soon, others began to see in the flesh what she saw in the mirror.

One day, she could not take it any longer. Picking up a bottle of French perfume that could no longer mask the stench of her being, she hurled it at the oval mirror, ferociously cracking the priceless antique. As she watched her image shatter, she grabbed a shard and slit her own throat. Lying there, with the piece of glass that reflected only her blood, she died a slow, agonizing death.

"They," who have remained anonymous for time immemorial, say that we dislike in others what we most dislike in ourselves. The sins from my days of privilege are few and long ago, and for years, I thought I might never find the fortitude to cease to punish myself for having been a part of that world. Though my sins are the smallest by comparison, they were the greatest because I committed them, but my allegorical mirror story was not about me. I have never cheated anyone but myself. But my hatred for those with whom I once consorted had eaten away at me, and because of this, there were many days when I felt deserving of punishment. Thankfully, I still judge the sins of others to be greater than mine. And there are some who I deem to have sinned less. I am nobody's judge and jury. Court is in session only in my mind. I feel no guilt for that.

When I looked at the ravages of time on my unaltered face and my sagging body, I wondered if I was being punished or blessed. Was my life of solitude in the Hotel Obscure a punishment that I had chosen? Or was it a blessing? By letting everything go, and no longer having to worry about looks or social status, had I been freed to be me, to move about the world without recrimination or restriction? Or was I letting a glorious life go by the wayside? It took me years to find that answer.

I don't go out very often. When I do, I don't look my best. To dress up in this neighborhood is to be discordant with everyone else.

I do not wish to be noticed. On the occasion that I go out with the night clerk, I do improve my appearance, but only a bit.

Most days, I go only to buy food or supplies, see a doctor on the odd occasion, take in a movie, or walk over to the park and sit … if I can find an area free of drug addicts or alcoholics. Sometimes I do, but I am never alone for very long. So I leave. I trudge back here to my room. Even traveling from the lobby to my room, I see things I don't wish to see. It is like watching the people from my former life in raw form without money to disguise them. There are also people here who exemplify humanity. I am not one of them. My greatest contribution to society is not to disrupt it.

I will tire of punishing the vacuous fortune hunters one day. I have already tired of it, but I let anger drive me. I must learn to stop that. Perhaps I will write stories to champion the poor, but I must take care not to turn them into monsters. That is my fear.

I have just learned that there has been an overdose on the third floor. I heard people talking outside my door. He was thirty-six. Someone said he was a writer with a big old desk. I remember him now. I used to see him in the park talking to the wrong people. They will be coming to pick him up soon, I'd imagine. It will probably be his first ride in a limousine.

I need to go out to buy food for Obbie. But I cannot pass through the lobby until I know they have taken him away.

There are more shocking things than a dead addict in a body bag. Many years ago, in the crippling chill of winter, back from a quick trip to the corner grocery, I was headed up the stairs to my room and saw something horrific as I approached the third floor. Holding his Brooks Brothers pants up with one hand and clutching his profusely bleeding genitals with the other, a man hobbled down the stairs in excruciating agony. Sweat and fury dripped from his face, his torture all the worse as he could not free up a hand, even for a second, to wipe so much as a trickle of it away.

He did not make eye contact with me as we passed. But as soon as we had, he let loose with a deep guttural moan. I wondered where he would go. It was twenty-nine degrees outside … cold enough for his blood to freeze on his body. I was certain he had left a warm coat behind. I even knew what it looked like: a rich chestnut-brown leather trench coat, lined with a taupe-colored fur. There were leather epaulets on the cuffs, classic buttons, and a zip chest pocket. The design of the stitching and cutting were the epitome of well-worn prosperity. A pair of brown Ralph Lauren leather driving gloves was stuffed in the left pocket.

Two minutes later, a young male prostitute, one whom I'd seen only once before, came whistling down the stairs, smiling as he shimmied in his new acquisition. With one hand, he pulled the gloves out of the pocket, clutching a fat wallet in the other. I noticed some traces of blood on his hands, but they were soon to be elegantly covered.

The last time I had seen my son-in-law's coat was that final day in court, when the judge had admonished him, my daughter, and their attorney.

As I climbed the stairs, reflecting on who I had become, I discovered that not a speck of motherly love had remained within me. I felt smug and vindicated. My daughter had not shopped wisely. She had attached herself to the first man who fit her superficial and self-serving needs. She had ignored the no-return policy, and she had failed to read the labels carefully. I had tried so hard to prevent such a misfortune, but she was her father's child and had seen me as an outlier with little to offer. On the day she was born, I loved her unconditionally. I thought I always would. And I did. Until one day I didn't.

Nestled within the depths of my psyche, perhaps there is some vestige of maternal affection. Perhaps, had she been the one bleeding on the stairs, I might have shown concern. But had that been so, I don't believe it would be any greater than I would have shown for a complete stranger. Probably less, as I would have had to steel myself into a place of invulnerability before tending to her wounds or calling for help.

As for him, I imagine he claimed to have been attacked on the street, but his sliced genitalia told a different story, and not one I cared to write or mull over too intensely. I did wonder how severe the injury was, but the thought lingered only as long as it took me to reach my door or as long as it takes a bird to flutter by a window. I paused on the landing to catch my breath. Six flights up isn't an easy climb, but I was used to it. Once inside, I opened my bag, grabbed the box of apple cinnamon tea I had bought, and prepared a cup in the microwave.

Three months later, I heard the male prostitute had been shot to death in an alley. A year after that, the man who pulled the trigger cut a deal by naming the person who hired him. I don't know what happened to my daughter after her husband moved into his prison cell. When I read about it in the paper, I was reminded how little I cared and how little I had been cared about. And then I let it go.

There is no joy in my life. Yes, there is momentary physical pleasure and tranquility, but not joy. The closest I come to that is my love for Obbie. I am content with him by my side, and his frequent purrs tell me that the feelings are mutual. Some may see my life as a sad journey, coming from wealth and so-called privilege, only to live among the misfits of humankind. But I see the journey in reverse. I have left the misfits behind. I have extricated myself from the plague of pretending, the punishing pangs of persecution, and the indignity of inauthenticity. I have shed my thin skin and replaced it with impenetrable armor. Losing Obbie would be my only Achilles Heel. And if that were to happen, I would likely travel alongside him.

I exist without any rules or expectations by others, and I give the same in return. I covet nothing and fear little. Disappointment, deception, disillusionment, and despair are unable to destroy me anymore. I feel a calm in my soul that few can claim. I am exactly who I wish to be.

I MISS HIM (The Great Sabotage)

I only knew him for a few months, but I miss him with a passion that I don't have the ability to describe.

Right before we met, my boyfriend of three years left me after learning I was pregnant … and then I had a miscarriage. I was devastated. I was so consumed with grief I thought I'd never be able to care about anyone or anything again. But I did. As my soul was unraveling, I met someone who became my best friend. I had barely begun to heal when I lost him too.

I guess there are lots of reasons why we bonded: We were both in our own private hell and both in need of companionship … and love. We each had unique ways of sabotaging ourselves too. Still, I thought we would make it work … eventually. I wasn't under any illusions; I knew he was damaged and incomplete, just like me. But in my flawed thinking, I figured it would be okay, because he would be the one man who wouldn't judge me.

I was wrong, only not in the way that I anticipated. He *did* judge me, and he decided I was too good for him. Isn't that the kicker?

Everything changed after the first kiss we shared. Even though I knew he felt the same way I did, I'm afraid I killed him. I didn't think I pushed that hard, but I think it scared him to know he could be loved and that we could have worked out. He self-medicated himself right out of this life. I keep wondering … if we hadn't met that day in the park, if I hadn't been so distraught and so desperate for another human being to hear me, would he still be alive? I will never regret meeting him. But if I'm responsible for his death, I will regret it as long as I am able to process a lucid thought.

But even that won't be easy because he awakened something in me ... he made me feel. And while he couldn't come to terms with his emotions, he loved me. That is nowhere near enough for me, but it is all that I have. I really believed I was helping him to live again. But now I feel like I am an accomplice to murder ... or maybe assisted suicide. Another kicker.

The day of his death was a waking nightmare. After trying five times over six hours to reach him, I was sure something was wrong. I called the front desk and asked the clerk to check on him. He did. Nearly an hour later, the clerk called back to say he had found him slumped over his desk ...dead. I hung up and screamed until my throat was raw. Finally, I called back and asked to come see him, but they had already taken him away. I started to ask where, but then I decided it was better to remember him alive.

Because I was the only person who seemed to know him, the police had several questions for me. They wanted to know if he had parents ... or any other family.

His parents were in their early twenties when he was born. When he was two, they decided to see the world ... without him. They left him with an aunt and flew to London. They sent a postcard from Paris saying they hoped he was okay, and that was the last of any communication. When his aunt died three years later, he went into the system. He told me he had more foster parents than he could count. He said that any time someone would ask about his parents, he'd say, "which ones?"

I told the police his childhood led to abandonment issues that led to substance abuse. That was all I really wanted to tell them. Ha! I say that like I had great restraint or something. That was pretty much all I knew. Except that he was afraid to be loved. But they didn't need to know that.

Two days after he died, I moved into his room, surrounded by everything he owned. I didn't do it just to be near him; I did it because I couldn't afford the one-bedroom I had shared with my ex. Not if I wanted to eat, too.

So now I live in his room with his desk … the Victorian Mahogany Kneehole that he cherished so dearly. He was a writer, and this was where he created people and the worlds they live in.

I'm not a writer. I'm a cashier at a grocery store. I ring stuff up, and I scan a lot of coupons. And if no one is around to help me, I bag, too. I'm good at that, although some days I feel like I've lived my life by always putting heavy cans on top of egg cartons. But that's me: too much weight in the wrong places. I tear up every time I see an elderly person buy cat food, and I know they don't own a pet. Or when I see shame wash over someone who has to remove a much-needed item or two from their order because they don't have enough money. Once in a while, I "forget" to ring things up, but I'm watched too closely to do that often. I can't appear too sympathetic or I'll be fired. Then I'll have to eat cat food too.

My job is as boring as it sounds. I wish I could write about the time I had an alien in my line buying snacks to take back to his ship, but of course that never happened. Yeah, sure, I've had some crazy customers, and their antics would probably fill a book, but who cares. As far as I know, none of them are aliens … just miserable people trying to survive. I have no more to say about them. When I leave work for the day, I leave all of that behind me and try to focus on things I enjoy.

I love crafts. I think scrapbooking is fulfilling, only I have an empty life, and I don't think the point of scrapbooking is to preserve nothingness. So I cut up magazines and make collages of things that make me happy—like big rolling waves, babies, puppies, kittens, orange poppies, and dream homes. Sometimes I paint little flowers on glass boxes and saltshakers. And when I find just the right kind of rock, usually in the park, I paint animal faces on them. They make really cute paperweights. I've sold some of my work to people I know, but it's really not worth mentioning. I'm only doing so because I long to have even a speck of the creativity he had. Just to feel worthy.

What I don't want is his almost psychotic fear of success that waged constant war with his desperation to be some kind of legend; the thought of being ordinary slayed him.

I thought I could be his muse and take him away from his demons. I know a muse is supposed to have an interesting life, but I really wanted to elevate his consciousness to a place where he could look beyond his fears. I wanted to be a part of something special.

I love creative men, even if they're difficult. I love minds that see more than my eyes do. I shouldn't reiterate this, because it's the dumbest thing in the world, but I thought I could fix him. Not change him—I'm not that lame—but maybe glue some of the cracks together to keep him from falling apart. I didn't know he'd fall like Humpty Dumpty.

I am almost done reading the novel he left behind. I have one chapter to go. He just called it *Jack*. There are a bunch of question marks after that, so I'm thinking he wasn't real sure of the title. I do remember, however, he told me that he named the character Jack because jack was all he really had.

He had to have been writing like crazy. I remember when he met me, he told me his novel was sixty-thousand words long and barely half finished. Now I can see he's written one hundred and thirty-thousand words. So why did he leave the world when he was so close? This novel … I just love it. Not just because it's a very human story, but because it brings him back to life. I can almost touch his words and see him before me, speaking them. He put a piece of himself in every character. Even the ones who are nothing like him show his influence. That really blows my mind.

His book … it's about this man, in his sixties, who had been estranged from his family because he's spent his whole life touring as a jazz musician. Out of the blue, his daughter calls him. She wants to reconcile and asks him to come live with her and her daughter. The guy didn't even know he *had* a granddaughter. He agrees to come. And the "yes" is barely out of his mouth when a member of his former jazz quintet asks him rejoin the group on a world tour.

And that's when his life falls apart ... like mine did the day I found out I was pregnant. It sucks how getting something you've always wanted turns into your biggest nightmare.

I've been afraid to read the last chapter. (Funny, since I read well over a hundred thousand words in one weekend.) But after writing this and getting my own feelings out, I think I've got the strength to plow through the rest. At least I hope I do.

> "The Party's Over" was always the last song of the closing set. As soon as the final lyrics left his lips, his purpose fluttered away as it twirled upward with the ambient smoke.
>
> He was no longer a jazz vocalist. Only a lonely man with this nose pressed up against the plexiglass of an ersatz civilization. If he loved no one, there was no hurt to be had. He had tried to make himself believe that but had neglected to consider the wretched pain of isolation, masked by the temporary presence of stage lights and an appreciative audience.
>
> This night, like every night, Jack watched as the drummer hopped off his throne to meet the woman in the short skirt who scurried over to fling her flesh against his. This night, her movements, perfectly angled, offered him a peek of what treasures she would soon bestow on her lover. The view taunted when it should have titillated. It was like seeing a trailer to a goddamn movie that was never coming a theater near him. But how would he know what was playing? He always stayed home and never checked the listings.
>
> Then there was the sax player. He loathed commitment as much as Jack did, but his sex addiction gave him far less time to mull over the gaping hole in his soul. Besides, playing sax gave the

illusion of a powerhouse, bursting with a vital, unrestrainable force. And thus, he regularly attracted a virtual buffet of pussy. Every night, they lined up like bar shots that he couldn't possibly down in one night. Individually, they were lonely women with low self-esteem who willingly tossed their self-respect into the nearest trash compactor. He would walk over, order a drink, make small talk, then like a game show host waiting a long beat before announcing the winner, grab the chosen one with a flourish and whisk her off to a private table. After a few more drinks, and whatever foreplay suited him, he'd take her next door to his hotel room.

The unchosen remained seated at the bar and fired death stares at him and his *femme du jour*. But despite their grievous pain, they had no trouble cutting loose their distress if he chose them the next night ... or sometimes, when he'd had a triple shot of macho juice, later that same night, humiliating the chosen one he'd just shot his first load into.

At one time or another, he'd fucked every last one of them. They all knew it, but something had inoculated them against maintaining a modicum of dignity. There were always other men at the bar, waiting to pounce on them, but most nights they refused, and somehow, doing so made them feel respectable. And when they did go off with another man, they labored under the fantasy that they were sparking jealousy in a man oblivious and utterly apathetic to their existence, save the rare moments he was finding utility in their body parts.

As Jack studied them, he pitied them through his revulsion. Walk the fuck way, he thought as he watched them primp and cheapen themselves. Licking their lips, lowering their necklines, and raising their already too-short hemlines, they were only a hair's breadth away from being displayed in the raw in the store window of life ... with all goods deeply discounted and marked for fast clearance. Indeed, rejection was the chosen aphrodisiac at Chlamydia Central.

Meanwhile, Jack watched as the piano player slipped out

the back door. It was well known that he frequented a gay bar down the street … often with the bass player, who on alternate nights hung out at the club post-gig to pick up women. Jack had no desire to delve into anyone's proclivities, but he still felt compelled to observe what was in front of his face. No different from reading the newspaper, really. You read shit, but you don't get involved. You just turn the page or throw the thing in the trash.

It didn't seem to matter what city or what country they were in. Geography had little say in personal preferences, and patterns easily replicated themselves. There's a reason they call it baggage: you drag it wherever you go. He should know; he had a ton of it. If he could only send it to the lost luggage room of some mythical airport, he'd be making progress.

He let his recent past flash before him again. Before he left on tour, he'd enmeshed himself in an affair with his married ex-girlfriend who he'd found by accident when he ambled into a Port Authority diner one night. Despite his best efforts, he started to fall in love with her again, but when she wanted to leave her husband and come on tour with him, he couldn't escape fast enough, ignoring the crackling sounds of her shattered heart that he stepped on as he hurried away.

He couldn't let himself continue to feel anything for a person who was in a position to hurt him … abandon him. Yet, nobody was doing any abandoning *but* him. He didn't trust anyone … not even the daughter who wanted to give him a second chance or the granddaughter he'd never met. Fuck people for loving him; it messed everything up every time. And fuck people for not knowing that if they only fought for him one hundred and one times, instead of only one hundred, he might stay.

He didn't know how to acknowledge other people's feelings. Not in a way that mattered.

Truth. He had fallen in love with a girl he met at the park. He loved her so much he didn't want to hurt her. He knew how unwittingly callous he could be. She was being too respectful of his space because she didn't want to lose him. She didn't even know that she had become his muse.

The way that she loved him filled him up like a hot-air balloon. He felt like he could float over mountains, lakes, oceans, and deserts, and never come down to earth. Her love was so immense, and there was enough of it to last into the beyond. The connection was multi-layered; she was someone he could spend hours in bed with and someone he could expose his vulnerable side to, as well. She showed him her tears, and he knew he was safe to do the same. But he was too cowardly to cry, and let his faux machismo think it had won ….

And that was all he wrote. Except for this bullshit note that he scribbled under the last line. It must have been meant for me. Who else did he expect to see it?

I cannot finish another man's story when I am unable to finish my own ... I hope Jack is better at fighting his demons than I am.

I am devastated. I am so furious that I wish he would come back to life so I could kill him for being so stupid and so cowardly. I was right. He did love me, but the yellow-bellied weakling chose death. He poured his soul into this book the same way he poured whiskey into a glass. Then he stopped. Why was he so afraid to even try and have a good life? He wrote one hundred and thirty thousand words, then slithered away to die. He could have done something transformative for Jack, whether good or bad, but he bailed on him and bailed on himself, letting his thoughts wander to me. Was he trying to make this my fault?

Thirty-six years and one hundred and thirty thousand words later and there is no ending. Not one that's worthy. Not one that's brave, heroic, or admirable in any way. This ending is the great sabotage ... perhaps that would be a worthier title for his book than *Jack* ... and for his life as well. I hate him right now. And I hate myself because I love him. I want to beat his chest with both fists and rage at him. I want to slap his face and scream at him. And I want to cry my eyes out with my head buried in his chest and have him stroke my hair as I do so.

I hate him so much.
I love him so much.
I'm over him.
I have to be.

When I was eight, I wrote a poem. I was so proud of it. It was about the house I lived in, my mother, and the pretty flowers that she grew. My mother was thrilled, and she encouraged me to write more. I did. I made the mistake of showing them to my father. He told me that writing poetry was the most useless thing I could do. He said I had no talent at all and that I'd better learn that sooner than later. From that day on, if he even heard me singing so much as a one-line song I'd made up, he'd tell me to stop.

My mother told me that he had been hurt so he was hurting me the same way, without even realizing it. How could he not realize it? That made no sense to me. But I didn't want his ugly words to hurt me again. I didn't want to hear that I had no talent. So I buried my creative aspirations, embraced the mundane, and without realizing it, I found myself attracted to people who wouldn't let anyone wrest their dreams from them. And I let that satisfy me as I continued to suppress my own creative desires and pretend that painting rocks would satisfy my soul. I had rocks in my head.

I'm determined to find out if I'm any good. I'm going to give it everything. And even if I turn out to be the most unremarkable writer in the world, I'll keep trying. I won't be afraid to succeed or fail.

I know I can do so much more than ring up groceries and mourn for the dead. I can take all of the broken pieces of myself and create someone new. I'll be someone with a purpose who can help other lost souls, rather than just be one, but not someone who will allow herself to be dragged into their darkness.

I know I will have bad days, and I may even have moments when I feel that an unfinished life is my best option too. But I won't let those thoughts take over.

I was thinking that maybe in another life, if there is one, we just might be able to give this thing another go. But that's delusional. There's someone better for me in this life.

But I still miss him.

NOT THAT LONELY

"Addicts. They all die early one way or another. Even if they don't OD, they kill themselves some damn how. I seen it too many times," said the seventy-something-year-old man in the dark gray wool cap, green flannel shirt, and well-worn jeans. He looked over at the front desk clerk as two uniformed men wheeled out the bagged body on the cart through the small hotel lobby. "Who was it, Henry?"

Henry didn't bother to look up as he turned the page of his newspaper. "You worried one of your kin's in that bag, Johnny?"

"Hell no. None of my kin live anywhere near here. You know that."

"Exactly. Which is why I ain't tellin' you shit. None yas."

Johnny swatted the air as if to disqualify Henry's remark. "Most the business you stick your nose into ain't none yas either, but that never stopped you from pryin'."

"Quiet, Johnny. This is my reading time."

"Ah, checkin' the ponies ain't readin'." Johnny pulled a piece of dried beef out of his pocket and put it in his mouth. "Man, these things are hard to chew."

"'Cause you hardly got no teeth left, brother man," came the voice across the room.

Johnny looked up at the forty-something-year-old man with the red bandana around his head and the unzipped gray hoodie that revealed a dull white T-shirt underneath. "You're not my dentist, Clyde. You don't know nothin'."

"I got eyes," Clyde said as he pulled an iPod out of his backpack and connected it to a pair of earbuds.

Johnny started to answer him but stopped when Clyde put

the buds in his ears and turned on his music.

Annoyed, Johnny refocused his attention on Henry. "So how'ya know he'd passed?"

Henry turned another page of the paper. "Got a call from some lady asking me to check his room. I did. He was dead. Made a call. That's all. No need for you to know anything else. My horoscope says so right here: 'Avoid lonely old men asking too many damn questions.'"

"Bullshit," Johnny said, sticking the dried beef back in his pocket. "You probably don't even know your ass-ter-whatever-they-call-it sign."

Henry shrugged and turned another page of his paper.

Looking down at his lap, Johnny stared at a grease stain on his jeans. He rubbed it with his forefinger, but nothing happened. The grease was as embedded into his jeans as loneliness was into his soul. He looked down at the beige-and-black speckled linoleum, taking particular notice of the missing pieces. He noticed that the space closest to him was shaped like a mandolin and about a foot away was the head of a cat … with one ear.

He glanced up at the large clock on the wall. "Ain't no damn eight-thirty," he yelled over to Henry.

Henry looked up, barely meeting his eyes. "That damn clock's been stopped for years. You know that. Too lazy to take out your phone?"

"I ain't got no cell phone, and you know *that!* I can barely pay to live in this dump. So damn stupid to use a phone for a clock anyway. Remember when we was growin' up …. If we needed to know the time, we sure as hell didn't look at the damn phone. Be like hearing a ringing sound and answering the clock. When we wanted to take a picture of something or somebody, we got a camera and stuck a roll of film in its ass. Sure as hell didn't take the receiver off the hook, point it at someone and say 'cheese.' Person probably would've thought you was gonna take them out … would have whooped yer ass 'fore you whooped theirs. Or maybe, they would've strangled you with that curly-ass cord that looked like a lock of Shirley Temple's hair. Hmm, kind of looked like that curly-ass Italian pasta, too." Johnny pulled a pack of tissues out of his shirt pocket, plucked one out, then blew his nose. "Hell, I remember when you could call the damn time up. Nice lady recording would say, 'At the tone, the time will be four thirty and ten seconds.' You could call the weather too. That was a downright normal way to do shit.

"And when people took a damn video of you, a big-ass camera would be pointing in your face. No way you could miss it. Now, people be slippin' shit outta their pockets and recording ya pickin' your nose. And same with all of those damn spy gadgets—hell, you can look at a mofo and their shirt button be recording everything you do and say. They could be transmitting everything to Mars … you know, where a bunch of alien motherfuckers with big black eyes sit in a control room and communicate telepathically. Yeah, they watch you and then make plans to annihilate your ass next Tuesday. Bullshit, man."

"Man, you really are bored today," Henry said. "You wanna write sci-fi, get a pen and paper. This is how it works: thoughts go from your brain, what's left of it, to the paper. No audio. Nothing for anyone to hear while you think this crazy shit up."

Exhausted, Johnny exhaled as if he was spitting air into the room. After a minute, as if tranquilized, he looked at Henry. "Just don't know why the damn clock has to stay broke."

"You wanna know the time. Wear a watch."

"The clock just needs batteries," Johnny told him.

"Batteries ain't in the budget," Henry said, still reading the paper. "You wanna buy them, then stand on a chair and install 'em, be my guest. Double As."

Johnny laughed. "My ex-wife was a double-A cup."

Henry slammed his paper down. "Do I look like I give a rat's ass about your ex-wife's little titties?"

Hurt, Johnny looked away, brightening as he saw Gloria Tan, one of the hotel's regular residents walk into the lobby. "Shine, little glowworm, glimmer, glimmer …"

Gloria, not quite five foot tall, stood in front of Johnny in her bright lime green muumuu with lemon yellow flowers and a matching infinity scarf around her neck. Wrapped around her pinned-up gray hair was a purple-and-pink scarf. A pair of black reading glasses rested on the top of her head, threatening to slide down her forehead. Her hands, covered in liver spots, pushed a cart with a large bag of groceries in it. "I told you, shut up with that song already."

"Aww, c'mon, Glowworm."

"No call me that. I no worm."

"You're a love bug, then," Johnny said.

Gloria reached into the large paper bag in her cart and pulled out a rectangular box of plastic wrap. "I no damn insect," she said, smacking his upper right arm.

"I'm sorry," Johnny said, rubbing the spot where she'd hit him. "Let me make it up to you. No sense you dragging that cart to your room. I can do that for you."

As he began to rise from his chair, Gloria gave him a reminder smack with the long box she was still holding. "Sit down, worm singer. Stay down, you."

"You missed the dead man being wheeled outta here," Johnny said, determined to engage with her.

Gloria stopped and looked at him, dropping the box back into the bag. "What you mean?" She looked over at Henry. "Somebody die? Not Mr. Chang!"

"No. Not him. One of our younger guests has taken a permanent vacation to the great beyond. They came for him right after you left. And that's all I'm saying except you've got good timing, Gloria. You missed the whole thing."

Gloria looked down at her bag of food. "No appetite now. So who die?"

"No names," Henry said. "Next of kin hasn't been found."

"Kind of makes you appreciate folks while they're here," Johnny said.

Looking hard at him, Gloria pondered his words. "Maybe some people."

"Shine little glowworm, glimmer, glimmer …"

"I said no sing that song to me!"

"It's a Mills Brothers song. 'I got a gal that I love so, glow little glowworm, glow.' Don't you remember?"

"You no listen to me!" Gloria grabbed the box of plastic wrap out of her cart and held it up.

Taking the earbuds out of his ears, Clyde, who had been minding his own business, stood and walked over to Gloria. "Would you let me help you to your room, Ms. Gloria?"

Gloria smiled. "You no sing worm song to me?"

Clyde looked confused. "To a lady like you! Never!" he said, winking at her. "Only love songs."

"But I *was* singing her a love … oh, never mind," Johnny mumbled.

"You charmer," Gloria said to Clyde, putting the box down. "Yes, please. I appreciate you help me with cart."

As Gloria and Clyde walked away, Johnny looked defeated. Reaching into his pants pocket, he pulled out a thick silver disc with an embossing on top. Staring at it, he began to caress the image of a runner, smiling as he did so.

"Lucky charm, Johnny?"

Johnny looked up to see Margaret, a tall woman with dyed red hair, wearing a black miniskirt, sheer black top, long gold-tone earrings, and fire-engine red stilettos. "Damn you look hot! Hope there ain't no firemen around. Don't want nobody puttin' you out!"

Margaret laughed. "So whatcha got there?"

"Silver medal won by my daddy. For high school track and field. I keep it in my pocket so he's never far from me."

"Been a long time since he passed?" Margaret asked.

"Oh, yeah. Nineteen years. Lost my mother four years after that."

"Sad thing, death."

"Sure is. Speaking of, guess you know they wheeled someone outta here just a while ago."

Margaret's mouth fell open. "No, I had no idea. I was too busy tending to … well, you know." She looked at Henry. "What the hell happened?"

"Someone died," Henry said, turning on the small television that sat on the desk in front of him. No more questions from anyone."

"He won't say shit," Johnny told her.

"No, but I'll find …." Margaret reached into her red shoulder bag and pulled out her phone. She read a text, then looked at Johnny. "Got another job. You know how it is, sugar. Wish I could stay and chat."

"Yeah, me too."

"You take care, baby," Margaret said, rushing toward the door.

Nearly colliding with the wild-haired woman wearing three layers of clothing, Margaret looked disdainfully at her, as the woman had nearly knocked her over in a rush to enter the lobby.

Frantically, the woman looked around the lobby, her eyes settling on the only one seated there. "They came for the dead man!"

"They sure did," Johnny said, putting his father's medal back in his pocket. "Did you see them?"

The woman sat down next to Johnny. "I see everything."

"I see most everything too. But I don't recall ever seeing you. You got a name?"

"The devil!" she responded.

Johnny puckered his lips and blew out a loud puff of air accompanied by a whistle. "I don't know what you've done in your life, but I can't believe you're the devil. What's your given name?"

Her eyes narrowed as they scanned the room. "That man behind the counter; I know what he's doing."

"Watching TV."

"He's getting instructions from the devil. But Satan ain't coming to get me because I'm gonna get him first!"

"Henry isn't very friendly some days," Johnny said, crinkling his brow. "But he's not in cahoots with no devil."

The woman looked around the room again and pointed to the clock. "Idle hands are the devil's playthings. Those hands aren't moving because SATAN doesn't want them to!"

"Well," Johnny said uneasily, squirming in his chair. "It's actually because the batteries in the clock are dead."

"DEAD! Satan turns the living into the dead. He turns our daily bread into poison. He hunts us down ... disguised as forces of good, then spits venom into our souls. He laughs as it flows through our veins and warts appear on our skin." She stared at Johnny. "You got the devil's warts. I see them!"

Rattled, Johnny touched his face. "Nah. A few moles. A few skin tags. No warts. And sure as hell ain't got no devil's warts."

The woman jumped up out of the chair and began running around the lobby. "Satan has been here! I saw the dead man. I saw them take him away." She pointed to the floor. "The devil's footprints!" She walked over to Johnny and pressed her nose against his. "The devil leaves footprints everywhere he goes. But I'm the only one who sees them. I got devil vision!"

Johnny sighed with relief as she backed away and resumed pacing. "That or you been watchin' too much *tele*vision." He straightened his shoulders defensively as he saw her moving toward him again. "Stay back, will ya."

"I got devil vision!"

Henry looked up. "All you got is crazy, Shirley. Now go on … get the hell out of here."

"The devil told you to say that!"

"No, he didn't," Henry said, standing. "But he left his pitchfork behind and unless you want it where the sun don't shine …"

"Evil!" Shirley screamed at him. "Pure evil!"

"Out!"

Glaring at him, Shirley thrust her hand forward as her two forefingers pointed at him. "Be gone with you, Satanic demon!"

"OUT!"

As she begrudgingly left the lobby, Johnny looked over at Henry. "How did you know her name? I sure as hell never saw her before."

"She's been around for years. Gets put away somewhere, then let out. Can't imagine why you would talk to her. Fucking nutjob."

"Nobody else to talk to," Johnny said. He brightened as he saw James walk into the lobby. "About time a friend came along!"

"Hey, man … Can't talk to you. Got to get ready for a date tonight."

Johnny's eyes looked upward. "You got someone coming to your room?"

James shot him a dirty look. "No. I'm taking a lady out for a few drinks. Maybe we'll have something to eat at the bar. What the hell would you know? When's the last time you had a date?"

"I was married for thirty-four years. Macie was my date."

"She passed, right?"

Johnny looked uncomfortable. "Not exactly."

"What does that mean, man? Either a person's alive or they're dead."

"She's alive," Johnny said, embarrassed.

James laughed. "All this time I just thought … shit …kicked your ass to the curb then, did she?"

"Say whatever you want," Johnny said. "Not that simple."

"So you left *her*?"

"After she started cheatin' on me. Yeah, I did. Then the younger guy she left me for dumped her, and I sure as hell wasn't gonna stick around and be used until she found someone else. Macie didn't wanna give up the nightlife. Drinking, dancing, smoking … those were her favorite things to do. Maybe still are. Hope not." He sighed. "I outgrew the streets by the time I was forty. I tried to keep up the life for her sake, but it just wasn't my thing anymore. She said she was making up for the time she stayed at home being a mother. And she made it clear that if I wasn't gonna do her thing with her, she'd find a man who would. So good-bye marriage."

"Well, good for you, then," James said. "Doesn't sound like she did much for you."

"She did okay by the kids when they was growin' up. Before she became one herself again."

"Glad to hear that."

"And she was one hell of a good housekeeper."

James shrugged. "Well, I guess that's something."

"Oh, yeah. She was good at keeping the house when we got divorced."

"Oh! And you ended up *here*."

"Not right away," Johnny said. "Took me some time to work my way up." He laughed.

"Whatever, man."

Both men turned their heads as a well-dressed man hurried

down the stairs and across the lobby, refusing to make eye contact as he did so.

"One of Margaret's regulars," Johnny said to James.

The man turned, angrily looking at the two, but instead of saying anything, ran his hand over his gelled hair, snarled, then headed out the door.

"He's got a wife for sure," James said. "They don't slum it if they're not afraid to run into someone they know. Well, I've got to go make myself handsome for tonight."

"What time you meeting her," Johnny asked. "Three a.m? 'Cause if looking handsome is part of your game plan, it's gonna take you about that long to get there."

"Ah, shut the fuck up, man."

"I'm not much of a looker myself," Johnny said.

"You got that much right," James said as he walked away. "Later, man."

Johnny looked over at Henry. "You done with the paper yet?"

Staring at the small TV, Henry responded without making eye contact. "Why? You wanna read it?"

"Nah, ain't got no glasses with me. Ain't got none anyway. They broke."

"Then what the fuck do you care if I'm done with the paper. You need to line a birdcage or something? You can get a pair of reading glasses at the Dollar Store," Henry said.

"Those don't help. And my prescription ones bit the dust."

"Well, you need to find something better to do than sit in the lobby all day."

"I'm a lobbyist," Johnny said, chuckling.

"Then you're lobbying for bored, lonely old men," Henry said.

"Least I'm not nasty."

"Look, I'm paid to be here. Not much. But I'm paid. You on

the other hand … ah, what the hell."

Frowning, Johnny couldn't help but feel the anguish. "Other people get paid to work here, too. And none of them as unfriendly as you are some days."

"I'm no babysitter."

"And I'm no baby." Johnny could feel the humiliation run through him. Putting his hand in his pocket, he pulled out the medal again. "Sure wish I could run like you, Pops. Run far away from here." He stared at the medal for a few moments, almost as if hoping it would answer him, then put it back in his pocket.

"There you are," said the woman walking through the front door.

"Eleanor," Johnny said.

The older woman with the strange bleached hair sat down beside him. On the top of her head, a large portion of her hair, appearing matted and molded like a Sherlock Holmes flat cap, sat on her head while the rest of it hung past her waist. Wearing dark glasses that hid her eyes, her lips grabbed all of the attention, lined with a dark pencil and filled in with a frosted pink that imperfectly matched her light-pink acrylic nails.

Wearing a blue-and-red patterned shirt, her breasts sagged past the waist of her black pants. She complemented the outfit with a long mink wrap that came down to her knees. Around her neck was an oversized turquoise and silver necklace, but her wrists and fingers bore the greatest burden of metal. Every finger and every thumb donned a large silver ring with some kind of stone. Going a quarter of the way up her arms were large silver cuff bracelets pinching her skin. To ease the discomfort, she had paper towels stuffed under every one. Completing her ensemble were a pair of orange running shoes with red laces.

Sitting next to Johnny, she put her large green faux leather bag on the other side of her. "Boy, what a day from hell I've had.

Took special care to put myself together today and first thing that happens when I go next door to the diner was Addie, that damn dinosaur, spills a half cup of coffee on me. Thank the Lord it wasn't hot. She was clearing the cup off the counter as I sat down, not looking at what the hell she's doing, picking up too many plates, and she spills that damn coffee on me 'cause she was too busy looking at some stud walking through the door. Damn coffee landed on the bottom of my shirt and my crotch. Never so glad to be wearing black.

"Addie-saurus mumbles out an apology, then didn't even take my order. Rushes over to the stud and bats her eyes at him like he's Prince Charming gonna take her away on his horse waiting outside. Blah bleh blah bleh blah. And I'm sitting there thinking my empty stomach is telling my fists to punch her in the mouth if she doesn't stop flirting and take my order."

"Well ..."

"Finally get my order taken about an hour later and—"

"An hour later? Somehow I doubt that."

"Well, it sure as hell felt like it. The toast wasn't even buttered like I asked, and she brings me a dish of butter squares wrapped in foil sitting on some chipped ice. Damn things frozen solid like bricks and I ask her how I'm supposed to spread them on my toast without reducing it to crumbs. She don't even answer me because the stud wants his coffee refilled. Don't spill nothing on him. Hell no. No coffee on his crotch that she thinks she's got dibs on ... in your dreams, Addie-saurus, you old addled diner relic. They should have 86'd you a long time ago."

"How old is she?" Johnny asked.

"Sixty-eight," Eleanor said.

"But isn't she younger than you—"

"My eggs were okay, but I like me some crispy bacon ... not no undercooked slabs of fat. When I say something about that, she tells me I didn't 'specify,' and I told her as many times as I've eaten in that place, I shouldn't be needing to 'specify' how I like a damn thing. You hear me, Johnny? So finally I'm eating my food and Hester the Whore comes in crying because a john stiffed her, and she didn't get her money up front like she should have. Whatever. Like I care about a whore's problems when I got butter bricks, undercooked bacon, and a crotch full of some stranger's old coffee. Fuck that. You know?

"Then Addie's daughter, Doris, that black-haired, roots-showing loudmouth who works the night shift, comes in crying because she caught her boyfriend cheating on her with some bitch. And I'm thinking if the raggedy dame kept her hair one color, stopped stinking of cigarettes, and quit gossiping all the time, maybe her boyfriend wouldn't have gone looking elsewhere. I don't really care. But then the two of them start mixing it up when Doris says she's too distraught to work the night shift and wants the dinosaur that hatched her to work a double.

"Addie goes on and on about how Doris has no respect for her, how she's fucked up her kids—"

"I don't need to hear any more."

"How about this?" Eleanor asked, raising the stakes. "I think Addie's on coke."

"Nope. Don't think she uses."

"Hell yeah she must," Eleanor continued. "She gets these bursts of energy sometimes … and I hear that's a telltale sign."

"Believe it or not," Johnny said. "Sometimes I get bursts of energy, too."

From behind the counter, Henry burst out laughing and said nothing.

Johnny shot him a dirty look.

Impatient to continue her story, Eleanor went on. "And if you think what I just told you about them two fighting is bad, that was nothing. After Doris got through bitching at her mother, it comes out in conversation that Doris's so-called boyfriend was the one who stiffed Hester. Holy damn hell broke loose! Those two bitches start whatcha call a physical altercation, slapping each other, pulling hair … a real catfight over some pussy of a man. Then—"

Johnny put one hand on each arm of the chair as he prepared to stand.

"Sit down," Eleanor demanded. "This story is far from over. I had a very long day!"

"I really need to go," Johnny said softly.

"But you've hardly heard anything!"

"Been a busy day. I need some peace and quiet. But you know … I'm thinking Henry would really like to hear all about your day. He's kind of lonely. That's why he stares at the TV like he's doing."

"I think I'll talk to him."

"Oh, he'd *really* like that."

"Well fine, but first I'm gonna tell you everything and then I'll tell him. What I just told you is only about two percent of my hellish day."

Johnny stood and looked at her, before turning toward the stairs. "You take care, Eleanor."

"But I'm not done talking … this is some real interesting stuff … damn you …"

As he walked away, leaving Eleanor with a scowl etched on her face, Johnny mumbled to himself. "Not that lonely. Oh hell no. Not that lonely. Not me."

First Date

"I think this might be your lady friend," Marvin said to James as he wiped the bar with a damp rag. "A snazzy lady in red just walked through the door. How long have you two been seeing one another?"

"We haven't. She takes tickets on the train. We exchange a few words here and there. Got up my nerve this morning to ask her for a date."

"Well, here she comes."

James turned around to see Shayna, snuggly in a low-cut cherry-red dress, walking toward him. Standing, he greeted her warmly, then held out his arms, but dropped them to his sides when he realized a hug was out of the question. Oddly reserved, she smiled as she took the seat next to him at the bar.

"Hello, there," Marvin said, putting a cocktail napkin in front of her.

Shayna, dipping her chin and raising her eyes, winked at Marvin. "A screw … driver for me, please."

Marvin's eyes widened as he tried to sneak a look at James. "Be right back."

James looked at his date. "Not even a hello?"

"Hello, James."

"You look beautiful. I was wondering what you looked like out of your uniform … I mean … in a dress. I'm glad you could meet me tonight."

Shayna nodded but said nothing, smiling at Marvin as he put her drink in front of her.

"Didn't figure you for a vodka lady."

"Oh," she said. "Okay."

"How long have you been working for the Transit Authority?"

"I've told you before. Too long. I'm retiring in five years."

"Oh, right. What do you plan to do then?"

"Uh … not work." Shayna looked at Marvin. "Hey, baby, want to shove those nuts down my way."

"How about traveling?" James asked. "You must have some dream destinations on your bucket list, huh?"

"I'm just trying not to kick the damn bucket," she said, smiling at Marvin as he put a bowl of salted peanuts in front of her. "Besides, I'm not a list maker."

"I'm not really, either. Someone told me once that making lists was a habit of highly effective people. Guess that's why I never do it." He laughed but stopped as his attempt at a joke landed with a thud. "So, are you a music fan?"

Shayna looked at him with interest for the first time. "You a musician? Do you sing? Play? Both?"

James sighed. "I'm afraid I'm just a listener … an aficionado. Jazz and R & B mostly."

"Oh, you and a million others," Shayna said, looking away. "I'll bet that bartender is a musician."

"Uh, yeah. Matter of fact, he is."

She smiled. "I could just tell. He's got that vibe about him."

"I guess."

"What's his name?"

James tried not to show his disgust. "Marv Jackson. Plays jazz piano. Used to have a regular gig at a place called The Blue Lights in Philly. But that was several years ago. Now he tends bar and does the occasional gig. Work isn't always easy to come by."

Shayna licked her lips as she ogled Marvin. "But he's got that certain something going on. You know?"

"If you say so."

"I do say so," Shayna said, glancing to her right. "Can you excuse me for a moment, baby? I see one of my co-workers across the room. I'm just gonna go say hey."

"Sure thing," James said, standing as Shayna got off the barstool. "See you in a few."

Marvin, who had been talking to someone at the end of the bar, saw Shayna had stepped away, then hurried down to him.

"Where's the fire?" James asked. "You look like you're in a hurry."

"Just wanted to talk to you. You know Billy, yeah? Security. He's the off-duty cop who moonlights here for us once in a while. One of the best on the force."

"Yeah, I know him. It's been a while, but yeah, I've seen him around."

"Well, he was just telling me one of your neighbors was taken out in a body bag today. Only thirty-six. Lived on the third floor."

"Oh, shit," James said. "So that's who it was. I was just talking to him last week. Told me he was going to get his act together, get away from the drugs, hook up with some fine lady he'd met, and move out of the Obscure forever."

Marvin grabbed a glass and filled it up with soda water for a customer who was signaling him. "Well, looks like he got that last part down."

"Yeah. Sucks to be him."

"Folks gotta be careful what they wish for," Marvin said as he walked away.

"I'm back," Shayna said, sitting on the barstool. "Boy, this place is filling up."

"It's a popular club." James took a sip of his drink. "So, that was quick."

"You think? Just as I was getting near her table, she and some guy started in with the tongue gymnastics. I wasn't going near that."

"No, I wouldn't either."

"I saw the bartender walking away just as I was coming back," Shayna said. "Was he asking about me by any chance?"

"Not even close." James thought before continuing. "A guy who lives at my hotel was carried out in a body bag today. Was only in his thirties. Damn shame."

"Oh. Really? Dead people scare me. But they fascinate me, too."

"Have you ever seen one?"

"About ten years ago. I had just punched the man's ticket. In less than five minutes, God punched his ticket too. Aneurysm, I heard. I was standing only three rows away when he checked out. I was a wreck, and passengers were freaking out every which damn way. And that sure as hell didn't help nothing."

"What did you do?"

"Asked passengers to remain in their seats and stay calm. I really wanted to tell them all to shut the fuck up. But I got to be professional and all that rot. Luckily, the next stop was only a few minutes away, and some men boarded the train and took him away. That shit shook me up. I've never punched another ticket without thinking about that man." Shayna took a healthy swig of her screwdriver. "Where do you work again?"

"Retired," James said.

"So how come you ride the train every day?"

"I help my daughter out. Babysit my grandkids. Visit friends sometime."

"Oh." Shayna looked bored. "What kind of work did you do?"

"I was a big-rig driver."

"Guess you never saw any dead people … not unless you ran over someone with your truck." She laughed.

Stone-faced, James looked at her. "No, I never killed anyone.

But there was one night I saw more dead people than I ever want to see again." He motioned to Marvin to bring them a second round. "So, you like jazz? 'Cause I know a joint that jumps, just like that Fats Waller's song, every Thursday through Sunday. Maybe we could go some time. There are five guys that jam, and some of the best vocalists in the area come by to sing with them. 'That joint is jumpin'; it's really jumpin'....."

"Tell me about the dead people."

"Aw, that's not a good story for a date."

Shayna looked at Marvin, who was now standing in front of her. "Hit me up, baby." Winking at Marvin, Shayna turned back to James. "Tell me about it."

"Hey, if having a guy die on your train upsets you, you might not want—"

"Tell me, for fuck's sake."

"Okay, then," James said, catching a sympathetic glance from Marvin. "If you're sure...."

"I'm sure already!"

"Okay then …. Well, it was like this. I was working then for a big-rig towing company. I used to tease the guys that I worked with about how the coroner's vans were all county and that our company had just gotten a county contract. 'Cause you see, not a one of us wanted to go anywhere near a van with a dead body.

"So, about a month later, I get the first call. Lucky me. The dispatcher says that a coroner's van broke down and is at a hospital. He said the van was empty. I was married then, having dinner at my mother-in-law's place, so I asked Ken, my brother-in-law, to ride along with me. He was game and so we headed toward the hospital. I even called the dispatcher from the road, you know, just to confirm the van was empty. And she said it was. So, when we got there, I'm wondering why a coroner's van is outside of the ER."

"What made you wonder that?"

"Because coroners don't drop people off; they pick them up. You know?"

"Oh, right. Go on."

"Sure you want to hear this?"

"Oh, for fuck's sake," Shayna repeated. "Yes!"

"Okay, then. So to be specific, the van was headed down the emergency ramp toward the door. I see this dude come walking out. I figured him to be a sheriff. Couldn't see his badge because he had a sweater on. Kind of a cold night. Anyway, I go to the nurse's station to ask for the coroner, and the nurse tells me he had just walked by me. I don't know why I didn't put two and two together. I just figured the coroner would be some old guy.

"So, I catch up with him and tell him who I am. Tells me his name is Alex. I explain that I'm gonna rear tow the van—you know, pick it up from the back and be on my way. He tells me I can't do that. And I'm thinking, how the hell is this guy telling me how to do my business, when he tells me that there are two people in the van. Ken and I look at each other, and I'm thinking, oh shit, well, this is gonna be interesting."

"I'll bet."

"So, moving on here, I positioned my truck to the front of the coroner's van. See, you're not supposed to tow anything with the drive shaft, so I had it in my arms. I didn't wanna forget it and leave it in the back of my truck, so I asked the coroner to store it in the back of his van."

"So you gave the coroner the shaft," Shayna said, laughing.

"I guess so," James said, trying to smile. "Anyway, Alex opens the door to the van, and I see two gurneys. One is about the size of a backpack … child in there … and the other was an adult. They were covered, so I couldn't see their faces. Alex sees my face and asks me if I'm afraid of dead people."

"Were you? How about Ken? Was he?"

"Ken was waiting in the truck. Had hopped in with me when I moved it to tow the van." James exhaled. "But as I told Alex, I'd rather not come in contact with any of the dearly departed. At that point, I laid down the shaft, and before I know it, Alex uncovers their faces to show me that there was nothing to fear."

"Didn't that freak you out?"

"Only when the dead guy winked at me."

"Wow, telling a story about dead people isn't really the best time for a joke."

"But you just made … yeah, right. Anyway, I called back my dispatcher and told her that there were indeed bodies in the van and that I had to take them to the morgue before I could tow the van to the mechanic."

"Get to the good stuff," Shayna urged.

Exasperated, James continued. "We get to the coroner's office, and it was tough to back up to the doors because the tow truck was thirty-two feet and had the van attached. I got the truck halfway up the ramp, backing it in, when Alex tells me that he can get the bodies from there. He opens the door and pulls out the adult body. Then, he picked up the kid, who was wrapped in sheets, just like you pick up a damn suitcase. He takes the kid and places him on the guy's lower legs so he only had to pull the one gurney."

"A guy could get a gurnea doing that," Shayna said, laughing.

Baffled, James continued speaking. "So, on the ride to the morgue, just talking, Alex and I discovered we only lived a mile from each other. That being the case, Alex asked if I could drop him home after he dropped off the bodies. I said I would and that we'd wait for him.

"Next thing I know, we're at the morgue. Alex removed the bodies, handed his bag to me, and asked Ken and me to come inside. I gotta tell you, that was already way more than we'd bargained for. Neither one of us had a mind for that kind of adventure, but Alex insisted. So, we thought, what the hell."

"For sure, who gets an offer like that every day?"

"Not many. But who wants one?"

"I would have been up for it."

"Really? I thought you just said you can't punch a passenger's ticket without thinking about the guy who died."

"I don't see the connection," Shayna said. "Just go on with your story."

James shook his head. Behind Shayna's back, Marvin put his hands up in the air as if to say that he was confused as well. Taking a breath, James continued. "So after the bodies come off the van, Alex puts them on these blue tables outside. There were several tables, about waist high."

"Really, what if it rained?"

"Oh, there was an awning over all of the tables, so they had that covered. So to speak."

Shayna had no visible reaction as James shifted on his barstool. "Okay so moving right along, after the doors open automatically, the blue table is taken in. Inside, there was this big desk and a couple of people standing behind it. Someone takes the kid and puts him right there on the desk. Then, a guy dressed like a doctor, covered in plastic and wearing rubber gloves, wheels the blue table away while Alex fills out some paperwork.

"The doctor guy takes the body maybe twenty feet and puts it on a scale so he knows exactly what the guy weighs. Alex explained that the scale automatically deducts the weight of the table. You know ... so it's accurate."

"Hell," Shayna said, "I hope I'm at my goal weight when I die ... or less. God forbid the last thing that happens to me on this earth is to have a damn scale be accurate ... or add even so much as a pound. You know?"

James twisted his mouth. "Somehow, I don't think the guy

was worried about his weight." He took a sip of his drink. "Anyway, I'm still standing in the reception area with Ken. We can see maybe four bodies from where we are. That's when Alex talks us into watching how they examine a body. So, we're thinking we've come this damn far and we might as well go with him.

"The guy on the table was Hispanic. He had on brand-new Nikes, nice Levis, and there he is … lying dead as a doorknob. Been killed in a car accident. They cut his clothes off and we're just standing there watching."

"How did that make you feel?" Shayna asked.

"Not great. Like I was violating the guy's privacy. I started to say something, but then the pathologist is talking to Alex while he's examining the body. He's turning it on both sides to check for foul play, GSWs, and things like that. The dead guy's legs went forward from his knees to his chest. Then the pathologist says to Alex, 'Well, I know that's broken.' Then he says the guy has dried sperm all over his body. They turn him over and damned if he did have a washcloth stuck up his butt."

"Seriously? Wow, is that kind of thing normal? I don't stick things up my nether region, but if I knew I was going to die, I'd make sure to give my ass the all-clear." Shayna chugged her drink. "That's bizarre. But who knows. Maybe they see that kind of stuff all the time."

"Don't think so," James said, "because the pathologist called everyone over to take a gander. They were making all kinds of jokes—"

"You mean they were making the dead guy the butt of their jokes," Shayna said, snickering.

"Yeah, whatever. But they're also trying to come up with a plausible explanation. The only thing they could think of was that he must have had sex, wasn't wearing any underwear, and for some reason shoved the washcloth up there afterward." James stopped to make sure Shayna was still interested. "It was about then that another coroner had just gotten back from McDonald's. He's still eating his damn Big Mac, a damn onion hanging out on his shirt, looking at the guy. When he finished, he toe-tagged the guy and took him to the freezer. Ken and I are looking at each other when Alex says, "You two look squeamish; let me show you something."

"Oh, intriguing. But what happened to the onion?"

"For real? Hell if I know or care. His back was turned to me when he took the guy away. Anyway, Alex, Ken, and I go through another automatic door. When we get past it, there's a long corridor with bodies in the hallway. There's a lady in a plastic bag that was unzipped. I swear, she looked like Marilyn Monroe. We counted seventeen stab wounds on her body. Her throat was cut and her eyes were wide open. She was found in a park, completely naked. Man, that just slayed me. Ken too. Just hurt like hell to see that."

"Wow," Shayna said.

"Guess you've heard enough."

"Not if there's more to the story, I haven't."

"I just don't feel right—"

"Finish!"

James picked up his drink and took a few good sips. "Okay, then. Well, Alex was determined to de-squeamify us. That's the word he used, too. De-freakin'-squeamify. He says he wants to show us something else and takes us to this freezer. There were like sixty bodies in there. All of them were naked except for two who were fully dressed. I couldn't believe it. This guy is wearing a suit and tie, shades, and dressed to the nines. In a damn freezer. So I asked Alex why that was."

"What did he say?"

"It was a homicide, so they had to preserve the clues. I told Alex that he sure looked intact to me. That's when Alex turned the guy's head to one side, and right behind his ear was a bullet hole—"

"Sure as shootin'." Shayna laughed.

Trying to ignore her, James continued. "After that, we walked around and saw several bodies that were nothing but skeletal remains. You know, like parts that had been discovered in different places throughout the city."

"I'll bet the coroners were trying to get a leg up on all of this. Maybe get ahead in their investigation."

"Is this funny to you?" James asked. "I thought you said—"

"No, what kind of ghoul do you think I am?" Shayna burst out laughing. "Oh, come on. Tell me more."

"It gets worse. I don't know if I should tell you."

"Oh, please. Just finish already."

"Well, okay then. So, we get ready to leave that area, after Alex does some more paperwork, and then he says that he's got one more thing to show us … in the same building, but outside. The place was called 'decomp.'"

"Bet you had to really compose yourself to go in there!" Shayna said, grinning.

Shaking his head, James kept talking. "There was a woman who worked there, covered one-hundred percent in plastic, even down to her shoes. She acknowledges Alex and he asks what's going on. He asks if she's busy, and she barks back, 'Whattya think?'

"She then shows us someone completely dismembered. Couldn't even tell if it was a man or a woman. On the next table, there's a white guy who over time had turned really dark … splotchy. He had been dead for a couple weeks in his home before anyone found him. He had blue eyes, still open, and maggots coming out of every orifice on his face. The decomp lady said it happens all of the time. Her job is to go out in the field, so to speak, and prepare any decomposed bodies by wrapping them up in plastic so there is no contamination when she gets back to work. Then, when she brings the remains back, she goes over the body again. She was spraying it with bleach when we were talking."

"Yeah? What else?"

"How much more do you want? That's all I got. End of story."

Shayna made an exaggerated sad face. "Nothing else?"

"Just what Alex told us when we finally left. 'After a while, you just become desensitized to it all. But never with the kids. That still gets me every time.'"

Reaching into the bowl in front of her, Shayna grabbed a small handful of peanuts. "They always make the peanuts in bars extra salty so you'll order more to drink."

"Why don't you tell me something about yourself? I know you've got grandkids. You mentioned them to me once."

"I probably did. What can I tell you? They're three, five, and eight and always covered in mud. Two boys and a girl. I keep telling my daughter-in-law not to let them play in the backyard. But hell, she don't listen. They're good kids. But I hope they'll be cleaner when they grow up, you know?"

"Kids get dirty. It's part of what being a kid is all about."

"That's what she says," Shayna said, her eyes turning toward Marvin as she soaked in his physique. "I'll bet he works out. You can tell."

"He does. His wife manages a health club."

"Oh," Shayna said, her disappointment obvious. "I see."

Frustrated, James forced a crooked smile. "Look, you want to go somewhere else? That club I told you about isn't open tonight, but there's a place three blocks away where they've got a great jazz pianist. Marv told me about him. Might be nice to hear some music. Relax. Chill. Get to know one another."

Shayna twirled the long gold chain around her neck. "No, I don't think so."

James bit his lower lip and thought for a moment. "You

know, you seemed a lot more interested in me on the train than you do now. You want to call it a night? No hard feelings?"

Shayna sighed, her agitation obvious. "I need to use the little girl's room, sugar. I'll be right back."

"Whatever," James said, watching as she hopped off the bar stool and walked away.

"There might not be as many fish in the sea as there used to be," Marvin said, standing before James as soon as Shayna was out of sight. "But what you got here is a perfect case for 'catch and release,' my man. Let this one go."

James reached into his pocket for his wallet. "Oh, I hear ya, brother. She's not interested in me, and I damn sure have lost interest in her. You're probably wondering why the hell I even asked her out."

"Crossed my mind," Marvin said, putting his palms down on the bar.

"I'm wondering too." James picked up the check, took a look, then put some money down on the bar. "I'm outta here."

Marvin picked up the money and nodded. "Thanks, my man. I'll let the lady know."

As James walked out of the club, Billy, who had been standing at the end of the bar, walked down and sat in James's empty seat. Billy turned, looked around the now-crowded club, and satisfied that all was well, turned back to face the bar.

About five minutes later, Shayna returned to her seat, startled, but not upset to see Billy in James's seat. "Hey, baby. What happened to the man who was here?"

"Paid the check and left, I think."

"Oh. Really? Nice of him to not even say good-bye. He was a rotten date anyway."

"Why's that?" Billy asked.

"All he talked about was this time him and his brother-in-law got an impromptu tour of a morgue. Nasty stuff, you know? Hardly first-date talk."

"I see," Billy said, locking eyes with Marvin who had already told him all about Shayna. "Oh, well."

Pouting, Shayna looked at her near-empty drink that she didn't want to pay to refresh. "Didn't even buy me another drink before he left. And I'm so thirsty."

Billy just looked at her, refusing to take the bait.

"I just don't know what kind of a man makes jokes about going to a morgue. If you ask me, that's sick. Especially after I had just told him about a man dying on the train where I work."

"I didn't hear the conversation. So I'm not in any position to judge."

"Well, how's this: when he asked me out, he said we'd have drinks and probably a bite to eat. Here I am on an empty stomach … not to mention thirsty … as I just said … and he's gone."

"He is."

"Do you know if he's a regular here? I'm thinking he has to be since he seemed to know the bartender pretty well."

"I believe he is. I see him fairly often."

"Good. Because I'm gonna order a steak dinner and a split of Piper Heidseick. Next time he comes back in here, he can damn well pay for it."

"Don't think so," Billy told her. "The man isn't here. What he doesn't order, he doesn't have to pay for. You can pay with plastic, though."

"Oh, honey, my credit's been in the crapper for years. No, I think I'll go ahead and order up everything my heart desires. I'm gonna get what I deserve!"

Billy smiled to himself. "I think you will. Just remember, it's on you. Not the man who just left. You hear me?"

Shayna put her hands on her hips and stared at Billy. "Listen, baby, I'm not worried about that shit. Do I look worried?"

"No, you don't."

"Exactly. Now, you see any po-lice uniforms around here?"

Billy made a cursory glance around. "Can't say that I do."

"Exactly!" With a smug smile on her face, Shayna raised her hand to get Marvin's attention. "Oh, bartender, baby, can you bring me a menu?"

TWENTY-SEVEN

I ain't such a good talker. I coulda been, just never wanted to be. A part of me was just lazy, I guess. Another part just didn't care. But still, I didn't like following all of them grammatical rules … or any rules. Maybe because they all got broke the day I was born. I used to mumble a whole lot, too. I thought that if people couldn't be sure what I was sayin', then maybe, I'd get credit for sayin' something awesome. Only it usually worked in reverse, and people would think I was cursin' them out under my breath. Most of the time, I wasn't, but I sure was thinkin' stuff they wouldn't have wanted to hear.

My birth mom tossed me on the doorstep of the local firehouse like I was a newspaper on her route to "hell no, I don't want a kid." My father was a cop then, and that's how my parents learned about me and decided to take me in, seeing how they wanted a kid and all. Especially a son. He was the first one on the scene when the firehouse called.

My parents never told me all of this; I just thought I was adopted, the same way other kids usually are. I had to learn the real story from some church lady at my house. One day, she came over to bring a casserole after hearing my mother wasn't feeling well. She blabbed to my mother about a bunch of mindless stuff. Then, after moving on to gossip about some couple in the church, she couldn't wait to let my mother know that she knew all about "the boy's wretched beginning" 'cause her brother was a fireman, and he was at the station the day I got abandoned. She went into as much detail as she could … just to show off. My mother just sat there, shaking and looking around to make sure I was nowhere I could hear. But I was hiding behind the draperies, peeking through the fabric. And I heard everything. Called me a spawn of Lucifer and his crack whore. That's when my mother kicked her outta the house right quick. But soon as the front door was shut, my mother, well, she cried for hours, and when my old man got home, she asked him what if the lady was right. She wanted to know what if I did have a demon in me, and he just hugged her and patted her hair like you would with a pet. Then he told her to go make dinner. And that was the nicest I'd ever seen him be to her.

I was maybe eight then. I ain't all that sure. Coulda maybe been seven.

But I do remember what happened right after my ninth birthday. Some lady from the Rotary Club was visiting our house. When my mother went into the kitchen to fetch the hag some tea, the lady told me I could benefit from some elocution lessons. Next day, I asked my teacher what it means for someone to "benefit from electrocution," and she sent me to the principal. After a whole bunch of bullshit and calling my parents in, I got suspended for lying and threatening to fry my teacher. I never did understand what happened until about three years later. I was watching this show about them royals in England where I heard the word "elocution" again. I realized I'd gotten the word wrong and figured the whole mess out for myself. But it was too late. I didn't give a damn anymore. I already knew they didn't give a rat's ass about me and never would. I was pretty sure they were wishin' I'd come with a return policy. Money-back guarantee. But I didn't.

Lots of stuff happened to me, but it was them two things that—well, I guess they had the most impact if you're psycho … um … logically inclined to think about stuff like that. Yup. I just wanted to vaporize from their world into one of my own. I never belonged in theirs, 'cause in my case, with that whole nature versus nurture argument, nature was the clear winner and not by no damn nose. By a long stretch. I figured I wasn't more than a stone's throw away from the sperm donator and the baby-tossin' incubator that made me.

When I was in the third grade, I had the nicest teacher ever. When Mother's Day was coming, she brought in art supplies for all of the kids to make cards. Pretty much everyone had no problem knowing what to draw, but I just sat there and looked lost. When my teacher saw me struggling, she asked me to walk over to the window with her. It was real green outside … lots of trees, birds, and even flowers. She asked me did I see anything I wanted to draw. Just then, a dragonfly landed on the windowsill outside. I pointed to it. She smiled and asked me did I need her to pull up a photo of a dragonfly on the computer because the real one probably wouldn't want to pose for very long. I took a good look at it and told her I could memorize it. I remembered the first time I'd seen one on our back patio when my mother told me what they were called and that she thought they were so pretty. I thought she was kidding me because they didn't look anything like the dragons in my storybooks.

Giving my mother that card was probably the happiest I ever made her.

About a month after that, it was her birthday. As he always did, my father just shoved some money her way and told her to pick out something. He said he didn't know her taste, but he just couldn't be bothered taking the time to pick something out.

She took me with her to this jewelry boutique in town. As soon as she looked in the case, she cried out when she saw this silver dragonfly cuff bracelet. It had four dragonflies carved in the silver and a space in the middle to put your initials. She was so happy. She told me this would always remind her of the first time we saw the dragonfly and of the beautiful card I made for her. After she gave the shop lady her initials, we went and had lunch while they got her bracelet ready. She loved it. Wore it every day.

I thought maybe things would change after that, but nothing

did. I didn't flunk out of school or wreck the house, but that didn't matter. I think they just hated the way I talked. It reflected bad on them, and it reminded everyone I was adopted, which reminded my parents that they couldn't conceive a kid. Never was told which one of them had the problem. But I'm damn sure my father had a low count 'cause when nosy people asked why they adopted, his eyes would go black, and my mother would jump in and say she had lady problems. Then he would sigh with relief but still look pissed. And she'd get all damn trembly and look like she was afraid of him. I always wanted to try and make her feel better, but I felt like he'd hit me if I tried.

    I was a loner. The only kids who talked to me were kind of loners, too. Once, I overheard a teacher on her phone call us "'the misfits'" when she thought we'd left the classroom. Only I was going back in 'cause I'd left my hoodie on the back of my chair. And she gave me an "oh shit" look, and I didn't say nothin', but I gave her a real steely-eyed look so she'd know I heard her all right and wouldn't be pretendin' otherwise. After that day, she never made eye contact with me again. I think she gave me better marks than I earned, being afraid I'd say something to get her fired. I just didn't care enough. Not about anything. Letting her know I heard her was good enough for me.

    I can't ever remember a time I didn't hurt in some way. But I didn't know how to unhurt, so I didn't try. I didn't follow the rules, but I didn't try to break them on purpose. I just kind of did that naturally. There were times when I hurt worse than ever and hoped that maybe my mother would show real love for me. All I wanted was a hug, for her say that she loved me, and everything would be all right. And even though she didn't do that, though it sounds strange to say it, I often believed that she really wanted to comfort me. It was like her eyes spoke when no other part of her could. But I must have been wrong. Every time even my body language, which I 'spose was as off-putting as my spoken language, showed me to being open to some attention or affection, she'd turn away.

I gave up. I figured they weren't gonna love me until I sounded and acted like they wanted me to; I wasn't gonna try to love them until that didn't matter. So yeah, that's what ya call an impasse or a standstill. They probably would have loved to hear me use them words. Ain't that ironic? I learned a whole lot of words I never used. Guess that's sort of like saving money you ain't never gonna spend and still livin' like you're poor. I dunno.

I wasn't close to the kid they wanted, even though I never got in much trouble. Not the kind where your ass ends up in jail and someone has to bail you out. Until I was eighteen, the three of us lived in the house like we was strangers. As I got older, I started to realize that my parents were like strangers to each other too. I never saw affection between them. The most I can remember is that day he comforted her with that damn pat on the head. When he was gone away on business, I'd hear muffled cries coming from their bedroom. Like she was sobbing into a pillow so I wouldn't hear her. I worried she might suffocate but she always survived. I never ever thought she was crying 'cause she missed him, neither.

More and more, I'd hear her cry when he was home. Them sobs was never muffled. I knew he must have been saying something to her that wasn't very nice. As the years went on, I could hear his voice get louder and louder. Man, did he scream at her. Some nights I heard her cry so bad that I half expected she might have a black eye or a broken leg the next morning. Too many damn times I was worried he'd just pull out his gun and shoot her. And then come for me.

I never knew what he said to her; I just know he did a number on her head, and she was scared to death of him. When I was in a really bad way, I would blame myself. Like thinking I wasn't the kind of son he could be proud of and so he had to be angry as fuck that she just didn't leave infertility alone instead of adopting someone's throwaway garbage. Forget the irony of him being the one to discover me at the firehouse. That wouldn't stop him from blaming her for wanting a kid so bad.

The older I got, I just watched my mother disappear from herself. I'd see this vacant look in her eyes. I always felt like she wanted to talk to me, but she never did. And despite that, I wanted to help her, but I had no idea how a person even does that.

When I made it to fourteen, I came to the conclusion there wasn't much worth livin' for. I was thinking of doin' myself in and relievin' my parents and me of the damn fakery we all lived.

But while I was mullin' over my demise, one of my "misfit" friends got a new Gibson guitar and gave me his old Martin. He started me off learning some chords, and the rest I learned on my own, watching videos. I took to it real good. Like I'd been playing forever. One day, some friend of his brother's asked if I had taught him how to play. He sure didn't like that. He was embarrassed, not to mention pissed, but he put all that aside 'cause he figured my talent would be useful to him when we formed our group. Only I never wanted to be part of a group. But I didn't think I needed to tell him that until push came to shove it up his butt.

And shove came as soon as we got outta high school three and a half years later. By that time, I was way damn better on my worst day than he could ever be on his best. I told him I was going solo, doing a whole different kind of music than the pop he was down for, and he told me I was a fucking ingrate. I hurled a "whatever" at him and walked away. Last so-called friend I ever had.

Leaving my parents' home was harder than I thought. Not because of my father, but 'cause my mother had this pained kind of pleadin' look in her eyes. She was tryin' to say a whole lot to me. But when he'd glance her way, she'd go back to just staring straight ahead like a mannequin. My father said good-bye to me like I was a long-term guest checkin' out of his hotel. One he was real glad to get rid of! He refused to leave my mother alone with me, and I could tell how bad she wished he would.

I used to read about how aliens would abduct people and take them aboard their spacecraft. The whole point was to extract sperm from the men and put alien sperm into the females. They did this stuff to create hybrids of aliens and humans. Hell, maybe that's what I was. Never thought of that before.

Anyway, I ain't gonna go off into that, but I bring it up 'cause all of the abductees would report that they communicated with the aliens through some kind of mind-speak. Nobody said a word, but they were still talkin' and understandin' each other. So that's sort of how I communicated with my mother exceptin' that I never really knew for sure what she wanted to tell me. Not really. All she said aloud was for me to take good care of myself and keep in touch. My father sort of grunted like that went for him, too. But we all knew that day, we'd never speak again.

I moved into the city. Into this here room in this end-of-the world hotel.

I got a job at a warehouse two blocks away. I didn't have to talk a whole lot. I just did my shift and came home to my guitar and my music. I coulda lived somewhere better on what I made, but I knew the warehouse was closing down in a few years, and I thought I'd better save what I could. The best thing about livin' here was that nobody looked down on me. Nobody gave a damn about how I talked and didn't hardly nobody even know the word "elocution," much less worry about anyone benefittin' from it. That to me right there was freedom. I was nobody's burden anymore.

I'd be lyin' to say I never thought about my mother, 'cause in actuality, I did. I called her several times, but when she would answer, I would just hang up. I just didn't want to burden her, and I was afraid if my father was nearby, she'd be punished for talking to me. I never had any proof of anything, but I felt this in my gut like a sucker punch from a playground bully. I hoped that she would know it was me on the line and that would be enough. And if she didn't want it to be me, then maybe she could just shrug it off as a wrong number.

To be honest, I didn't always come home to my guitar and music. Sometimes I brought a girl with me for a completely different activity. Not different girls, just this married one who worked at the warehouse in the office. Her husband was a truck driver who had a chick in every town. It had been a couple of years since she felt anything for him, and she sure didn't want to catch whatever diseases she figured he must've been picking up in his travels. She couldn't afford to divorce him 'cause they had two little kids. So, a couple of nights a week, her mom stayed late to watch them, and we'd do our thing until she had to get home. And then I'd grab my guitar and dissolve into my own world.

Anyway, right on schedule, three years later, the warehouse closed and we all lost our jobs. The girl—guess I should call her a woman—that I was messin' with, finally got a divorce and met a good guy who knew how to love her right. I was happy for her. When she told me, I couldn't help but wonder if maybe my mother wouldn't want to do the same. I wondered if he still yelled at her. Did he threaten her? I think that's one of the reasons I'd call and hang up. At least I'd know she was still alive. It was hard for me not to remember that his gun was never too far away. And that he had a bad temper. But maybe with me being gone, he'd have less anger and not think about using it. If he ever did. I don't know. But it was just real hard not to speculate.

I had plenty of money saved so livin' in this dive wasn't a problem. But playin' only for myself was a problem. I got up my nerve and went to an open-mic night at this coffeehouse on the outskirts of the city. They really liked me there. The only problem was that all of the bands and singer/songwriters who played there had followings to fill the room. And hell, nobody followed me. So I couldn't get past being an opening act, even there.

It was a start, though, and every time I played, people came up to me and wanted to know where I would be next and why didn't I have my own show. After about five people asked me if I was gonna play this club called Turbulence, I decided to go there and check it out.

My hair was way long past my shoulders, and I had enough grunge and angst to look the part of a headliner. The manager still didn't want to be bothered because he never heard of me, but this foxy chick that worked there, and just happened to be the daughter of the owner, said she wanted to hear me.

She fell for my music hard. For real. And I booked a solo gig right then and there. Yeah, I got lucky. Another act had to cancel, and I was in the right place at the right time. I went back to the coffeehouse and told all my new fans I'd booked at Turbulence.

Honestly, I didn't expect but two of them to show, but a whole damn group did. Word got around, and I played to my first full-ass house. Turbulence booked me regular after that, and the chick that fell hard for my music—well, she fell hard for me, too.

I didn't want to, but damned if I didn't fall for her too. It wasn't nothin' like the fling I had at the warehouse. Not that I didn't care about that person, but this was love. And it felt good. But damned if it didn't scare the livin' daylights outta me at the same time. I really believed I was immune from having these kinds of feelings. I thought maybe there was something in my genetic makeup to keep that from ever happenin'.

What else really surprised me was how much I wanted my mother to know. So many times, I came so close to callin', but I never got past that fear of her gettin' hurt because of me somehow. Then, one day, I got my nerve up and did call. But when she answered, I couldn't talk. She even called my name for the first time, and I knew it was safe. But then I realized it wouldn't stop there, and I was so damn sure I'd be puttin' her in danger. I could never shake the shit my gut told me about what my father might do to her. So I hung up. But she knew it was me. I never did figure out if I was a coward or a hero.

Puttin' that aside, life was better than I ever thought it could be. Who knew that baby left on the door of the fire station would be such a damn musical genius, but I was. Hell yeah, and in love with this beautiful woman, too. At Turbulence, I was a real draw. I felt more like a rock star every day. Left this raggedy-ass place and moved in with my woman. I recorded three CDs during those years, started playin' bigger venues, and we whooped and hollered together the first time we heard one of my songs on the local rock station. I knew my mother wouldn't hear it, but maybe someone who knew us both would tell her that I'd made good. And if that didn't happen, well then, hell, she'd know when I became a star. I was on the grind and nothin' was gonna stop me. Only it did. Like a big steel door coming down from the skies … the kind of heavy that you walk into, knock yourself the fuck out, and didn't see comin'.

I was with my woman at the nicest damn restaurant I'd ever been to. It had glass chandeliers and these hideaway booths with dark purple velvet curtains. The wait to get one of them was months, but I had booked one, and the day had finally come. I couldn't wait. And I couldn't believe it, either. I was actually gonna ask someone to marry me. Damn.

I knew something was wrong the minute we walked into the place. She looked around at how fancy it was, and her face went pale. When the dude in the tux sat us in the booth, she looked sick to her stomach, then said she had no choice but to blurt it all out. I don't think she barely took a breath before telling me she was tired of playing second fiddle … or maybe ukulele to my acoustic guitar. I dunno. Some damn thing like that. I just know it was a fucked-up musical cliché that wasn't true. I started to ask her what I'd done to make her feel like she wasn't important to me, and she rattled off how I was obsessed with being a damn rocker, and she didn't wanna be my star groupie and wait for the day when I ditched her for younger ones. Didn't matter to her one damn bit that I'd never cheated. She had it all figured out.

She also had another man. So, yeah, maybe she just told herself all that so she wouldn't have to feel guilty and could just put the whole damn thing on me. When the waiter came over, she told him to just give us a few more minutes. The dude nodded politely and went away.

And that's when she told me I needed to be outta her condo the next day. Oh, yeah, and that Turbulence had a new owner and was closin' at the end of the week for renovations. It was gonna be a jazz club. And it was getting' a new name. As if that even mattered.

It had all been fun while it lasted, is what she said, but she was burnt out on the life and on me. Oh, yeah, and she deserved better.

The next day I moved out. Never did have a lot of stuff. I hauled ass back to this godforsaken hellhole and even got the same room. My gigs at Turbulence were gone. I fell into depression and stopped tryin'. I guess it would make sense that I started takin' drugs to ease my pain, but despite them bein' a big part of the music scene, I never used anything stronger than weed. But I did know where to get shit. You couldn't live where I lived or do what I did and not know that.

Despite being miserable, I kept tryin' to make my life work 'cause I had proof that it was possible. I booked random gigs here and there, but nobody went crazy over me like they once did. Maybe it was because I felt so dead inside, and it showed on the outside. I don't know. I felt like a hollowed-out Easter Bunny that had melted in the sun … just a big mess that needed to be cleaned up.

On the day I turned twenty-seven, I had reached the end of my road. I felt lonelier than I'd ever felt in my life. That's when I thought that joinin' Jim Morrison, Janis Joplin, Kurt Cobain, Jimi Hendrix, Brian Jones and all the rest, in the damn 27 Club, would be my legacy. I'd always had a morbid fascination with that club. It seemed right for a mess like me.

I mean, seriously, how did a throwaway baby ever think the world, much less any woman, would want him? How did he have the damned nerve to think he could make somethin' of himself? That little bit of success and good living was just the universe teasing me.

At least I had put out them CDs. I wasn't leavin' no great legacy like the other guys, but I was still a rocker turnin' off the lights at twenty-seven, and I'd be in an exclusive club. That would be somethin'. Maybe I'd even be discovered post-mortem. Whatever. It was the best I could hope to do in my miserable life. The more I thought about it, the better it sounded. And the angrier I got at myself for ever havin' thought I could have a good life. Even the people so desperate for a kid hadn't wanted me.

And so, I went down to the local park with a fistful of dollars, bought me some pills, and came back here to take them. I took all twenty-seven pills … fitting, huh … and I died. My rent was due in two days, so when I didn't pay it, the desk clerk came to look for me. He saw me, muttered a bunch of shit to himself, then made a call. Some men came and carried my body out on a gurney. But see, the thing is, my soul never left this room. I've been trapped here for years. I've seen more sorry-ass shit than you could imagine. Just watchin' people like I've been doin', I realize my life wasn't as bad as I thought. Maybe I should've tried harder. But now I'm dead. I don't get another chance. And I'm trapped here forever. The afterlife ain't like an after party. You never get to go home. You are home.

The only reason my words are reaching paper is because

someone sitting in this room is into automatic writing. That's where spirits guide the hand of the living, and they write down everything the spirit is saying. Yeah, I'm being channeled, and I'm all too happy to spill. I had a whole life of keeping my pain inside. So if this poor soul wants to know about me, she can keep on writing.

Her hair is all tangled and wild. Her face is streaked with makeup under the hair. I can see blood and scratches now. Her body is shakin' so hard I ain't sure how she can keep on writin'. Now I'm seein' a gun next to her, and right away I know she's killed someone with it. She's writin' with her right hand, so that's probably the hand she used to pull the trigger. I can't touch her; I can only keep spillin' my guts so she doesn't feel alone.

I look at her left hand. Here in this fuckin' purgatory, I start to cry. I haven't seen this silver dragonfly bracelet with the initials in years. It's even prettier than I remember it. Her wedding ring is gone. I can't believe I've been goin' on and on like this and didn't even recognize her.

She's lookin' at the gun with a hunger in her eyes I ain't never seen.

I always wanted us to be together, but not like this …

TO BE PERFECTLY FRANK

Frank Mullins was mesmerized as he watched the flickering "DI...E..." outside his hotel window. He'd been in his hole of a room for exactly three minutes when the loneliness and shame of his wrecked life squeezed him like a favorite shirt that had shrunk two sizes in the dryer.

Who the hell was he? A fifty-three-year-old man who had lost everything he'd ever had: a wife, two children, a good-paying construction job, a home, and his sobriety. He'd stopped drinking two years, four months, and six days ago, but it was far too late to regain anything from his former life. Not even his self-respect.

There was no one left who cared that he was now sober. He'd hurt too many people with his lies, infidelity, recklessness, and angry ways. And the irony was that he had accomplished such a long list of failures while wrapped in a fallacious blanket of perfection. His mother, in her selfishness, had whipped Frank into state of delusion where nothing less than being the perfect son and stand-in husband was acceptable. Setting him up for failure made him a volatile man, subject to outbursts when things didn't go exactly as planned. Ellie, his wife, had given him so many chances to get things right, and each time, he'd let her down. Over and over again, she pounded him with the point that she wasn't looking for a perfect husband, and that the harder he tried to be one, the more he screwed up.

The smallest things made him furious … especially when precipitated by his own shortcomings. If he made even the tiniest mistake, he'd lie about it. He'd create grandiose scenarios just to cover the smallest infractions. He was consumed by his quest to be the perfect husband.

And so, he never so much as left a sock on the floor for Ellie to pick up. Every day, he would compliment her outfit when he got home, praise the meal she'd prepared, ask after his in-laws, and tell her he loved her. He never failed to remember trash days. And every Friday night, without fail, he would bring her flowers. He'd never forget an anniversary or birthday, did the yard work, and even cleaned the bathroom on weekends when he wasn't playing with the boys.

While some women would've seen Frank as the perfect husband, Ellie saw him as a robotic figure that never deviated from the ill-founded model of the flawless man he'd designed for himself. His compliments, delivered by rote, lost their meaning, and his lack of spontaneity, adventure, and humor drove her to the brink of despair. She begged him to remember his humanity, to take chances in their relationship, even if it meant failing, and to remember that variety, not perfection, was the spice of life. But Frank had no faith that he could succeed without the invisible blueprint his mother had rendered for him at an early age. It was too daunting. He had to be everything his father had been. He heard his mother's voice and he heard Ellie's. But he had lost his own.

When Ellie's appreciation for his efforts dwindled into nothingness, he would explode with rage, then calm down. Then, back in perfect-husband mode, he would buy her more flowers.

Even his lovemaking, exactly the same every time, lost all meaning. Ellie was done. She told him her days of having sex with a one-trick robot were over.

Desperate to fix their problems, he decided to work on the sex issue and sought a prostitute to practice on. Only his lover-for-hire, paid to make a man feel good, praised his sexual prowess so much that he started to believe Ellie was the problem, not him. It was then time to seek women of the unpaid kind, in bars, to test out his new skills and see how they enjoyed what he had to offer. After a little more than a year making the worst possible choices, Frank now had a serious drinking problem. His life became more complex and muddied by the day. Ellie, who had endured the smell of alcohol on his breath and his increased outbursts, tolerated it all patiently. Having ceased to care a long time ago, she had bided her time and knew exactly what was coming. One day, she casually asked him why his very predictable behavior had deviated from the norm, not to a place of joyful spontaneity, but to a dark place of anger and addiction. He was too far gone to understand that she was done with him.

Panicked, Frank became enraged and concocted over-the-top lies that exposed the very behaviors he was trying to hide. That's when Ellie found out that he'd been taking his whiskey with a side of slut. Unlike most wives, she was not unhappy. She was, in fact, overjoyed to have a valid reason to take the boys and leave him. Her plan to wait until he self-destructed had worked beautifully. And now, he had handed her a Get Out of Jail Free card.

"Bitch," Frank mumbled as he looked around the shabby room. "Damn bitch."

Ellie was now happily married to some environmental attorney named Charlie … good old fucking Charlie … and his kids were both in college, courtesy of their stepfather.

He'd tried many times to call his sons, but every call went straight to voicemail. Somehow, his boys must have known he was calling. It wasn't easy for him to keep trying, either. The only time he had a chance to call was when he could pick up an odd job and use the nearest landline or borrow a cell phone from a kind soul. Maybe his children only picked up from numbers they knew. Who the hell cared anymore? He wasn't trying to stalk them; he just wanted to be their dad. But they had no use for him.

To hell with them; they were someone else's kids now. Fuck their little-league coaching, take-them-to-the-zoo-and-buy-them-ice-cream sperm donor. And damned if he didn't teach them all about dinosaurs, steam trains, and help them with their homework when they needed it.

The flickering lights were beginning to grate on him. He was certain he'd have a goddamn stroke if he kept looking at the schizophrenic dance of luminosity. He wondered why different letters had different life spans. No matter what sign it was, no matter where it was, some letters always burnt out before others. But this … DI … E … had to be planned. It was too sadistic to be coincidental.

From his sixth-floor hotel window, he looked away from the diner and to the east at the rooftops of the decaying neighborhood below him. The abandoned warehouse across the street had an orange fence around it that was covered in graffiti. It was surprisingly well lit at night, but that was to keep squatters and addicts out. He'd heard the property had been bought but didn't believe it. He'd heard those rumors before. Nobody would want to rehab the buildings on these ramshackle streets unless the entire neighborhood underwent gentrification. Those windows would stay broken, blackened, and boarded way longer than he could wait. There would be no jobs for him, and if there were, by the time the work was done, the neighborhood would be too expensive to live in. The yuppies that moved in would probably spit on him.

He was down and out, goddamnit, but he wasn't homeless. Seven-hundred-and-eighty-five dollars a month from his aunt Lydia's trust fund and a string of odd jobs saw to that.

He wondered if he could get a gig sitting at the front desk of the dump he was staying in. The old man who gave him his key looked dead. And if he wasn't, he sure as hell wasn't long for this world. Frank knew a fellow drunk when he saw one. The only wisdom Frank had left came in the form of precepts learned from his late grandmother at an early age and had been spouted to whatever dribbling drunk happened to be at the next barstool.

He'd asked the old man if there was a spot for him. Nope. Seems there was a regular night clerk. Had the night off. Date night, the guy called it. As if he cared.

Still looking out the window, his eyes fixed on the weather-beaten, wind-shredded canopy of the junk store next to the warehouse. The last woman he'd been with, some pill popper he'd picked up inside a Denny's at 2 a.m., had scraggly unkempt hair exactly like that canopy. But damned if that canopy wasn't prettier.

He thought to ask her name after thrusting himself between her thighs for as many minutes as he could hold out, but she was fast asleep when he finished and had only a sticky souvenir to remember him by when she woke up. High-as-a-kite-pussy-not-worth-a-damn bitch. He'd bought her a Grand Slam breakfast in an unspoken exchange for some wham-bam-thank you-ma'am sex. What a joke! He'd plugged his old electric drill into more attractive orifices.

He vowed never to go down that road again. An old copy of *Penthouse* would be a better companion. Frank didn't want to admit that he wanted a decent woman in his life. Pie-in-the-sky wishes were for fools. And so were pill-popping sluts.

Frank had stayed in the Obscure many times. All of the other rooms, no matter how seedy, had some kind of halfway-comfortable chair to sit in. Even covered with wretched floral fabric that stank of everything it had ever come in contact with, the bloody chairs were there. Broken footrests and all. Not in this room. Aside from the toilet, the only other thing Frank could sit down on with any back support was a stiff-backed chair with a vinyl seat and chrome legs. It was the kind of chair used for big functions in hotels, then stacked against a wall afterward.

If an important ass sat on one of these chairs, you'd better believe it was going back to an office to sit in an executive lounge chair with fucking lumbar support that was ergonomically designed.

Yeah, a bunch of overeducated brains worked hard to pool their knowledge so that asses of privilege could protect their backs while other poor slobs, especially ones in construction, broke their backs to erect big buildings so that fucking ergonomically engineered chairs would never be homeless.

Frank sat in the lousy chair that was placed next to a crappy round table that was about the size of a large pizza. He would have preferred a large pizza, especially one with pepperoni and mushrooms, to the laminated composite board table stained with the imprint of every round—or square-assed—bottle that ever spent time there.

Sticking out from underneath the table was a wastepaper basket, standard issue black metal. Ugly as the nameless pill popper he'd banged.

So much for housekeeping. If the dead-looking guy at the front desk had a wife, emptying trash was probably her job. She was probably wiped out by the time she'd finished the fourth floor. Who knows? Maybe, she made some cash banging guests on the side. Or maybe she paid the guests to pump *her* a few times. Or maybe it was a mutual consent thing. That was a distinct possibility. All he knew was that her cadaverous spouse had nothing more to offer her in this lifetime.

He stopped thinking about the nameless woman who probably didn't even exist. Fuck it. It didn't matter if she existed or not. Frank was certainly correct in his supposition either way. He stared at the trash-filled bin. Looked to be all paper of one kind or another. Well, Frank sure as hell hadn't brought any reading material with him. The old relic of a television sitting in the corner with a pair of broken rabbit ears on top wasn't going to provide any entertainment, and he'd already experienced the view outside the window. Why not read the trash? Damned if he had any better ideas.

Uncrumpling a balled page of newspaper, he saw a marked-up section from the classifieds. Someone was looking for a job. No, maybe not. This was from the Personal ads. Circled in red, under *Women Seeking Men,* Frank looked at the ad: Pretty, but lonely. Widow. 51. Big heart. Just wants to love and be loved. Any good men out there?

Well, wasn't it just like Frank to be a day late and a dollar short once again? No doubt the last poor slob to stay in this room had answered the ad. Wasn't a long ad, didn't say too much about her, but sounded like she didn't want much more than he did … just a little piece of the happiness pie.

Frank looked at the top of the page to see the date on the paper. Two weeks old. On the opposite page, he saw some more circled ads under the heading *Men Seeking Women.* About fifteen ads had been circled, then X'd out.

His curiosity awakened, Frank put the paper on the tabletop and continued to rummage through the trash. Seeing a handwritten note, he eagerly grabbed for it, but the paper it had been written on had been torn into pieces. Momentarily alive with purpose, Frank's fingers furiously scrambled to find the remaining pieces. Rewind forty-five years and there he was, a child, sitting at the dining room table, putting together a 500-piece jigsaw puzzle of an old steam train traveling through the Colorado Rocky Mountains. Boy, that was a pretty place. Frank remembered the moment he put the last piece in. He felt a sense of accomplishment and loss all at the same time.

"How'dya like to ride this train someday, Son? Just you and me on a father-son trip to the Rockies?"

"Won't Mom be upset?"

"Heck no. Having us out of her hair will give her a vacation. Maybe she and your aunt Lydia will take their own vacation."

"When can we go, Dad?"

"Well, not this year, Frank. But one of these days soon. I promise. Just got to work out my vacation time at the job. One of these days, for sure."

But "one of these days" never came. Frank's dad died two years later when a drunk driver hit his car on the way home from a late night at the office. Frank's mother barely clung to sanity, telling Frank that the only way to honor his father was to be perfect in every way. Under no circumstances was he to do anything to upset her life further. And if he did, she would have to send him away. She couldn't afford a boarding school. No, he would become a ward of the state. If he wanted to remain at home, he had to be perfect. And, she reminded him, his father was looking down from heaven, and he would know if Frank disobeyed.

It was then that his quest for the impossible began to take over his life. Frank was too young to understand that becoming a carbon copy of his father was illusory, and his mother had descended too far into mental illness not to let her son go through life wondering why he failed so often. But his Sisyphean attempts kept him going, and at twenty-five, he married a woman his mother approved of, worked a blue-collar job she considered beneath him, and eventually became a father to two sons she adored, but was rarely allowed to see. Even Ellie, his ex-wife, agreed that her mother-in-law was not someone she wanted messing up her boys the way she'd messed up their father.

Frank missed his father terribly. He still dreamed about visiting Colorado. But as much as he wanted to make the trip, the greater part of him vowed to never set foot in the state. Just wouldn't be right without his dad.

When his boys were seven and nine, he reconsidered. He wanted to take them to Colorado in honor of his father. It would be the perfect vacation. But they weren't interested in leaving their friends for any part of the summer. The last thing Frank wanted to do was force an expensive vacation on them and to dishonor the grandfather they'd never known. Besides, if they didn't care, why the hell should he?

They were just kids. He shouldn't have been hurt by their rejection. But he was. He was clearly not even close to the father he'd wanted to be. And it wasn't just them …. it was right around the time Ellie refused to have sex with him. And that's when he began drinking and sleeping around. He became a drunk just like the man who'd killed his father. His sons, repulsed by him, turned away.

And now, in some misguided allegiance to the do-gooder paying their college tuition, and their now deliriously happy mother, they'd rejected him forever.

Looking down, Frank saw his balled fists looking back at him. Only they looked more like assholes than fists. He didn't want to get any angrier than he already was. Anger threatened his sobriety, although he didn't know if it was worth preserving anymore. But that delusional piece of him still aimed to be as his mother had wished him.

He hated it when he let his mind wander so far away. He needed to focus on the trash and find the other pieces of the handwritten letter, not travel back in time to relive his childhood or his marriage. He found the second piece of the letter quickly and laid it on the table.

Next, he pulled out a store receipt. The fucking Dollar Store. A haven for crap. Did people really buy those plastic figurines they sold by the hundreds? Ugly shit. Especially the ones with glitter. And really, how much can anything be worth if it's only being sold for a dollar. Two cents? Piece-of-garbage store. He'd shopped there many times. But only for shaving cream, disposable razors, and candy bars. Not for anything he'd ever display in his home, if he had one.

Wonder what this guy bought there. He looked at the receipt. Lipstick, nail polish, and pantyhose. Is that the cost of being a woman: three bucks? Well, to each his own. Frank didn't care if a man needed to dress like a woman. He was just grateful for not being one of them. Bloody crooked wigs, five o'clock shadow, cheap clip-on earrings, brassieres stuffed with God knows what, bright red nail polish on hairy mitts, ugly discounted size-11 shoes that were never walked in properly, and a big-assed problem with public restrooms. Frank shook the thoughts out of his head. He knew he didn't know what the fuck he was talking about. Damn, he hated it when his mind stepped in bullshit.

Aha! That was better. A little bit of concentration, and within minutes, all six pieces of the torn-up letter were reunited on the tabletop.

Before he read the words, Frank saw the liquid stains on the letter. Tears or vodka. Who knew? The room had a prevalent stench of alcohol anyway. He wasn't going to sniff the letter to find out.

Dear Maria:

You've been a really good wife and I'm a louse. No man in his right mind should leave a woman like you, but I'm with someone else now. She isn't half the woman you are, but she's what I need. She's my addiction. I don't want to hurt you more by telling you all the reasons I love her. You just need to know that there's nothing wrong with you, my sweet. It's all me.

Find yourself a new man who can appreciate you. Tell the whole world I died. I remember how you used to tell me how devastating it would be for any woman to say her husband left her for someone else. So don't do it. Just say you're a widow. I'm heading out of Dodge anyway. Nobody will know. There's $5600 left in the savings account for you. Sorry I had to take the 30K. I'm a bastard. Maybe someday I can put it back. Sad thing is that I feel proud for leaving you that much. You're better off without me. I'm a dick. Have a good life.

Eddie

Frank closed his eyes and shook his head. What a fucking idiot he was, assuming that the previous guest was a man dressing as a woman. Only a bloody asshole with an overactive imagination would pick up a receipt for women's items and surmise something different from the obvious.

Sadly enough, he knew why. He was a jaded bastard who saw through pretense, even when it didn't exist. Nobody was going to put one over on old Frank Mullins. The ad circled in the paper was her ad, Maria's ad. The ones crossed out were all of the men who didn't work out. For one reason or another. Maybe she just changed her mind about them.

Maybe he had assumed something different because he didn't like the idea of a woman being alone in a dive like the Obscure.

Sifting through more trash, he found a photo, ripped in half, but still hanging together by a shred. He turned it over. It had been taken in Atlantic City, four years ago. She looked damn good to Frank. Long dark hair, big brown eyes, and a real sweet smile. Real genuine and all. Just like his grandmother's smile. The kind of smile even bitches can't fake. Boy, wouldn't he be happier than a pig sloshing around in shit to have a lady like this smiling at him.

Taking another peek into the trashcan, Frank noticed something shiny to the side of it. "Well, I'll be …" he said as he picked up the gold wedding band. Did she toss her wedding ring in the trash … and miss? Did she lose it? Why would someone with so little money throw away a gold ring? Was she looking for it? Maybe he could find a way to return it … and to meet her.

He wondered if she'd found anyone. Logic told him there was a good chance she might still be looking. Most people don't find true love in a lifetime, must less in two weeks with an ad in the local paper as their primary means of searching. Even if she were available, what the hell did he have to offer her? Seven-hundred and thirty-eight dollars a month barely kept him off the street. Who knows? Maybe with a renewed interest in life, he might find a job.

Who was that asshole guru he'd seen on a late-night infomercial touting some half-cocked 21 Days to a More Spiritual You? Cockamamie bullshit. In just twenty-one days, for only $29.99, he, too, could have his inner light shining bright. Yeah, he'd be a goddamn money magnet and lady magnet rolled into one. His fucking chakras would be aligned and balanced, and he'd be cooking with guru gas. Except he didn't know what a fucking chakra was, and damned if he wanted to know. He'd wasted too many years trying to be his father, and damned if that futile quest would fail on the spiritual plane, too.

But maybe, just taking the new age doubletalk out of the equation, there might be something in it for Frank. If he could find Maria, maybe she could bring him happiness. He'd sure try to bring her some.

Frank stood, put the photo in his pocket, and walked to the bathroom. A quick wiz and a shave later, he was off to find Maria. And he knew just where to start. The nearly departed desk clerk might know something. After all, she'd stayed in the same room no longer than two weeks ago.

Frank put this gold wedding band in his pocket, hurried out of the room, then closed the door behind him. He scurried down five flights of steps until he reached the front desk.

Glassy-eyed, the clerk stared at the small television on his desk.

"Hello."

The clerk looked up at him. "Yeah … can I help you?"

"I hope so. It's really important."

The clerk turned down the TV. "Who the hell are you again?"

"Frank Mullins. Staying in room 33."

The clerk sighed. "Oh, yeah. The guy who wants to work here. Ya always aim so high in life?" The clerk sniffed. "Well, what's the problem? Carpet not plush enough for ya?"

"What carpet? I didn't see anything but an old rug. Look, I'm not here to complain about anything or to ask for a job again. I'm just looking for a lady."

"Yeah. Should have guessed." The clerk grabbed a nearby tissue and wiped his nose. "Margaret comes in here least once a day. We got some others, but I don't know them one's names. If ya …"

"I'm not looking for a hooker. I'm looking for a fine, classy woman."

"And you're askin' me? In this place?" The clerk howled with laughter, then sat up straight in his chair and leaned forward. "Look, mister. I may not look like I know jack shit, but I do. And I know when I'm being played here. Just don't know why. A close look at my face will tell ya I don't give a damn and that it's been a real long time since I did."

Frank nodded. "You're not understanding me. I'm not here asking about how to meet a woman. I'm looking for a particular woman. Her name is Maria. She stayed in the room I'm in about two weeks ago. She left something behind, and I want to give it to her."

"Oh, yeah. I'll bet ya do! How's 'bout a cold shower. That oughta take care of ya."

"No, really! Please, I'm being serious."

"Okay, oh serious one. Ya got something that belongs to her? Let me have it then. I'll hold onto it for her."

Frank studied the clerk's face, taking special note of the way his eyes shifted. Looking to the right, he saw an old leather-covered flask on the desk. "No, I need to give it to her myself."

The clerk leaned back in his chair and crossed his arms. "Oh, I see. So ya don't trust me, eh?"

"Yeah, but …"

"Think you're better than me, huh? Got one up on me." He took a drink. "For one, ya wouldn't be standing here talking to me if ya were."

Frank began to protest, but the clerk put his hand up to stop him. "Oh, Lord! Save me from another one." He looked Frank dead in the eyes. "I don't wanna know how many damn years, months, days, and minutes ya been sober. Go tell it on the mountain. Fuck you, your sobriety coins, and AA too."

"I'm not trying to—look, what if I describe her to you?"

The clerk grabbed his flask and took a large swig. "And what if I describe my ideal woman to ya? Hell, I can show you." He pulled open a side drawer of the desk and pulled out an old magazine with a naked woman touching herself. "Yep. I like 'em like this! Turns me on to see a woman who knows what she's got. Makes her all the more delicious, ya know?"

Frank sighed. "What if I show you a photo of the woman I'm looking for?"

The clerk laughed and stabbed the photo multiple times with his index finger. "Unless she looks like this here babe, I ain't seen her. Didn't I tell you earlier that I'm only fillin' in for the night clerk? Only people I know is them ones been here a long time. But I sure as hell don't see classy chicks come and go. And sure as hell not at night."

Frank frowned and looked down at the floor. After a moment, he looked up at the clerk, who was taking yet another swig. "Look, so just do me this favor. I'm gonna be stayin' in this room for the time being, so if a lady comes by who says she lost something, can you at least tell her I have it? And tell the regular guys, too, okay?"

The clerk wiped his mouth with the sleeve of his flannel shirt. "Yep. Sure. Got it. Classy lady comes in here looking for something she lost, I'll send her straight to ya." He chuckled as he turned back to his television.

Disgusted, Frank walked away and headed for the stairs. As he reached the sixth floor, he was breathless and depressed. He walked into the room, locked the door behind him, then stared at the flickering sign until it made him dizzy. When it did, he lay on the bed and stared up at the ceiling. There was absolutely nothing left to live for. He had lost everything and didn't have even one paltry iron in the fire. Not a friend in the world. Despite his sobriety, everyone had turned away from him.

By some miracle, despite the sorry state of his existence, he hadn't given in to the booze. That was pretty damn amazing, actually. There wasn't a soul around to pat him on the back, not unless he went to a meeting, and he hated those fucking things. He remembered the first time a roomful of people said, "Hi, Frank" in unison, right after he said, "Hi, I'm Frank, and I'm an alcoholic." He felt ambushed, naked, and exposed. Those who noticed his discomfort told him it would get easier. But it never did. He wasn't interested in hearing other people's stories. He thought other weak people were pathetic … most of them, anyway. The last meeting Frank ever attended, he stood up and told everyone that he hated being there, and he'd sobered up just so he never had to listen to their whining again. Then, before he could take in the mixed reactions, he hurried out of the room, left the building, and never went back again. He also never took a drink again, and hey, that showed strength of character, willpower, determination, and drive. If only he could apply those characteristics to something else out there, maybe life wouldn't be so bad.

But most importantly, he had come to understand his weaknesses and limitations. He knew he didn't really hate the people in the meetings; he hated everything they said that reminded him of himself. And he didn't want his alcoholism to be the glue that bound him to others. He just wanted to be Frank.

Five days later, Frank stood in the small bathroom and looked at his lathered face in the cracked mirror. He looked down at the razor gripped in his hand. He glanced at his neck, then at the razor. He sighed. No, he would use the razor to shave the five-day growth on his face and nothing else. At least for the time being.

He hadn't planned to stay at the Obscure more than two nights. That was his way: to make the rounds from place to place in hopes of finding something new, something worth living for. But here he was, holding on to a glimmer of hope he'd found in the trash.

Absorbed in his thoughts, he almost didn't hear the soft knock on the door. Well, thank God for something. Someone was finally bringing him clean towels. As crappy as they were, at least they'd be clean.

He opened the door and looked with wonder at the woman standing before him.

"Oh, how funny!" she said.

"W-what's that?"

"Well, I came back here looking for a ring I'd lost. I never expected to find it again, but the man at the front desk said that the guy staying in room 33 had something of mine. I'm hoping what you have is my wedding ring. Not because I want to wear it again. I just need to sell it."

"Right. So ... um ... why is that funny?"

"Because you're all lathered up like Santa Claus. Who better than to give me a present!"

"Oh!" Frank said, suddenly self-conscious. "Please come in. I can shave later."

The woman smiled. She hesitated for a moment or two as she sized him up, then walked through the door. Hurrying to the bathroom, Frank wiped off the lather with the dirty towel and walked back to greet her. He pointed to the only chair there was, across the room, by the window. "Please, have a seat."

"I'd better not. I'd really just like my ring, if you have it."

"Is your name Maria?"

Her mouth fell open as she stared at him. "How did you know that?"

"Please," Frank said. "I'll be glad to tell you. Can you just sit for a few minutes?"

"I don't think so. I really shouldn't even have come in …." She turned toward the door. "I know better than to come into a stranger's room. You just seem so … I don't know. Okay, I guess. But still."

"I understand. We can talk in the hallway, if you wish, or in the lobby. I don't want you to feel uncomfortable at all."

"Well …"

"Really, I mean it. Would you like me to meet you downstairs?"

"No. Too many prying eyes. I guess it's okay." Shaking off her unease, Maria walked over to the stiff-backed chair and sat down. "Why do you have my ring, anyway?"

"See, here's the thing," Frank began, leaning awkwardly against the nearby wall. "I started writing a letter to my ex-wife, just about my boys, nothing personal, and then I decided to forget about it. That's when I ripped the paper up and threw it in the trash." He paused to run the story over in his head before continuing. "Soon as I did so, I realized that I really should send it after all. I couldn't send the letter I'd ripped up, but I could copy it onto a new piece of paper. I'd worked really hard to get the writing just right. And that isn't easy for me." He paused to gauge her reaction. "So, I reached into the trash to pull out the pieces, and that's when I came up with a letter written to someone named Maria. And then I found a photo torn in half … your photo."

"Oh," Maria said. "I see." Her face reddened. "I guess they don't empty the trash too often in this place. Please, go on with what you were saying."

Frank was pleased he'd told a plausible lie. He didn't want to be a liar anymore, but he couldn't tell her he was so bored he had been rummaging through the trash.

"Well, when I looked down again, I saw a gold ring right by the trash can." He pointed to the spot. "I wondered if there was anything else of value left behind that might be there, too. That's when I found what I assume was your classified ad."

"Oh, that stupid thing." She looked away for a moment, then back at Frank. "May I have the ring?"

Frank reached into his left pocket and handed her the ring. "This is yours, yes?"

"It is," Maria said, inspecting it with disdain. "I don't know what I'll get for it, but it will be worth more than the loser I married. That's all I know."

"I can relate," Frank said. "May I ask you something."

Maria tensed up. "Uh … yeah … I guess."

"Why did you call your ad stupid? I didn't think it was stupid at all."

"Because the only responses I got were from dirty old men and two who were only looking for … well, you know. I was going to answer some ads myself, but I chickened out and put a big X through every single one."

"I saw—I mean, why did you do that? Why didn't you get in touch with any of them?"

Maria frowned. Because the last man who answered my ad told me that the classifieds were for losers."

"Oh, really," Frank said. "So, if only losers read the classifieds, I wonder how he come across your ad."

"Exactly!" Maria said, relaxing her shoulders. "I wanted to say that, but I didn't want to prolong the communication … or the agony." She smiled uncomfortably as she stood. "I really think I should go."

"Well, I can tell you this," Frank said, his voice lassoing her back in place. "If I had seen your ad, I would have wanted to answer it. But I don't have a cell phone or an email address. So there's that."

"Well, we're talking now," Maria said, inspecting him with her eyes. "So, how would you have responded to me?"

"I would have told you I'm 53 years old and looking for a woman with a good heart. And I would have invited you to meet me for coffee."

"Would that have been a ruse for something else? Be honest."

"No, it wouldn't have been. And I know you have no reason to believe me, but I've sowed those oats a long time ago. I would have just wanted to get to know you. I'm not in a place right now where I care to look too far down the road. For now, I just take each day as it comes. So yeah, I really would have meant coffee … just getting together to get to know one another and see if there was any connection."

"I would have liked that," Maria said, putting the ring in a side pocket of her purse as she walked toward the door. "I probably would have agreed to meet you."

Frank followed her at a distance, then stopped and smiled. "Probably?"

She turned to face him. "The world is a scary place. Too many people have bad agendas, even when their offers seem enticing."

"I've made a whole lot of mistakes. Especially with my ex-wife, but I never set out to harm anyone. Never."

"No," Maria said, looking at him. "I believe you. I don't know why I do, either … because my trust in men is pretty eroded." She turned and walked to the door.

"Wait, please," Frank said, watching as she put her hand on the doorknob. "Would you like to go for coffee now? Maybe a bite to eat at the diner across the street? My treat."

Maria considered his offer as an uneasy smile played on her lips. "That sounds *perfect*."

Frank's countenance went limp, as if all hope had eluded him for the last time.

Maria let her smile fall away. "Oh, my. Did I say something wrong?"

He took a moment before responding, then stepped toward her. "No. It's just that word: 'perfect.' There's nothing perfect about me at all. I wouldn't want any woman to think there was. If I've learned anything in my life, I'm no good at trying to be a perfect man. All I can do is be Frank."

"Good. I'm so glad to hear that because perfection doesn't exist, and those who seek it are only looking for fool's gold. I don't want anyone looking for perfection in me, either. I always try to do my best, but I'm flawed like everyone else. I'm just so happy you brought that up. Thank you for being frank with me." Her mouth curved upward into a shy smile. "By the way, I don't think I caught your name."

Just One of Those Days

His chin in the palm of his hand and his eyes looking downward at his daily newspaper, Henry could feel his lids getting heavy as he tried to read the day's headlines. Catching himself just as he nearly dozed off, he sat upright in his chair, gasping as his eyes took in the sight in front of him.

"What the …." Smiling at him was something he'd never seen before in all his years as desk clerk at the Obscure. Wearing a bald cap painted the same bright white color as his face, sporting an enormous receding hairline with reddish-orange hair frizzed out on both sides of his head, half a bright red ball on his nose, red lips, and bizarre black lines accentuating his bloodshot brown eyes, a clown, in a colorful suit with four layers of ruffled collars, looked endearingly at him with a fixed gaze that made Henry's stomach flop.

"Don't smile at me like that, mofo," Henry said. "And that's for starters." He looked over and saw Johnny and Clyde, the hotel's most frequent lobby-hanger-outers, looking as dumbfounded as he was.

Despite the admonition, the clown's expression remained exactly the same.

"Well, damn," Henry said, nodding toward the lobby area. "You wanna stare and smile like that, check out those two clowns over there—brothers from another mother and all that. They just don't look like you is all. But they need some excitement, especially the older one, Johnny. Me? I'm good."

The clown looked straight at Henry, his gaze intensifying.

Henry rolled his chair back against the wall, noticing, as he did so, that the corners of the clown's mouth turned ever so slightly upward. "You're freakin' me the fuck out, clown man. If you're packing heat and planning to rob me, I'm telling you now, this place ain't exactly Fort Knox. Turn right on your way out the door, go down to the end of the street, make a left, then keep on walking until you get to Kentucky."

The clown continued to smile.

"Listen, if you're hell-bent on doing something, then do it and get it over with now. Gotta be better than this creepy staring smiling shit."

"He looks like he's in love with you," Johnny said.

Henry turned slowly to Johnny. "You wanna deal with this? You're the one who's always desperate for company, not me. So why don't you make yourself useful for a change?"

"You always tellin' me to mind my own business," Johnny retorted, laughing. "That's what I'll do."

Clyde, who was rarely without earbuds, took them out of his ears to hear the exchange, but said nothing.

"Do I need to be calling the boys in blue?" Henry asked the clown. "To take away your multicolored ruffled ass."

The clown took a step closer to the counter that separated him from Henry. Smiling, he slowly reached inside a hidden pouch in his suit, watching as Henry turned almost the same color as the clown's face, and pulled out a white card and held it up. Written on it were the words: I'm a mute clown.

Henry grabbed a pen and scribbled on a piece of paper: I'm a talking man. Then, he held it up for the clown to read.

Never breaking his gaze, the clown reached in for another card, holding that one up: I'm mute; I'm not blind or deaf.

"Well, aren't you the clown … I mean … oh, fuck. Got a card for everything, dontcha?"

The clown held up a third card that simply said: Yes.

"You want something," Henry said. "Or did you just come in here to gaze into my baby blues?"

The clown pointed upward.

"If you wanna get to heaven, you need to stop freakin' people out."

Placing his white-gloved hands in a praying position, the clown then tilted them to the left and rested his head upon them.

"Oh, you want a room," Henry said. "Tired?"

The clown nodded affirmatively.

"Room for one?"

The clown held up two fingers. Then three.

"Room for two? Three? What, you planning to have some kind of—"

Pulling a whistle out of his pocket, the clown blew on it, the shrill sound nearly ejecting Henry from his chair. Within seconds, a female clown, wearing an oversized clown suit, came waddling into the lobby, dragging a large duffel bag across the floor. Her eyes were painted with teal blue arches over her lids and a thick black line that ran under her eyes and beyond. The two clowns looked at one another; then the female clown looked downward while the male resumed smiling at Henry.

"Gee, I don't know if I can rent a room to unmarried folks. We have a pretty strict moral code here," Henry told him as a fifty-something man in a suit came down the stairs and hurried through the lobby, his shirttail sticking out of his fly. He cleared his throat. "Things do get by me, though."

The female clown reached into a pocket and pulled out a netted bridal veil and placed it top of her frizzy red wig.

"So, you two are married?"

She nodded.

"You're mute too?"

She nodded again, looking away. Henry noticed that her face

was contorted in pain.

"You okay ... Mrs. Clown?"

She looked at the male clown, her eyes begging him to do something.

The clown pulled a bunch of scrunched-up bills out of his pocket and put them on the counter. Henry counted out the money for one room and gave the rest back to him. "Lady Clown looks to be in pain. I got a room on the second floor. I'm giving you that one." Henry grabbed a key hanging on the wall behind him and put it on the counter.

The clown, his smile gone, nodded thanks, grabbed the key, looked at his partner with concern, then put one arm around her to help her walk.

Clyde jumped up from his seat in the lobby and walked over to the clowns. "Why don't you let me carry that duffel bag? You take care of your ... lady."

The clown nodded appreciatively as Clyde grabbed the bag and led them toward the stairs.

"No way they're both mute," Johnny said to Henry.

"I wish *you* were."

"I'm serious," Johnny said.

Henry dipped his chin and raised his eyes as he looked at Johnny. "And you think I'm not?"

"There was a mute kid down the street where I grew up. Quiet Quentin, they called him. I remember my aunt telling my mother that it was rare for someone to be mute if they weren't deaf. But we never did find out what the real deal was. My aunt—she was a nurse—said that maybe Quentin had a reason for not talking. Selective mutism, she called it. Yup. I still remember that. Quiet Q moved away when his parents split up. He went with his dad, as I recall, so something bad must have gone down with his mother. Always wondered what happened to that kid. I just hoped that nobody made fun of him, wherever he ended up."

"Hope not. But life is filled with sad stories." Henry turned to Clyde as he reentered the lobby. "Everything all right with the clown folk?"

"I think she's …. Nah, not saying anymore. I'm not the blabbermouth here," Clyde said, nodding toward Johnny.

"Ah, bull," Johnny said.

Henry laughed. "You do gossip like a woman sometimes, Johnny. There's a reason people call y'all 'Bonnie and Clyde,' and it ain't 'cause you're criminals or lovebirds. It's because you gab like an old woman."

Clyde put his earbuds back in and got lost in his music.

"Hey, Henry," Johnny said. "Actually found me a pair of glasses I can read with now. The Dollar Store got in a brand that works for me."

"Well whoop dee doo, hullaballoo, tell Mary Sue, and hooray for you!" Henry said, going back to his newspaper. Now if you only had something to read."

"Got me a newspaper," Johnny said. "Just been sitting on it."

"Only man I know who thinks he can read with his ass," Henry mumbled.

"Aw, cut me some slack," Johnny said, grabbing the newspaper and opening it up. "Didn't want it to fall all over the floor until I was ready to read it."

Fifteen minutes later, a woman in her mid-sixties, wearing a red and black sequined miniskirt with a skimpy matching top, tromped into the lobby. The flesh on her skinny legs sagged like tights that were three sizes too big. The weight of her heavy, beaten-up red leather Hobo shoulder bag rendered her lopsided, but nonetheless full of confidence. She sashayed over to Henry, singing: "Doctor, doctor, give me the news … I got a bad case of lovin' you." She touched the rhinestone tiara pinned precariously on top of her sloppily piled-up hair to make sure it was still there, and then curtsied.

Visibly out of patience, Henry scowled at her. "Can I help you?"

She reached into her bag and took out a bottle of water. To Henry's shock, she twisted off the cap, then poured it on her head. "I'm singing in the rain, just singing in the rain. What a glorious feeling, I'm happy again."

"What the ever-lovin' ...." Annoyed, Henry opened the bottom drawer of his desk and pulled out a roll of paper towels. "Now I gotta go wipe the damn water up so nobody slips and falls." He looked at her with disdain. "Get the hell ...."

With a smile on her face, she skipped out of the building. "I'm off to see the wizard ...."

Clyde rotated his forefinger by the side of his head as Johnny burst out laughing. Not amused, Henry tore off several squares of paper towels and walked around the counter.

"You're a real chick magnet," Johnny said. "The babes love you."

"Cut the crap," Henry said, carefully kneeling down to wipe up the water." So tell me. Have you ever seen that fruit loop before?"

"Nope. Thought she was a friend of yours."

"Much more your type," Henry said, his free hand massaging his right side as he stood up. "Same kind of mouth as you. Too much coming out of it."

"Bull," Johnny said. "I don't talk that much. Most times, I just say hello. But if you're in a bad mood, it's too much for your ears. Then, you tell the whole damn world I'm a blabbermouth, and I've got to explain to everyone I'm not. But hell, by the time I'm done, I sound like one." Johnny huffed in annoyance. "Be glad I don't sing to you, man."

"Don't be getting any ideas," Henry said, tossing the wet

clump of towels into the trash before sitting down again.

Johnny shooed away his words with a wave of his hand and went back to his paper.

Twenty minutes later, a tall young man with spiked, gelled hair, his eyes glazed and disoriented, walked into the lobby and waved a large red spatula. "Hear ye, hear ye. All rise. Court is in session! The honorable judge Schlippendiller presiding."

Henry stood abruptly. "Outta here, Nathan! Take your drug-addled, cockamamie bullshit somewhere else. Preferably to rehab."

"Do you swear to tell the truth, the whole truth, and nothing but the truth?" Nathan said to no one in particular.

"Do you wish to have your ass kicked, your balls kicked, and your face punched in?" Henry pushed down on the arms of his chair as if he were getting up to confront Nathan.

"I direct the jury to disregard that," Nathan shouted as he left. "Will the defendant please rise?"

Once out on the street, his voice was still loud. After "let the record reflect" was heard, his voice quickly trailed off.

As Johnny stifled a laugh, Henry shot him a look to be quiet.

An hour and a half later, with only a couple of regulars having come and gone silently, nobody said a word until Clyde noticed the latest visitor.

"Yo, Henry!" Clyde indicated the front door with his eyes.

"Officer Dodeen," Henry said. "What can I do you for?"

The officer leaned over the ledge and spoke softly. "This might sound strange, but I'm asking seriously. You seen any clowns around here?"

Henry nodded toward the lobby.

"I'm talking about real clowns. In full get-up."

"You think the runaway circus comes to the Obscure? Yeah, I gave an elephant a room on the fourth floor. He had a hell of a time getting up there, though. The giraffe wanted to help him up the stairs, but the elephant told him not to stick his neck out."

"Funny, not funny. And yeah, can't think of a better place for a runaway circus than this dive, actually."

"Why you lookin' for clowns?"

Dodeen shifted to one side and put his hand on his hip as if he was doing a bad impression of a sheriff from an old Western. "Well, these two suspects in particular volunteer at the Children's Hospital. The male clown used to work as an EMT somewhere, don't know anything about the female one. All's I know is that for the past sixth months, they've been going to the hospital, trying to cheer up the sick kids and their families. That's all good, but now these clowns are suspected of robbery."

"Like in robbing a bank?"

"Nothing like that," Dodeen said. "No guns involved. But we got a call that a lot of newborn supplies were stolen, including some painkillers. Got a complaint from Ellen Dee at County. Turns out, after searching the directory, there's nobody there by that name, but the lady at the desk was laughing real hard and said maybe I meant L & D, you know, Labor and Delivery."

"Hilarious, not hilarious," Henry said, stone-faced. "Sorry, I'm not up on anything having to do with babies."

"You only need to be up on whether you've seen any clowns. Anyway, they can't prove anything yet, but a staff member saw these clowns lurking in an area where they didn't belong. So, odds are they're the culprits. Can never be sure, though. Just need to find them. The sooner the better."

At that moment, a woman's wailing cry rang through the lobby.

"What the hell's that?" Dodeen said. "Sounds like someone's having a baby upstairs."

Henry leaned forward. "Last time you were in here with that little blond hoochie of a secretary, she screamed just like that when you plugged her. Ask Bonnie and Clyde if you don't believe me."

Officer Dodeen blushed as another scream filled the lobby.

"Guy must be awfully—"

"They call him 'Boppin' Bobby Big Dick,'" Henry said. "Every lady he brings in here cries like that. Sometimes I put cotton in my ears soon as I rent him a room."

"Well, now maybe you understand why you heard that scream coming from—I hope you keep your big fat mouth shut, Henry. I'd hate to have to glue it shut for you."

"I mind my own business. Wouldn't be here all these years if I didn't."

"All right," Dodeen said. "But you call me if you see any clowns or get wind of them from anyone who did. You hear me?"

"Will do," Henry said with a salute.

"Told you they weren't mute," Johnny said once the officer had left.

"The lady is having a baby," Clyde said. "Even a big-ass clown suit couldn't hide that … not once I was up close and personal. Her water had already broke, too. I wasn't gonna say anything, but since the secret is out …."

Another screamed filled the lobby. The three men exchanged glances and said nothing.

☠ ☠ ☠

The next day, shortly after noon, Henry was finishing a ham-and-cheese sandwich at his desk, while Johnny scarfed down a tuna-salad sandwich on white bread. Clyde, as usual, was lost in his music. But he was the first one to see the young couple walking down the stairs into the lobby: the man, with shoulder-length scraggly brown hair, carrying a duffel bag while the woman, a dirty blond with purple hair extensions, wearing a pair of elephant-themed harem pants and an old brown hoodie, held a newborn in her arms.

"Well, hey!" Clyde said, getting the attention of Johnny and Henry.

Henry stepped out of the registration area to greet them. "Well, who do we have here?" As he looked at the woman, his gaze intensified. He could feel his heart beating faster.

The woman just looked up at him, as if she were trying to memorize every part of his face.

"So, um … does this beautiful baby have a name?" Henry asked.

"Scarlett," the woman finally said softly, as she looked nervously around the reception area and small lobby.

"She's a real stunner," Henry said, looking at the baby's sleeping face, then into the woman's eyes. "Just curious: does this pretty baby have a middle name?"

"Um … it's Kate.

Henry inhaled an unexpected breath. "Scarlett Kate. Now that's a real pretty name."

"Um … yes. Thank you," she said.

Choking up, Henry waited a moment until more words came. "In fact, I'd say that's the most beautiful name for a girl I've ever heard."

The woman looked into his eyes, then at her baby.

"Officer Dodeen," Clyde said loudly, to alert Henry. "We're only used to seeing you when someone dies."

His eyes wide with purpose, Dodeen looked at Henry, then marched over to him and the couple. "Yesterday I asked you if you'd seen any clowns. You said no. Since then I got six people telling me they were seen in the neighborhood and two more who say they saw clowns walk in here yesterday. From what I hear, the tall one came in first, then the other one a few minutes later. What do you say to that? You been lying to me, Henry? You better not lie to me … about *anything.*"

"Oh, those two," Johnny said, diverting Dodeen's attention. "Yeah, I remember. That was strange. The first one came in here looking around. Just kept pacing, you know, like he was waiting for someone. Then, the other one came in. I figured she wondered what was taking him so long. The big clown shrugged like he was in the wrong place or something. Then they left."

"Oh, really!" Dodeen said. "And you didn't find that *strange*?"

"Strange is what comes in here every damn day. Why do you think I sit in the lobby? Better than anything on the TV. You know what's really strange for this place?"

"What's that?" Dodeen asked suspiciously.

"When I *don't* see nothin' strange," Johnny said. "That's when I wonder if I died and went to a parallel universe."

Dodeen's eyes narrowed as he considered what Johnny had said. "Where was Henry when this happened? Or was he lying to me? This is a bullshit-free zone while I'm here. Truth, Johnny."

"He was off takin' a leak, I think."

"Really. Is that so?"

"Well," Johnny said, mocking Dodeen's authoritative tone. "That's so, from my recollection. Ain't got nobody else's to offer."

The officer returned his gaze to the front desk. "That true, Henry?" You didn't see them because you were taking a leak?"

A long puff of air escaped Henry's lips. "How the hell do I know what I didn't see when I'm not here to see it?"

"How about you, Clyde? Did you see the same thing?"

"I dozed off for a good while when Ella was singing Cole Porter. Just remember waking up to 'I Love Paris' and wishin' I was there. Sorry."

Furrowing his eyebrows officiously, Dodeen contemplated Johnny's words. "Hard to believe you didn't say anything to Henry.

You're not exactly the silent type. More like the Obscure's color commentator."

"Yeah," Henry interjected. "If I let him, he'll talk my damn ear off. But he's been putting a sock in it lately because I've had it up to here." He made a slicing gesture across his neck.

Annoyed, Dodeen turned to the young couple. "How about the two of you? Did you see any clowns?"

"Hell no," Henry answered for them. "Do they look like they've had time to see anything?" Henry looked at the man. "I think I charged you for an extra night. I need to refund you that money."

Dodeen braced for a big sneeze and walked away to blow his nose.

Surprised, the man watched as Henry walked back to his desk, opened a drawer, counted out some money, then returned to the spot he'd been standing, and quickly handed him a wad of cash. Henry spoke quietly. "You folks are going back to Saginaw; isn't that where you said you lived? Not too far from the Saginaw River, if I remember."

Surprised, the man nodded, his eyes wide with appreciation as he stuffed the money deep into a side pocket. The woman smiled as a few tears fell from her eyes. She looked at Henry with love and gratitude.

"Better get going. Take care of the little one."

Flustered, Dodeen walked back over and eyed the couple again, sniffing heavily, some leftover mucous taunting him. "You people one-hundred percent sure you haven't seen any clowns?" He sniffed again.

"For fuck's sake," Henry said. "Blow your schnozzola again, will ya? And leave them alone while you're at it. Haven't you noticed they've been preoccupied with something more important? If they saw any damn clowns, they'd remember." He looked warmly at the couple. "You folks take care now. It was very nice to meet you.

Maybe one day, you'll come back."

The woman took one last long look at Henry. Then, taking a moment to acknowledge Johnny and Clyde, the two walked through the lobby and out into the street.

"Never heard you so sentimental with strangers before," Dodeen said. "Or anyone, for that matter." He sniffed. "Old grouch that you are."

"Nothing wrong with being nice to a young couple. So in love, loyal to one another and all."

"Well, this is a waste of my time," Dodeen huffed, looking angry. Turning his back to the lobby, he whispered to Henry. "Listen here. You save me a room for tomorrow night. Third floor corner if you've got that one. And keep your mouth shut."

"Good day, officer," Henry said. "My best to the missus."

As Dodeen left, Henry's face fell. His eyes were watery with tears and his pain deepened every wrinkle on his face.

Johnny and Clyde, stunned by what they'd never seen before, traded looks, then focused their attention on Henry. Broken and shaken, he glanced at them, trembling.

"What the hell," Johnny said, walking over to Henry. "You're not okay, man. Not okay at all."

Clyde stuffed his earbuds in his pocket and walked over to join them. "What's up? I saw you hand that dude a wad of cash. The same guy who was dressed like a clown yesterday. I could tell they were strangers to you. Now, all of a sudden, you're giving out charity. You gone soft in the head? Or maybe you got a thing for newborns? Or clowns."

Henry tried to respond but the words wouldn't come.

"You look woozy," Johnny said. He turned to Clyde. "Let's help him sit down."

Expecting a protest, but getting none, Johnny took hold of Henry's right arm while Clyde steadied his left. Slowly, they walked him back to his seat behind the counter. Henry nodded thanks.

"Thanks for covering for me with Dodeen, guys," Henry finally said. "Appreciate it."

The men, nervous about leaving him alone, walked around and leaned on the front of the counter.

"You're welcome," Clyde said. "So tell me, why *did* we cover for you? Why did *you* cover for *them*?"

"Oh, hell ... young couple, obviously poor and just had a baby. Last damn thing they needed was to be harassed or arrested by Officer Dodo Bird."

"He's got a point there," Johnny said to Clyde.

"Yeah, he does," Clyde told Johnny. "And you and I have known this dude for how many years? And when did you ever see him on the verge of fucking tears, all shaky and shit? Answering for myself: never. Never ever."

"Never ever for me neither," Johnny added.

Henry, crestfallen, looked sorrowfully at the men.

"Come on," Johnny said. "What gives?"

"Yeah," Clyde said. "I'm all for minding my own, but you're not right, man. I mean, something's eating at you big time. You're acting kind of like that mute clown."

Lost in thought, Henry said nothing. Johnny and Clyde continued to look at him, waiting. But Henry, taking inspiration from Clyde's observation, answered them only in thought, as his eyes focused somewhere in the distance, far beyond the walls of the Obscure. *When I left Michigan, all those years ago, I left a lady behind. Told me she was pregnant, but that didn't stop me. I didn't believe her because she'd told me that same thing before, and it wasn't true. Twice. She even faked two miscarriages. So, when she told me the third time, just as I was leaving town, I was sure she was playing the same hand again. I loved her, but I wanted out of that town somethin' fierce, and she wanted me to stay and rot there forever. She never would've left.* He looked around at his desk and the lobby of the Obscure. *If only I'd known I'd come to rot here instead.* The expression on his face became more melancholy. *I would have stayed, baby. I would have. Greatest regret of my life. I know that somehow, we could have come up with a life that worked for both of us.*

"Man, your thoughts, whatever they are, gotta weigh a ton. I'm surprised your neck can still hold your head up," Johnny said.

"Word," Clyde said.

"C'mon, Henry. What's going on in that head of yours?" Johnny asked. "Share your pain with us. It divides the grief and all that good stuff."

My lady. Henry thought, his eyes trying to smile as he remembered. *She was beautiful. That young lady who just left here … well, she looked haggard and world-weary, but when I could finally see her face, she was nearly the spitting image of my Charlotte and had blue eyes just like some washed-up dry drunk she's probably better off not knowing.*

Clyde tilted his head. "Are you okay, dude?"

And that pretty young thing that just got carried out of here. Her name is Scarlett Kate. He swallowed a lump in his throat. *That's my mama's name. She died two years after I left Michigan. I was all she had left in the world. I broke her heart, Charlotte's too.*

Johnny and Clyde shared another look as they watched Henry tear up.

"Man," Johnny said. "You're having a hell of a loud party in your head, brother man." He paused to wait for a reaction but got nothing. "*Henry …* you okay? You're too lost in thought to even tell me to shut up. Those clowns did something to make you crazy. Damned if I can figure out what." He sighed. "C'mon, talk to us."

Forlorn, Henry stared down at his desk and spun a pencil, then watched until it stopped. He sucked in as much air as he could, straightened his shoulders, and looked at the men. "I'm fine. Sometimes stuff just gets to you in a funny way. Messes with your head. Nothing to worry about. You know how things go down here, Johnny. You, too, Clyde. Just been one of those days …."

WHERE THERE'S A WILL, THERE'S A WINNIE

Jepper, the brown-and-white terrier mix, jumped up on the tattered love seat and rested his head, along with his right paw, on the old woman's lap. Looking up at her with love, his sad eyes recognized that something was wrong.

"You always know, don't you, boy?" she said.

Jepper blinked in recognition.

"I don't have a good feeling," she said as the big fan whirred beside her. "Your dad left a note saying he was going for a six-month checkup. Only I've lost count of how many six-month checkups he's had lately. After sixty-one years of marriage, a person knows when something's wrong. And if they don't, then heck, they've been asleep at the wheel."

Before Jepper could respond with a sloppy kiss, the key turned in the door, and the dog jumped up and ran to greet the tall, handsome, and very tired white-haired man who entered the room.

"Hey, Jeps, you're just what the doctor ordered," he said as he vigorously rubbed the dog on either side of his neck. Walking over to his wife, he kissed her and then sat down beside her. "How's my Winifred, the love of my life?"

"You can call me Winnie," she said, trying to light the darkness she felt. "What's wrong, Will? You only call me Winifred when you're nervous about something."

He looked into her eyes and tried to form a smile on his lips. "Ah, just—"

"Don't you dare tell me you've just had a six-month checkup again," she warned him. "Because if you do, I'll scream so loud this rickety old building will crumble."

Will smiled. "It's managing to do that just fine without any screams from you. Besides, you don't scream."

"I'm only eighty-two. While I have breath in my body, I can always start. I've got plenty of energy stashed away from all of my non-screaming years."

The corners of Will's mouth turned upward, but he couldn't quite smile.

Jepper, content to see his parents together, walked over to his bed in the corner of the room, circled a few times, pawed his stuffed bunny close to him, then settled in for a snooze.

Will took Winnie's hand in his and put his other hand on top of it. "You always make my heart smile, even when my face is too weary." He sighed. "It's not that I want to hide anything from you, love. We've always shared everything and that will never change."

"Because we've always *had* one other. The one thing you can't bear to tell me is that our journey is coming to an end."

"Our journey isn't coming to an end," Will told her. "In the grand scheme of things, it's only just begun."

"One of the things I have always loved about you, Will Drexler, is that you never cease trying to make things better for me. You try to take the pain out of every hurt, even when you know it's impossible. Just knowing how much you want to right every wrong has always comforted me. But we're at a point where you can't do that." She took a moment to compose herself. "And now I'm talking in euphemisms about journeys because I don't want to flat out ask you if you're going to die soon and leave me and Jepper alone in this place."

"I hope I don't do that, Winnie, my love. But I know he'll comfort you when that time comes."

Her forehead creased with pain, and anger set in. "Nothing will comfort me if you're gone. Besides, our boy is fourteen, and he's not going to be around much longer, either. I can't bear it here alone;

I just can't. You have to tell me."

"When I know," Will said, squeezing her hand. "When I know, I will tell you. I have no definitive word. And that's the truth." A smile escaped his lips. "I have another 'six-month checkup' next week."

Winnie sniffled. "You're trying to be adorable."

"Is it working?"

"No," Winnie said. "Well, maybe. But it's not making my worries any lighter."

"Being adorable has to do some good," Will said. "We've had our darkest days when we couldn't find anything to laugh about. I don't bring it up much, because it's been easier for us to go on with what we've had than to bemoan what we lost, but damned if I haven't been thinking about what Scott did to us. It's on my mind every day. Especially now when …"

"When you're afraid your life is coming to an end? And you've got to leave me here … that's why, isn't it?" Winnie asked.

Will bit his lip, his face reddening.

"I haven't seen you like this since that day our son absconded to Venezuela with our life savings. Two weeks and two days after your retirement."

Will stood and began walking around the room. "That's the day we lost our son, our money, our home, and pretty near every one of our friends who had trusted our financial-planning offspring with their money. I was just going to say that when the shock wore off, I blamed myself for having done something wrong. Only to be honest, Winnie, I still don't think the shock has worn off. And I'm not sure what I did wrong, though I know it must have been something. How did we raise a soulless sociopath?"

"It wasn't you!" Winnie cried. "You've been a wonderful father. Janis will tell you that. She does often, I know."

"Thank God for Janis," Will said, wearing himself out from

pacing. "And you ... you chose to stay at home with our children. To give them everything."

"Being a mother brought me great fulfillment. Seeing how things turned out, maybe I should have gone out into the world. At the very least so we'd be living on two Social Security checks instead of one. I did enjoy being a wife and mother, though. Remember when I used to paint animals on the children's bedroom walls? That was so much fun. But I suppose I should have gotten a job when the children were older." Winnie exhaled. "Please sit down, dear. You're making yourself sick and walking in circles isn't helping. Especially when it's ninety-something degrees outside."

"It's almost the same inside," Will said. "But I can't sit down. At least if I'm moving, I know my blood's circulating. Isn't that a good thing? And no, you shouldn't have gotten a job, unless you'd wanted one. You enjoyed life at home, and we didn't need a second salary. Neither of us could have foreseen what was to come. How could we have?" He stopped to slow his breathing. "Despite making good money as a mechanic, I should have gone to school for mechanical engineering and had a job that would have provided a pension. If I'd done so, the last twenty years of our lives would have been spent in our home, not in this miserable room."

"But all of that money you saved, that money that Scott took from us, that *was* your pension ... for world travel, for a cottage in the country, or for whatever we needed or wanted." Winnie nodded toward the empty space next to her. "You did plan ahead—you just never imagined our only son would rob us blind. You can't fix how things are now, and you sure as heck can't fix the past. You just got to stop what-iffing, my love. It doesn't do a thing but wear you thin."

Will stood still and looked at her. "I think I will sit down." Taking the seat next to his wife, he tried to pretend he hadn't winded himself, but his breathing gave him away. He looked across the room at the painting in the polished wooden frame. A winding path in the

French countryside led to a thatched-roof stone cottage on the left, surrounded by trees. A simple cottage—it had beautifully crafted blue shutters and a heavy wooden front door to match. An old red pail sat on one side of it, as if someone had just put it there momentarily and was coming back to fetch it. Multicolored flowers ran along the length of the cottage, and a gray cat slept on the small lawn, soaking in rays. Soft puffs of clouds dotted the azure sky, as if to just laze and daydream, while the sun did all of the hard work to keep the day sunny and cheerful.

"You know, Winnie, buying this painting on our honeymoon in Normandy was the best thing we could have done. We've never ceased to get joy from it."

Winnie smiled. "So true, my love." She looked around the room, furnished with what few pieces of furniture from their past had been able to fit. "Who ever thought we'd end up here?"

Will's face sunk, and he put his hands on his stomach, as if he physically felt the pain. "I certainly didn't."

"That wasn't meant as a condemnation, my darling. Because despite everything, I've been happy being here with you."

Will bit his bottom lip. Darkness filled his eyes. "You deserved so much more. I should have seen the signs. Remember that Fourth of July picnic we had when you and Janis baked all of those cookies, and they disappeared? We thought the Wilson's son had stolen them as a prank, and two days later, you found them stashed in Scott's closet. Selfish bastard … he just swiped the whole lot of them. Didn't even want them. Just took them because you and Janis got so much joy out of baking them together. And he hated that and wanted to punish you for it. I should have known that an evil character was building. He is my son. I should have known."

"No, no, no, no!" Winnie got up and stood before her husband. "Are you still pummeling yourself with guilt, Will Drexler? Do you really think that even the most perceptive mind on this planet would conclude that a teenager stealing cookies was a precursor to a grown man stealing five-million dollars from his family and friends one day? Because that's absurd."

"I still should have known," Will said, looking down at his lap. "There were many signs … in hindsight."

"Hindsight isn't all its cracked up to be." Winnie sat beside him, nudging him to look at her. "You know what I love most about you?"

Will shrugged.

"I'll give you a hint," Winnie told him. "It's the same thing that also frustrates me the most about you."

"I'd imagine a lot of things I do frustrate you," Will said, dejectedly.

"Oh, no, darling. Please don't beat yourself up. What I love most about you is that you never cease trying to be Superman for me. And in so many ways, you are. But you can't do the impossible, no matter how hard you try. There are some things even you can't make better."

"Can't accept defeat, Winnie. I'll never stop trying. If I have to harness every last ounce of energy in this old body of mine, I'll do whatever I can to bring you every possible joy. I never thought I could be so deeply in love with one woman for sixty-five years, but I have been. I don't ever want to stop."

Winnie put her arms around Will's neck as he put his arms around her. For a long minute, they kissed deeply.

"You do something to me, woman," Will said. "You still turn me on." He thought for a moment. "If we had been kissing on a park bench just now, you know what people would say about us?"

"What's that?" Winnie asked. "That we're madly in love?"

"No. That we're cute. I don't know why people who have been in love for a lifetime are seen as 'cute' while young lovers are 'hot' and all of that rot. I think we're 'hot.' Don't you?" He smiled warmly.

"Darned right we are," Winnie said, initiating a second kiss.

Will looked over at the painting again. "Not a day goes by when I don't imagine us back there in France. That cottage beckons. What a wonderful life that would be."

"We really splurged when we bought that," Winnie said. "I think we knew it would be worth every penny." She looked at Will. "You look upset. What is it? Will you please tell me what the doctor said?"

"Honestly, love. There is nothing definitive. If my face is registering pain, it's because I am thinking about Scott."

"Don't let him invade your thoughts. God only knows how difficult that is, but you can't empower him by letting him take up space in your head."

"I don't mean to, Winnie. It's just that when I look at this painting, I get such joy. But sometimes, I think about how this painting gave me the biggest red flag to Scott's character there was. It was an unwitting accomplice in portending the future, and I dismissed it."

"You're scaring me. Tell me why you're saying this."

Will shifted uneasily in his seat. "Remember the young artist we bought this from, Henri Georges Charron?"

"Of course. I'll never forget him. He was just about our age. Charming. And he sat right in the town square with that blue beret on his head, painting the little shops as tourists milled around looking at his finished work. He was delightful to everyone. He didn't seem to mind being interrupted. I remember he was very surprised, and thrilled, of course, when we bought the painting. He said that most people just tell him how beautiful his work is and move on."

"Exactly," Will said. "I remember."

"So how does Scott fit into any of this? He wasn't even born then."

"Because it was Scott who told me twenty-something years later that Charron had become a well-known painter and that our painting was worth a lot of money. He said he would sell it for us."

Winnie gasped. "You never told me that."

"No," Will said. "I didn't. I foolishly wanted to protect you. If I had been honest, maybe you would have been able to see just how bad things were going to get."

"I don't think so, my darling," Winnie said, caressing his face. "He is my son too. I wore the same blinders you did. Tell me what happened."

"Well, when he told me he wanted to sell the painting, I could see the dollar signs in his eyes. It sickened me. He knew this painting was our most treasured possession, but still, he wanted to sell it 'for us.' He hadn't yet stolen all of our money, so it wasn't as if we were in need or on red alert. Our son wanted to sell our beloved painting for a fortune, then throw us some paltry sum. He'd already been in touch with an art dealer. I'll tell you, Winnie: he looked at every thing and every one to see what was in it for him."

"I'm horrified to hear this," Winnie said. "Though it almost seems trivial next to the crimes he has committed. There's so much I could say, but what's the use. What is most important is that you can't let this upset you now. It's not good for your heart."

Agitated, Will stood abruptly and walked over to the window. Looking out, he waved to two locals who were entering the bodega one floor below, then walked back to Winnie and sat down again. "My darling, I wasn't completely honest before. The reason I went to the doctor so early this morning is because I was having terrible chest pains during the night."

"No!" Winnie cried.

"It's okay. The doctor said I was having panic attacks, but of course, at my age, with the history I have, he's still concerned."

"I've never known you to have panic attacks. What in the world happened to induce them?"

Hesitating, Will looked around the room.

Winnie lightly punched his arm. "The answer is in your head, Will Drexler. Don't look around the room to buy time while you concoct some story to lighten whatever blow there is coming. I'm on to you, fella. This lass has been around the ol' corral way too many times to be fooled."

Will took her hands in his and kissed each one. "I don't intend to fool you, sweetheart. It's just difficult for me to find the words."

"Tell me," Winnie said.

"I got a call yesterday," Will told her. "From Janis."

"Is she okay? Tom? The kids? I just spoke to her two days ago."

"Janis and her family are fine," Will reassured her. "I'm sure she told you that our amazing granddaughter made the dean's list again, and just yesterday, our grandson was promoted to vice president at his company. Janis and Tom are planning a trip to Australia over Christmas. He's got a conference in Melbourne, and the company is footing the bill."

"How wonderful," Winnie said. "I do believe their lives are nearly picture perfect, just as I prayed ours would always be. So what in the world has got you so spooked?"

"I'll just come out and say it: Scott was released early from prison yesterday."

"Oh!" Winnie moaned, putting her hand over her mouth.

"I'm afraid so. He made a beeline to Janis and Tom's house yesterday. Had the audacity to ask her for money to get a fresh start. Didn't express one iota of remorse for the five-million dollars he stole and consequently spent on God knows what during his three years of living the high life in Caracas. No plans to pay anyone back.

Janis said it was all about his seventeen years in prison after being caught, extradited, and convicted. Poor guy suffered so much. Had to eat horrible food, suffer daily humiliation, and live with killers and all kinds of scum 'not fit to shine his shoes.'"

"He's learned nothing from all of this, except how to be more morally reprehensible. I hope she didn't give him so much as a dime," Winnie said.

"Oh, she gave him something all right: the boot. Told him to get the hell out of her house and never contact her again."

"We have one strong daughter."

"We do," Will said. "He didn't go without a fight, though. Jan said he kept looking around the house, like he was casing it, appraising her valuables. Then, out of nowhere, he asked about us. Just wondered if we were still alive but didn't ask how we were doing under the miserable circumstances he created for us. Didn't have a lick of conscience or regret. Just wanted to know if we still had that painting by the French guy who became so famous. Oh, and where did we live."

"Good God!" Winnie said, the panic in her eyes apparent.

"She didn't tell him, my love. It was at that precise moment she kicked him out, but she said that on his way out the door, he muttered something about how he'll find us in no time at all."

"He wants to steal our painting!" Winnie cried. "And probably kill us, too."

"Look at me, sweetheart. Scott will *never* get that painting. It is ours, and I've left a small will bequeathing it to Janis."

Winnie began to shake. "But what if he storms in here and takes it? What can we do?"

"I don't think he'll do that, love. At best, I think he'd try some slick talk to wrangle it from us, if we even let him in, which we won't. Don't forget, he's on parole. He steals so much as a pack of gum from the bodega and he's back in prison with all of those men he doesn't think are fit to shine his shoes. Only he's the one not fit to shine anyone's shoes. Every person who's ever come and gone from this place, no matter what their station, no matter what their story, has been a better human being than our despicable offspring will ever be. I never thought I would feel such antipathy for my own son, but I do."

Will buried his face in his hands and sobbed, then quickly pulled them away and wiped his tears. "How shameful of me. I should be comforting you."

Smiling through her pain, Winnie lay her head on his chest and took a hold of his hand. "It's always been the two of us. Here for one another." She looked up at him. "People always said, 'where's there's a Will, there's a Winnie.' Everyone who knows us understands how deeply we love one another. And we will until the end of time."

Stroking her silver hair, Will smiled. "Exactly. That's why you don't have to worry about being alone. I said earlier that Jepper would comfort you when that time comes. I shouldn't have said that. I had a momentary lapse. Forgive me. I promise you, Winnie; we'll always be together." He looked across the room at the sleeping dog. "With our boy, too."

"You know, sometimes I think you really are Superman, my darling."

Will looked over at the painting. "We walked that very path to that cottage. I wonder if it's still being rented out to tourists. We were so lucky to get a room for two nights. There was another couple that had gotten there ahead of us. Remember? They were overdressed rich folks with way too much attitude. When the owner saw us come in, so in love, she told them she had made a mistake, and that we had reserved the place months ago. The couple called her some very unpleasant names and stormed out."

"Ah, yes! Now I remember as if it were yesterday. We were so grateful to that lovely woman. Her name was Justine." Her head still on his chest, Winnie grinned as her memories became clearer. "You made the most exquisite love to me in that cottage, Will Drexler."

"And you to me," Will mused, remembering. "Which is precisely why we had to have the painting of the cottage when we found Henri in the town square. Having this painting was akin to immortalizing that time forever. We were so young, yet when I held your hand, walking down that path, I thought to myself that someday we would return and do it all over again. Honestly, I daydreamed about retiring there … that was until …"

Winnie sat up, her anger returning. "I can't believe our son would want to steal this painting from us. He's so arrogant; he might just think he could get away with it. Maybe he won't worry about his parole officer. After all, he didn't care when he took five-million dollars from so many of us. A painting might be small potatoes to him."

Putting his hands on her shoulders, Will looked at her, a cold sweat forming on his face. "I will *never* let that happen. You have my solemn word. As solemn as the day we stood at that beautiful altar in your parents' backyard, before God, our family, and our friends, and promised to love one another forever." He paused as his breath became labored. "I know we said, 'till death do us part,' but that … that was not promise enough. We will never be separated. I-I will see to that."

"Oh, Will," Winnie cried, as tears of love filled her eyes. "I love you so much."

"And I you—"

"WILL!" Winnie screamed. "WILL!"

Clutching his chest, Will's body jerked as his head went back.

THE NEXT DAY

"Never heard them mention a son," Henry said, as he stood outside of Will and Winnie's room with the impatient stranger. "And I've been the day clerk here for the past eighteen years. Met their daughter many a time." He scratched his head. "I'm having second thoughts about letting you in. You could be anyone."

"But I'm not anyone. I told you: I'm their son, Scott Drexler. Look, I pounded on this door ten minutes ago and nobody answered. I didn't bring you up here so we could get acquainted. I don't want to know you any more than you want to know me. I'm worried that something could be wrong. My parents are old. You get my drift, bud?"

"They could be out walking the dog," Henry said.

"Really? They've got a dog? Well, you're the desk clerk in this palatial nightmare. Did you see them leave?"

"Well, no," Henry said. "I usually see everything but most times have my face buried in the paper, or I'll be watching the TV. And I got the desk fan going on days like this … practically right in my ear too. Not that it's any of your damn business. Still not getting why I never heard of you. Not sure you're their son. What's your sister's name?"

"Janis Drexler Burns," Scott said. "She's about five feet, six inches. Brown hair past her shoulders with blond highlights. Two kids and a husband."

"Hmm," Henry said. "Well, you got that part right. So tell me why I never heard of you."

Scott thought for a moment, then softened. "I really wanted to avoid this, but I suppose I'll have to tell you the truth, despite the shame it will bring to my family."

Henry looked cockeyed at him. "They got a reason to be ashamed of you?"

"Hell, no!" Scott said as his face contorted with disgust. "It's the other way around!"

"Really?" Henry asked. "Hard to imagine. Will and Winnie Drexler are just about the nicest folks I've ever known. Don't know how they fell on hard times to get here, but I know their daughter and son-in-law offered to have them live at their house. Begged them, actually. Only they wouldn't have it. Determined to live on what they could afford, and, like Winnie told me, she didn't want to be a burden. Said she wanted her daughter and son-in-law to have their own love story, just like she and Will have."

Scott grimaced and made an ugly sound with his lips. "Isn't that just like my mother to play the martyr. And the romantic."

"Nothing you're saying sounds like the people I know. I normally don't ask people their business, but if you want me to open this door, you're gonna have to tell me why these fine people have done anything to be ashamed of. Because so far, you haven't convinced me of a damn thing."

Looking down at the worn carpet, Scott quickly contorted his face to show pain. Fully into character, he looked at Henry. "This isn't easy, but I'll tell you." He cleared his throat. "Seventeen years ago, I developed a mental illness. I won't go into detail because it's too painful to talk about. But what I will tell you is that my family had me committed to a state facility against my will. Wasn't much nicer than this place. I've been there all of these years, struggling to get better. Of course, the fact that neither my parents nor my sister came to visit me only made my recovery take that much longer. I'd say it damn well impeded it. But I worked hard despite the painful alienation from my so-called loved ones. After all of those years, the doctors finally recognized my progress and I was released. So yes, the reason you never heard of me was because my parents were ashamed to have a mentally ill son."

"Really? You kill someone?" Henry asked.

"Hell no!" Scott bellowed.

"What you're saying doesn't sound like the Drexlers at all,"

Henry said. "Two of the kindest and least judgmental people I've ever known. Can't imagine them turning their backs on their own son because he was sick, be it physical or mental illness."

"Well, people aren't always how they seem," Scott said. "People can seem real decent and turn out to be the scum of the earth."

Henry shook his head. "If you think your parents are the scum of the earth, then for sure I'm not letting you in. Because they're as far from that as people can get."

"I wasn't specifically talking about my parents," Scott protested. "Just making the point that people aren't always the saints they might appear to be. But nonetheless, I'm here to make amends with my parents. To forgive them for sending me away and pretending I didn't exist. Because I don't have room for any hate in my heart."

"Let me see your driver's license," Henry said. "Prove you're who you say you are."

"Gee," Scott said. "You know, my license kind of expired in the seventeen years I was locked away. Don't exactly have any credit cards, either."

"No, I guess you wouldn't."

"Look, bud, all I want to do is make amends with my parents. How 'bout this? Everyone always said I looked like my father. Can't you see the resemblance?"

Henry studied Scott's face. "Matter of fact, now that you mention it, I can. Very much so. Got your dad's face and eyes, but your mother's nose. Don't know why I didn't see it before. Guess it's just that I never heard of you."

"Well now you know why," Scott said, fidgeting with the change in his pocket. "Can you please open the door so I can see if my parents are okay?"

"I s'pose." Henry knocked loudly on the door. "Will, Winnie,

Jepper? Anybody in there?" He put his ear to the door to listen. "Not a sound. Not a soul in there."

"Not unless a couple of mimes are having at it," Scott said sarcastically. "But certainly not my parents, or their dog, not unless they're all dead. I'm really starting to worry. Can you please open the damn door? Or would you prefer I kick it in?"

"All right," Henry said. "Against my better judgment but you do look like them, and I must say, I'm worried too." He looked at Scott. "But I sure as hell ain't gonna leave you alone in here. You got that? Bud!"

Tapping his foot impatiently, Scott waited while Henry put the key in the lock and turned it. As soon as the door was ajar, Scott burst into the room as Henry followed behind him. Standing in the room, Henry looked around. "Nobody here. Everything is nice and neat, just like always. There's Jepper's bed in the corner. And that's the painting they love so much."

"Ah, there it is!" Scott exclaimed, rushing over to the wall where it hung. Putting his hands on either side of the painting, he lifted it gently, but quickly, off the wall. "Hello, baaaaa-by! I've been looking for you for a very long time."

"Hey! That ain't yours," Henry said. "Put it back!"

"The hell it's not mine," Scott barked. "Guess they never told you that I was an artist. I painted this before I got sick. After they put me away, they must have stolen it. I don't know what cockamamie story they told you about it, but this is my masterpiece."

"No, it's not. I know all about this painting and how they bought it on their honeymoon in France."

Scott scowled. "You think people who lied about locking up their only son wouldn't lie about a painting? You're one gullible SOB!"

"You wish," Henry said. "Okay, if you're telling the truth, let me see where's it's signed with your name."

Scott looked at the painting, his mind spinning to come up with an answer. "What the goddamn hell is this!" he shouted. "Stupid old fools! This is worthless now! I told them this was … oh, fuck! I can't believe they did this!"

"What are you talking about?" Henry asked.

"My mother must have done this. Gone and painted her and my father, and their damn dog, right onto the path of this painting. She used to paint zoo animals on my wall as a kid. But I never thought she'd desecrate fine art. This doesn't look like her style, though. She's not this talented. Not even close. But I can't think of any other explanation. Damn her!" Scott said, dropping the painting onto the bed with disgust. "When they come back from walking their dog, tell them Scott said they can burn in hell."

Ignoring him, Henry picked up the painting and smiled. "Well, I'll be. Ain't that beautiful. That sure is Will, Winnie, and Jepper walking along that path. And don't they look happy."

"Damn, damn, damn," Scott shouted as he stormed out of the room. "Stupid old fools."

Henry looked around the room. "Will, Winnie … you here? He's gone now. He won't be back. Just heard him stomp down the stairs. Must be in the lobby and out the door by now. You hiding in the closet? The bathroom? Jepper? You here, boy?"

Laying the painting on the bed, Henry walked around the room. "This is plum crazy. Something feels different. If y'all were out walking Jeps, you'd have been back by now. Especially in this crazy heat.

"If you're hiding, come out. I can understand why you wouldn't want to see that son of yours. He's a nasty piece of work. But he's gone now. Like I said: won't be back." Henry walked quickly to the closet, opened it, then closed it again. Hurrying to the bathroom, he poked his head in the doorway, then looked around the room in confusion.

Walking back to the bed, he picked up the painting. "Well, holy Moses. I must be hallucinating. I know Winnie, Will, and Jepper were walking down this path just a minute ago. Now, he's holding the door of the cottage open for her, and Jepper's playing with the gray cat in the yard."

Henry sat on the bed. "Maybe this crazy heat has made me crazy. Maybe I've got some kind of heatstroke. Because what I'm thinking … can't possibly be. Then again, I've spent way too many years in the Obscure. Eighteen years in this place has finally taken a toll on my sanity. I should have expected it, dealing with every joker on the trash heap of life. I thought all of the nice ones would keep me sane. Apparently not."

Pulling a handkerchief out of his pants pocket, he wiped the sweat from his brow, then looked at the painting again. "I don't know. Will, you always said, 'Where there's a will, there's a way … and a Winnie.' And Winnie, you always said Will was your Superman … would make the impossible possible. I thought that was just love talking. Maybe it was. But I'm thinking your love was even more powerful than even you knew. I can't figure any of this out." Henry paused to reflect on what he had just said. "Now, if you'll excuse me, I'm gonna go call your daughter …." He stood and looked around the room. "I sure am gonna miss you people something fierce. You, too, Jepper. You, too."

ONLY SIXTEEN

I rarely look in the mirror anymore because the woman who stares back at me rattles my nerves. She is every bit as confused as I am. Some days, I can barely picture how either of us look, but today, I know that her face and mine are one and the same. Tomorrow, I may not.

I know there are many lines on my face. I can feel them. They run across my forehead like the ruled paper I used to use in school. Between some of the lines are brown spots. On the days I dare to peek, they look like notes on a staff … right on my forehead. And I wonder what song I am wearing.

I know these "notes" are called liver spots. Only they're not on my liver. They're on my forehead, my face, my arms, and my legs. If they are on my liver, I can't see them. I don't like that name: liver spots. It is ugly. But I know it. My grandmother had them. She told me they gave her character, just like her wrinkles did. I believe I am of good character; I don't think it has gotten me anywhere.

Nearly everything I see reminds me of something I have seen long ago or can imagine in my mind's eye. The lines under my eyes are like crescent moons, turned on their sides, floating … always floating. Deep vertical lines run between my upper lip and my nose; they remind me of the rows of corn I ran through as a child on my uncle's farm. The corn never stayed all year 'round though. But those were beautiful years. I still miss the swing on the old oak tree. I almost felt like I could fly. My grandmother lived in that house with my aunt and uncle. She didn't like the swing. My uncle had fallen from it as a child and broken his arm. He mended okay, but my grandmother was always afraid one of her grandchildren would get hurt. She thought too much about the swing, I think. As she got older, it was all she talked about … even long after it was taken down.

When I grew into my teens, Sam Cooke was all the rage. Swoon is a silly word, but that's what girls used back in the day to describe the dizzy feeling a person gets when they feel attraction to someone sexy like Sam. I have always maintained that girls who swoon look like they are about to pass out or throw up.

There was this boy. And when I saw his handsome face for the first time, I came as close to swooning as I would ever get … without actually doing it. My best friend back then said I had butterflies in my stomach. I don't like that expression any more than I like the word "swoon." I guess that's because I take it too literally. Butterflies have four life cycles. They start being eggs, then larva … or caterpillars, then pupas … or chrysalis … and there they grow to be butterflies. I was very good with science, and I did not want to visualize all of these stages of life, multiplied in numbers, happening in my stomach. That is certainly enough to make anyone swoon … throw up. I just wanted to admire a boy.

I noticed him immediately. He looked like Sam Cooke. He was sixteen, just like me, and he went to a school in the next town. We met at a football game. He walked right up to me and said I was the prettiest girl he'd ever seen. We both left the friends we had come with and sat by ourselves in a corner of the bleachers, barely watching any of the game. That was on a Wednesday night; we had our first date that Friday.

We went to see *The Fly*. He had wanted to see it, and being so interested in science, I was all too happy to see some crazy science fiction. We loved it. It wasn't anything like a romantic movie … the ones that make you want to hold hands, but we did anyway. After the film, before we headed to the local diner, we sat in the car. Sam Cooke's "Only Sixteen" came on the radio in his father's 1953 Ford

Victoria. It was our story, he said after time passed. "She was too young to fall in love, and I was too young to know."

Four months later, our baby was conceived in the back seat. Unlike other teenage boys, mine did not want to run away. He said his heart had never been happier, and he had a plan. He would work part-time as a carpenter's apprentice until we graduated from high school. Then, we would get married and he would become a carpenter. I made the mistake of telling a friend how good he was with his hands. I showed her the wooden heart box he had made for me. But all she wanted to do was giggle about how talented he was with his hands and other parts. I guess I deserved the jokes that came … but not every day. I got sick of them fast. You might say I swooned every time she repeated her stupidity. I was sixteen, pregnant, and scared. But I was in love, and all I knew was that I wanted my baby and his father more than I had ever wanted anything in the world.

I kept my pregnancy a secret until I was in my fifth month. My father was a preacher, and my mother was the kind of woman who wore flower-print dresses that she had sewn and thought it was her privilege and her place to dutifully serve her husband. I'm sure my father loved her some kind of way, but it wasn't the way I had learned to love at such a young age. 'Round town, some people said some things about him, and I figured out that he actually preferred women who didn't wear flower prints with lace collars but plunging necklines and a whole lot of everything else my mother was always covering up.

From the time I was young, I knew I was nothing like her. She was weak. All she did was parrot his words and opinions. And that's exactly what happened when I told them I was pregnant. He spoke first. Once she knew what her opinion was supposed to be, they both insisted that I had to give up my baby for adoption. I said I would never do that, no matter what, not ever. They saw a fire in me they never knew existed. But they kept insisting I give my baby to strangers, and I kept telling them that I would die first. By the time I was in my eighth month, all of us so worn, they agreed I could keep my baby as long as I graduated high school. And then they reminded me that I had shamed the family … because maybe I didn't hear that the first thousand times they told me.

My sweetheart worked hard. No movies for us anymore. Our only time together was when we could steal it because they forbade me to see him.

I thought labor would be the most painful thing I'd ever been through, but it didn't compare to what happened next. My beautiful baby girl was born weighing seven pounds and two ounces. She had gorgeous golden brown skin, and right away, I could see that she had her father's eyes and my nose. I didn't hold her for very long, maybe ten minutes at best, when they said they had to take her for special tests. I wanted to ask them to wait, to give me a few more minutes with her, but before I could even protest, I was asleep.

When I woke up, I was back in my room. With grim faces, my parents were staring at me. They'd take a break to look at each other, then stare at me some more. It didn't take me long to get the sickest feeling ever. Worse than swooning, worse than anything I had ever known. I screamed for my baby.

They told me my baby's heart was not fully formed, and she died. I screamed louder and longer than I ever had in my life. The pain was indescribable. Tears flooded down my face as I called for her, then screamed again. My parents never consoled me. They just told me to be quiet. They tried to get me to sign some papers, but I refused. I just kept screaming. They told me I would have to be sedated if I didn't stop. I saw a big old nurse standing nearby with a needle, and she looked sadistic. I could tell: she was a lip licker. You know, people who lick their lips in anticipation of something that gives them pleasure … perverse as it may be. I didn't want her near me. So I quietly asked for my baby, and again, they told me she was dead. I screamed again and woke up in a strange place.

It was a bedroom in a house. It was very clean and had no personality. I felt very groggy. My head had never felt heavy like it did that day. I knew that mean nurse had injected me with something.

I was just about to try to get out of bed when I heard people talking. I closed my eyes and pretended to still be drugged. I heard a man tell a woman that my baby would have a happy life with her adoptive parents and that my boyfriend had been forced to move out of town. And then he reminded her to tell me that my baby girl had died of a malformed heart.

I wanted to get out of there and run far away. But I knew that if I did, I'd be put away in some place with locked doors. Even at the height of my youthful despair, I knew better. I kept my eyes closed and drifted back to sleep. When I woke up three hours later, a smiling lady was sitting in a chair, just staring at me. She told me she was my father's cousin; I was a long way from home, and I would now live with her and her husband. Their only daughter had moved away, and the room I was in once belonged to her.

Everything had been arranged. I would finish school nearby. I would work part-time at their sewing notions and fabric store. When I graduated, I would work full time. I would only be given a small stipend, though, as I would be paying off everything they were spending on me. The woman pulled a notebook out of her apron book to show me that my bill was already being tabulated … room and board from day one.

Aghast, I smiled pleasantly as if in accord. I soon realized that even if I paid off my expenses as they wished, I would still be incurring them. I learned that the original plan had been for their daughter to work in the store, but she had her own ideas on how to life her life, much to their displeasure.

When I spoke to my parents on the phone, they told me I was lucky to be where I was, "in such a respectable situation," and they said nothing about seeing me again. I had shamed the family and was sentenced to life in a sewing notions and fabric store.

In an instant, I became a different person. I learned how to hide my grief and to acquiesce for survival. As time went by, I fooled everyone. I let them think I was happy in my new life. I saved every penny I was allowed to keep. I even made friends so as to appear well adjusted and satisfied. Out of the three friends I made, I truly trusted and loved only one. And when I was nineteen years and three months old, this friend gave me a great sum of money from an inheritance she'd received and told me that I no longer had to wait until I was in my twenties. There was enough money for me to put my plan into action right away.

Each day, I would carry something to work that I wanted to keep, and she would stop by to get it, take it home, and put it in a suitcase. Less than two weeks passed and I was ready to go. With a smile, I offered to stay late at the store and do some inventory. I left a note on the counter, and once the dark had obscured the view of the store, I locked the front door and slipped out of the back one. My friend, who had been waiting behind the store, drove me to a bus station more than one-hundred miles away. I was a legal adult, and there was nothing my father's cousins or my parents could do … but I still didn't want them to find me. And they never did.

I found a modest studio apartment in the first city where I lived and got a job in a women's clothing store. My retail experience proved helpful, as did my knowledge of fabrics, although I did have to lie about the name of the store and the city I had come from. I put my money in the bank, and every extra dime I had went to paying a private detective and paying back my friend. The detective discovered that my baby's adoption had been very secretive, and all of the records had been sealed. My boyfriend, it seems, had changed his name, as there was no record of him after graduating high school. I was distraught by the news but never dissuaded from continuing my search. Every time I moved to another city, I left a forwarding address. I wanted to make sure that if any news came to light after I was gone, I could always be found. That dim hope gave me the only solace I had.

I remember living in six different cities. I moved to every city he had ever talked about, hoping I might see him on the street and be reunited. Or, that I would see my baby and recognize her immediately. Then, I would go to court and try to prove she had been stolen from me. I had never signed the papers they tried to force on me without explanation and had long since figured out that someone had forged my name. I'm very sure it was the man who preached about sin every Sunday, enjoying secret dalliances with women when not at his pulpit.

Life after the sixth city is not a vague memory. It is a nonexistent one. It's like another lip-licking nurse injected me with something to knock me out, only this time, for twenty years.

I am not very sure what kind of place this is where I live now. It is shabby, but the beautiful lady who takes care of me is always trying to make it nicer. Last week, or perhaps it was last year, she sewed a new slipcover for the chair I sit on. She is very talented. I have six watercolors on the walls, each one depicting a city I remember living in, and she painted them all, including the walls they hang on.

She cooks every meal herself in the small kitchen area she has set up. I feel more content in her presence than I ever have in my life. Her father lives across the hall, and he looks after me too. One day, he gave me a wooden heart and told me he had carved it just for me. It rests perfectly in my treasured wooden heart box. Some days, I take it out and hold it to my own heart. In those moments, I feel young again, but I worry that tomorrow, I will forget where the heart came from. When I first told him this, I saw tears fall from his eyes, and he said over and over again how sorry he was. I didn't understand; I told him he was mistaking me for someone else. That just made him cry even more. I know he loves me because of the great love I feel from, and for, him.

On the days when I am up for it, they take me out for a walk. The neighborhood, like me, has probably forgotten much of its previous life. Nothing is new and shiny, nor is it old and well cared for. I am different from the buildings I see, as I am well cared for by two angels who fill me with love.

Today, we went to the diner across the street to have a meal. Perhaps it was breakfast, or maybe lunch. I can't remember. The diner is old, like me, and on many tables, there are small jukeboxes. While she made sure I was comfortable in the booth, he looked through the songs, then stopped. Tears welled up in his eyes. He took a quarter from his pocket and put it in. Magically, Sam Cooke was singing "Only Sixteen." I remember being lifted from the darkness and transported into the light of clarity and back in time. It was glorious … euphoric … like nothing I had ever experienced. I felt radiant and young. As he took both of my hands into his own, tears ran down my face. Everything was clear; I knew why these two people loved me so much and why I loved them. As we all cried, I remember thinking that prayers truly work. My heart was so full. My two wishes in life had come true. I felt a boundless joy that I have never known before.

I am sitting in my chair now. This beautiful angel just brought some medicine for me to take. I don't like swallowing pills, so she always brings me chocolate pudding or applesauce to make it easier for me. She is so gentle, so kind. Just like her father.

I feel a bit agitated, though. I remember the joy I felt earlier, but I do not know why. I can only surmise that being loved is the reason. I want to ask them, but I feel certain I should know. And so, I pretend that I remember and they pretend that I do too.

JUNK TRUCK

Jayla let out a scream as her cell phone played "Leave Me Alone," startling her as the carton of files she was carrying fell to the ground, papers sliding out of their folders and creating a fan-like piece of Asian art on the old carpet.

Exasperated, she sighed and sat down on the bed, looking carefully to see who was calling before she answered the phone. "Hey, Derek!"

"Hey, Jaybird. I was concerned when I got your message saying you'd changed your number. You've had that number since mobiles came into existence or—should I say—since you got your first one."

"Yeah … I know."

"Okay. Something's not right. You sound worn and out of breath."

"I am. Score for the Oxford professor. How is life in merry old England, anyway?"

"Merry. No changing the subject. What's going on with you?"

Jayla plunked down on the bed. "You know, as much as I regret not leaving the states and moving to England with you all of those years ago, I'm glad I didn't. You have a wife and two beautiful children … and you're happy … and I couldn't have given you that."

"You're still changing the subject," Derek told her.

"Which was?"

"Which was that you sound more weary than I've ever heard you. Like you've just told the entire world to go to hell. Except for me, of course. Gee, I hope that's not why you wanted me to call." He paused. "No, if that were the case, you would have called on your old number, admonished me to take a downward trajectory toward eternal damnation, and *then* changed your number."

"Exactly!" Jayla said, laughing. "It's no wonder Oxford handpicked you for their prestigious faculty. Your intelligence—"

"So true. But come on. Spill. What's going on?"

"Okay. I'll tell you. Just don't say I'm a fool, or I'll never talk to you again either."

There was a brief silence on the other end of the phone. "Wow, so maybe my joke about eternal damnation wasn't such a joke after all."

"You know I didn't mean that, Derek. You're the only real friend I have left in the world." *I know you're in England, but you're embedded in my heart.*

"Talk to me. I'm not going to interrupt. Just give me the lowdown."

Jayla looked around at the boxes and the disarray in the room. "I know the thing that always drove you nuts about me was how I let my family and friends drain every ounce of energy from me. You used to say they squeezed my soul until not a drop of me was left. And I know, Derek, that if I'd been able to say no to them, you would have begged me to come to Oxford with you. But you didn't. Because you knew that even with thousands of miles between us, they'd take so much of me that there would be nothing left for you … just like for all of these years, there's been nothing left of me for me." She bit her bottom lip to stop herself from shedding any tears. "You can say something if you want. You won't be interrupting."

"I'd rather have you continue. Wait just a second … Fiona—hold any calls, will you? Thanks. Okay, Jaybird. I'm back. Keep talking."

"To begin with … my mother died two weeks ago."

"Oh, Jay … I'm so sorry!"

"Don't be. I'm not."

"Oh … okay."

"I took a demotion at work so I could care for her. I was too ashamed to tell you that. I let you believe I was sharing the work with my siblings. I'm so sorry for that."

"Whoa. Are you saying that you did everything? There are four of you … all within miles of one another. Why did you have to do everything? That's insane."

Because my two sisters and my wuss of a brother were all too messed up to so much as cook her meals, manage her medications, get her to appointments, or do fuck all for her. No taking turns in my family. *Everything* fell on me. I gave up my managerial job to make phone calls all day so that I could work from home. Her home. Yeah, I gave up my condo because I never got to live in it anymore. Not to mention that I couldn't pay for it on my new salary."

"So your siblings never came by?"

"Oh, sure, they came for visits all the time. And they always had a problem that only I could help them solve. My sisters never shut up about their messed-up relationships. Carrie was forever fighting with her ex about the kids, yet she always seemed more interested in making sure her current boyfriend didn't leave. And Missy kept getting fired from every sales job she had because she was either drunk or hung-over most days. Not to mention going through men like they were flavor of the week. Even the ones who drank didn't hang around. That pretty much tells you everything, doesn't it? But good ole me, I got her into rehab and encouraged her to be the person I knew she could be. That's me: Jayla the perpetual cheerleader. And now, she's sober and wants to be a model. I told her that models don't start their careers at thirty-two and that she needs to rethink her career ambitions, but she's not listening. She's just waiting to be discovered. Meanwhile, she's on the fast track to having an eating disorder. And Steve—well, he's just so dysfunctional that every single thing he does falls to pieces." Jayla sighed. "But that's a long story for another time. You probably can't wait for me to finish. You must be thinking I'm as bad as they are."

"Not at all," Derek told her. "Your biggest problem has always been your inability to say no to people."

"You'll be very happy to know that has all changed."

"Really? I'm chuffed to hear it. Tell me more."

Jayla got off the bed and walked around the room. Looking out the window, over the diner five floors below, to her left, she watched a man adding junk to a truck more worn than the refuse it carried.

"Jaybird ... you still there?"

"Sorry! I was just watching this man rearrange a bunch of crap in an old truck like he's doing some 3-D jigsaw puzzle. I'd say he's got everything but the kitchen sink in there, but I'll be damned if there isn't a kitchen sink right on top of that heap of crap he's driving around: metal shards, wooden pickets, old frying pans, an air conditioner, rope, old electronics, store mannequins, broken furniture ... you name it. And that's just what I can see from five stories up ... and I'm not even directly over the truck."

"Where the hell are you?"

"In an old hotel ... in the city. They call it 'the Obscure.' That ought to tell you something. I'm not even sure what the real name actually is." She sighed. "I'll get back to that in a minute. Anyway, taking care of my mother was sheer hell. Not an ounce of joy. She was demanding, entitled, critical, narcissistic, and mean. And if it wasn't enough dealing with her and my screwed-up siblings when they called or came over, my so-called female BFF always wanted me to show her how to work the laptop she's had for two years. I never could figure out why she couldn't learn, until one day it hit me; she never paid attention when I showed her anything. She just came to me whenever she needed help ... or money. Or advice, which I might add, that she never took. And not once did she ever offer to help with my mother or show me an ounce of compassion for the hell I was living in. Nah, it was all about her."

"Holy hell, Jaybird ... Things were a mess when I left seven years ago, but they weren't the kind of mess you just described."

Jayla watched as the junk truck driver shoved a battered hubcap between the sink and the torso of a mannequin. "Are you ready for the kicker?"

Derek sighed. "Tell me."

"She left every penny in her will to the three of them, including her house. Cut me out completely! Didn't leave me so much as one of her hideous Hummel figurines."

"Bloody hell!" Derek said. "For what reason?"

"Because my siblings are too screwed up to earn a living, and I've always been *so* good at figuring things out and earning a paycheck. They need the money because they might not survive without it, whereas I always land on my feet. Oh, and get this, she didn't like the way would get so flustered with her. I didn't answer her with a smile when she criticized every fucking thing I did to make her happy and comfortable. One day, I had to attend an important—and mandatory—all-day meeting at my office. It was a company-wide thing, and everyone was required to show or else. She was so angry that I chose to attend instead of keeping her company. Throwing away my career for her wasn't enough. No, she wanted me to lose the much lower-paying job I took so I could care for her twenty-four seven. And that's the day her neighbor, who heard her screaming at me, volunteered to take care of her while I was gone. And guess what her neighbor's husband does ... He's a lawyer. Oh yeah ... and that was the day she arranged to have me written out of her will."

"Oh, honey. I'm so sorry. That is horrible. I don't suppose there's any chance your siblings will do the right thing and divvy everything up fair and square."

Jayla walked away from the window, sat down on the floor, and started to clean up the mess of papers she had made. "Nope. Steve said it would be disrespectful to my mother not to honor her wishes. And of course, my sisters agreed."

"Of course they did. Bloody ingrates. Damn them. You need to contest this, Jayla. I really think you've got an excellent case. I'm a scientist, not a lawyer, but really, I think you would win." He hesitated. "I hope you don't mind me saying this, but your father would be furious if he knew this."

"I don't mind at all. You think that hasn't crossed my mind numerous times. He would be livid. But dead men tend to be extraordinarily quiet. Have you noticed that?"

Derek laughed. "You still make me smile."

Jayla righted the box on the floor and put a folder back into it. "How did I ever end up with a boyfriend like you? Everyone else in my life has been so needy, so destructive, so full of themselves."

"You have such a big heart, honey. I saw that the moment I met you. And I loved you for it."

"Yeah, you did. And eventually, it broke us apart. Like I said earlier, if I had known how to say no, both of our lives would have been so different. But at least you're happy, right?"

"I am. I feel very blessed. But right now, I'm worried about you. Why are you living in an old hotel called 'the Obscure?' Tell me that, at very least, it's obscurely nice."

Jayla laughed. "No, can't tell you that. Though there are some nice people here, and some not-so-nice ones too, I'd imagine. But nobody lives here who isn't down on their luck in some way, I'd imagine. If not, they're probably batshit crazy."

"But you work, Jay. Even with a lesser position, you can afford better."

"I can. But I want to live cheaply … very cheaply, so I can

save my money and travel the world when I have enough to retire early. Very early. I can't do that if I'm paying rent for a nice place. I'll always just have that 'nice place,' that isn't even mine, and nothing else. This hotel is a dive, but it's such a dive that the management is fine with tenants painting or doing anything they want to improve it … just no loud colors on the walls. And they allow pets here, so I'm going to rescue a dog. That's something I've always wanted to do. He or she will be the best company I've ever had. But more than anything, Derek, I just want to be alone. Stick me with a fork; I am so done with my family. I'm done with all of them, including that so-called miserable best girlfriend. I'm in the best place; I am. I'll fix this room up and it won't be so bad. I'm going to paint the walls taupe and make one a dark brown accent wall. And I'm going to get lots of plants … maybe some fake ones, so I don't kill them all. I've already ordered a mini- fridge, a double burner, and a microwave. Doesn't get any better than that, does it?"

A heavy silence hung on the line.

"Don't worry, Derek. I'll be free, and that's what I want now more than anything. And I'm not a hermit; I do have friends at work. And yeah, we actually go out together once or twice a month. But I'm good here. I can learn about all the places in the world I want to visit and make all sorts of wonderful plans for the future. I'll be happy because I'm away from the monsters that made me miserable, and I've got something amazing to look forward to down the line. And you and I will still talk, right? Like we always have."

"You'd better believe it. Listen, sweetie, I have a faculty dinner meeting in ten minutes, and I'm woefully unprepared. But we'll talk again soon … or email. Better than that, how about a video chat soon? Or doesn't that place have Wi-Fi?"

"It does. From the outside, looking at this elegant structure, you'd think it had nothing more than old black metal landlines, but it actually has Wi-Fi. If it didn't, I'd have moved to another dump that did. Sadly, I think a computer connection with the outside world is *all* that some of these people here have. Hmm … maybe I'm one of them now. For the moment anyway."

☠ ☠ ☠

Jayla could feel the thin metal handles of the paint cans digging into her palms as she walked into the small lobby. With her purse on one shoulder and a large bag of painting supplies on the other arm, she could barely walk.

A woman with curly red hair, who had just been speaking to the desk clerk, sidled up to her. "Hey, are you new here? Need some help with that? I'm Sandy. I just moved to the fifth floor last week."

"Oh, that's where I live. I just moved in too."

Without waiting for permission, Sandy reached over and took a can of paint from her. "Now, let me have that bag too. You're ridiculously overloaded."

"Really, I'm fine. I can carry everything."

Sandy grinned. "Well, I'm holding this can hostage until we get upstairs, so you might as well give me that bag with the paint tray sticking out of it."

Jayla hesitated, then reluctantly handed her the bag as the two women headed toward the stairs.

"So what's your name, neighbor," Sandy asked.

"Jayla."

"Oh, that's a gorgeous name. Very pretty! I like it a lot better than Sandy. Maybe I'll change my name to Jayla, too."

Feeling a chill go through her, Jayla continued walking up the stairs, tired by the time they reached the fifth floor. As she put the can of paint by her front door, she turned to Sandy. "Thanks for your help. May I have my stuff now?"

"I'd love to help you paint," Sandy said. "I once painted four bedrooms in my childhood home. Haven't lost my talent."

"Thank you. I'm good."

"You're gonna need a ladder, you know."

"Yes," Jayla said. "The desk clerk is bringing one up for me to borrow. Like I said, I'm good."

"Be sure you don't walk under the ladder," Sandy admonished her. "Bad luck. I must've walked under a whole lot of ladders in my childhood because I've had nothing but misery my entire life."

"I'm sorry," Jayla said as she turned the key in the door. "We all have our crosses to bear."

Sandy stood there, waiting for Jayla to open her door. Jayla stood there, waiting for Sandy to open the door to her own room.

Frustrated, Jayla looked at her. "Thank you for helping me carry the paint up here. I've really got to go now."

"Okay."

Jayla had no sooner pushed the door open, when Sandy strode in behind her. "Wow, your room is a good three feet larger than mine. I was sure they were all the same."

"Not this one," Jayla said, stunned by the intrusion. "It's a corner room. Henry told me it was a bit bigger when I moved in. Listen, I'm sorry; I really am busy."

"Whatcha gotta do?" Sandy asked playfully.

"Work, Sandy. I've got a lot on my plate. Okay?" Jayla gathered the painting supplies and moved them out of the way.

"I'll keep you company."

"No. I can't work with anyone here, and I'm not in the mood to socialize. You need to go, okay?"

"Oh, come on. We're just getting to know one another."

Jayla felt her nails digging into her palms as she balled her fists. "I'm sorry. I'm trying to be nice, but you make that really difficult."

"I'm just being friendly!" Sandy protested.

"No. You're not. Look, perhaps you're under the impression that my business is yours because we have rooms next door to one another or that because you helped me carry a can of paint upstairs, we're meant to be best friends. But you'd be wrong. You'd be very wrong."

"Oh." Sandy stood there, staring blankly, then burst into tears, collapsing onto the floor.

Fuck my life! "Is there something wrong? Can you please get up?" Reluctantly, Jayla held out a hand to help her up. Sobbing, Sandy stood and walked over to the upholstered chair and fell into it. "I'm sorry! I'm just a mess. My husband just left me. He told me he was leaving me for a man. He left that same day. That's why I moved here. I couldn't pay the rent."

"I'm sorry. I really am. It's a shame that society puts pressure on people to live as a heterosexual when they're not. Too many lives have been messed up because people didn't feel they were able to be open with their homosexuality. I'm sorry that you were hurt. I guess it's best you found out now."

"But he's not gay!" Sandy blubbered.

"But you just said …."

"It was a lie. I caught him with my best friend two weeks later! He moved in with her."

"Wow," Jayla said. "And she didn't think you'd find out if your husband was living there."

"Well, I only see her at the gym once in a while."

"But you said she was your best friend."

"We went to the movies together once … a couple of years ago. And she helped me learn how to use the treadmill. We used to talk at the juice bar. She was the best friend I had."

"Oh," Jayla said uncomfortably. "I see. Well, I'm sorry. That must be a bitter pill for you to swallow."

"You're not kidding! And he was my second husband. Well … sort of. My so-called first husband had our marriage annulled after one month. He said there was no point in not copping to a mistake. Especially the biggest one he'd ever made. Not a surprise, I guess, since my parents didn't even plan to have me. I was born when my mother was forty-three and thought her childbearing days were over. I was their mistake too."

"I'm sure they felt very blessed to have another child."

"Oh no they didn't," Sandy said emphatically, her eyes burning with rage. "With four grown children, the youngest one being seventeen, they sure as hell didn't want a to take care of a baby. They resented me my whole life. Nobody ever paid any attention to me. And I'm the only one in my family with bright red hair. My mother said it was a recessive gene at work. Just made me stand out all the more, but not in a good way. Like, 'there goes the ginger weirdo.' I tried dyeing my hair, but it just looked even worse. It's like my mother made sure her unwanted baby got flaming red hair so nobody would know I was a part of the family. She probably swallowed a bottle of red hair dye when she found out she was pregnant. Oh, I'm just being silly now, but I'm so angry."

"Many people have painful family memories. There's nothing pleasant about it. I'm sorry to hear that, but I really have things to do." Jayla walked to the open door and stood by it.

Sandy, looking morose and resigned, walked to it. "Okay, thanks, Jayla. And I really do like your name better than mine. I'm not kidding about changing it."

Jayla closed the door behind her. She looked upward. "Why are you testing me like this? Haven't I been through enough?" The words just out of her mouth, the cracked paint on the ceiling looked at her as a small piece fell, landed on her head, then hit the floor.

Her mouth open in surprise, Jayla blinked. "Well holy paint chip; I guess not."

☠ ☠ ☠

Three hours later, Jayla had just finished setting up her desk when the intense pounding on the door made her jump. She walked over to the door. "Who is it?"

"It's Sandy. I have something for you. Please open the door."

Shaking off her unease, Jayla opened the door. "Do you always pound like that?"

Sandy stood there, holding a large white bag in her hands. "I knocked lightly, but you didn't answer."

"I was breaking down boxes. I guess I didn't hear you."

"I brought you a gift: homemade chocolate chip and oatmeal raisin cookies from the bakery. It's about a mile from here. But I didn't mind walking there; you're worth it." She handed Jayla the bag. "Remember that old cigarette ad: 'I'd walk a mile for a Camel?' Well, I'd walk a mile for a friend. More than that."

"Um … uh … that's very kind of you, Sandy. But sugar and I don't get along so well. I try to eat as little as I can. I'm sure they're delicious, but you should take them. They'll just go to waste with me. But thank you." Jayla handed the bag back to her.

Sandy frowned. "What can I get instead then?"

"Absolutely nothing. Really. Nothing. I'm good."

"I need a huge favor. I'm so frustrated. Can you help me? Please!"

"I really—"

"It won't take long, Jayla. Please."

"What is it?"

"I'm trying to order something from a website, and it won't take my card. I keep running out of space before I can get the whole number in. I'm horrible with computers. Please!"

"Okay," Jayla said. "I just need to get my key and lock the

door." Sandy watched as Jayla grabbed her phone from the desk, put it into her side pants pocket, then grabbed the key ring that had been lying next to it.

"See," Sandy said as they entered her room. "Way smaller than yours."

"I guess it is," Jayla said, walking to the window. "I see we have practically the same view. You're a bit closer to the front door of the diner. And hey, you've got a bird's-eye view of the junk truck below. That's gotta be worth something."

"I was down there earlier," Sandy told her. "I applied for a part-time job. They might have a couple of days opening up, but they said other people were interested too. That's code for them saying they wouldn't hire me. People hate me."

"Um ..."

"I found out what the deal is with that junk truck. The driver is a scrap dealer. He collects all kinds of junk from all over, and he sells different materials for a profit ... to be recycled. He said he's had a lot of mannequins lately from a department store in the suburbs that just closed. I asked him who would want them, but he said this one big theater is using them as props."

"Oh, well, I did see a mannequin's torso yesterday. Maybe those legs sticking up are her other half," Jayla said. "Kind of gave me a scare. I wonder why he's parked here so often."

"I know why. His girlfriend works at the diner. He has two meals a day there, but sometimes he just stops in when he's in the neighborhood. I wish I knew what it was like to have a man love me that much. You should see the way they look at each other ... all lovey-dovey and all. Why can't a man look at me like that? Why was I destined to live in such misery? I'm a good person. Why am I always the outcast? Why, Jayla?"

Jayla walked away from the window. "You said you needed help on the computer. What can I do?"

"But I just want to know why …"

"Sandy, do you need help or not?"

Defeated, Sandy sighed in agony. "I'm trying to order some anxiety meds from this Canadian website, but it won't take my card." Sandy nervously twirled a lock of her curly red hair around her finger. "It's not that I'm a junkie or anything; I'm not. I just can't afford to keep going to the doctor to get meds. Besides, these are cheaper."

"I'm not judging you."

"I didn't tell you the whole reason that I had to move here."

"And there's no reason you should," Jayla said. "It's none of my business."

"But I don't mind—"

"And I don't want to know, either."

Sandy pouted and sat on the bed next to her open laptop. "Sit down."

Reluctantly, Jayla took a seat next to her.

"See, after my husband left me, I was really lonely. And he did leave me money. He left me enough to live on for two years. But then I met this guy online. He told me he was madly in love with me. He said the sweetest things. We only communicated through live chat, but you could feel the passion. It was so intense that my lady parts did a little happy dance with every word he typed. He totally got me the way nobody ever had. We were going to get married and live in Hawaii. He was—"

"A romance scammer," Jayla said, cutting her story short.

"I guess. But I know he really loved me. He just took my money out of desperation. I really believe he'll be back someday. You can't fake the kind of connection we had."

"Yeah, Sandy. Actually, you can. And he did."

"I know that's true in most cases, but this was different. He'll be back."

"No, he won't," Jayla told her. "He won't ever be back. Whatever name he gave you and whatever photo he might have showed you belong to some unknowing person whose picture was stolen from the Internet. I guarantee you that. Don't wait for him, and don't believe anyone you meet online like that." Jayla sighed. "Can you show me the problem you're having?"

Sandy handed her the laptop and pointed to the field where she had a partial credit card number typed in. "See how it stops right there? I keep trying, but it won't take my whole card number."

Jayla glanced at it. "See here. It says not to use any spaces. You've been typing in the spaces as you see them on the card. That's why you can't get the whole number in the field. Try it again without the spaces. I'm sure it'll work fine."

Sandy looked disappointed. "Oh, that's all it was? Well, can you just wait for me to try it to make sure?"

"Okay, try it."

Sandy picked her credit card off the bed and carefully typed in the number without spaces, then hit the "Submit" button. When her card information went through, she frowned. "Oh, silly me. Well, thanks, Jayla." Flustered, she dropped her card on the floor.

"I'll get it," Jayla said, getting up. As she bent down to pick up the card, her phone slid out of her pocket and onto the floor.

"And I'll get *that*," Sandy said, making a furious grab for Jayla's phone.

Putting Sandy's credit card back on the bed, Jayla held out her hand. "My phone, please!"

"Just a moment," Sandy said. Phone in hand, she ran to a corner of the room and quickly typed in a number."

Jayla's face turned red when she heard a ringing phone. "Did you just call yourself on my phone?"

"Yeah, I did," Sandy said. "I really wanted to have your number, and I was afraid you wouldn't give it to me. You're not as open as I am about things."

"Sandy, give me my fucking phone." Jayla grabbed it out of her hands. "There's no reason for me to be open with you or to have offered my cell number. I'm a woman who lives next door to you; that's all. I don't want you to help me paint my room, and while I'm sorry you're lonely, I can't help you there, either. If you want friends, go out into the world and make them. You had NO right to steal my phone number. And that's what you did; you stole it. And don't say another word about changing your name to mine because that's downright creepy as fuck! And don't ever call me or knock on my door again. Do you hear me?"

Sandy burst into tears. "I'm such a horrible person! No wonder people always leave me! Just like you're doing."

Angry, Jayla turned to face her before opening the door. "I was never any part of your life *to* leave you. Do you understand that? I'm a stranger you met in the lobby yesterday. You carried a can of paint and a bag of supplies up the stairs for me. And not because I asked you to help me … but because you pretty much took them from me. And then you came into my room, uninvited. I have tried to be nice to you, but you make it really difficult. No, you make it impossible! Now, I'm telling you: just leave me alone." Turning the knob, Jayla walked out, slamming the door behind her.

☠☠☠

"Oh, Jaybird. I'm so sorry to hear all of this. Did she really say she wanted to change her name to yours?"

"She did. And she's just needy and weird enough to do it."

"Keep your distance, honey. I mean it. I know she's only next door, but still. I must say though, I'm really proud of the way you handled her. You *have* changed. The old Jayla would have listened to her whole life story."

"The old Jayla is long gone; she really is."

"Well, I loved her, and I love the new Jayla. Did you say this happened two days ago?"

"Yeah. And so far: crickets. But something in me doesn't trust that things will stay that way. Thanks for listening, Der. I know you've got to run. I just had to call you and give you yet another new number. Ironically, yesterday, I was going to the give the lucky chosen few my new number, as well as update my banking and credit card information. But I got pulled into Sandy's bullshit and never got a chance." Jayla picked up the foam Earth stress ball on her desk and squeezed it. "Weird, huh? I've had one number for twenty-something years, and this week I've had three different ones. I hated to change it again, but the idea of her having my number kept me awake the last two nights."

"If you hadn't already gotten a new mobile number, I would have told you to do so. You don't need that barmy chick calling you."

"Say what?"

Derek laughed. "Oh, barmy! The Brits use it to describe someone a bit mad or crazy."

"That's her," Jayla said. "Barmy. Love you, Der. Thanks for listening. We'll talk soon."

"Cheerio, Jaybird. Next time, let's try to video chat!"

"For sure," Jayla said, smiling as she ended the call.

Just as she was laying the phone on the desk, the intense pounding she'd heard two days ago had returned. Grabbing her phone, she hid it in a file folder in her desk drawer, then walked to the door.

"Who is it?"

"You know who it is, Jayla. It's Sandy. And I don't appreciate you changing your phone number!"

Furious, Jayla opened the door and stood in the doorway to block Sandy from coming in. "Bitch, are you crazy? I didn't appreciate you *stealing* my fucking number. You had NO right to do that … none. You're damn right I changed it. Why the hell were you calling me anyway?"

Sandy sniffled. "I wanted to apologize. I'm thinking you might have thought I was a little forward. But it's wrong that you won't give me a chance to be friends. Just wrong."

Jayla tensed. "I have every right to choose who I want in my life and who I don't want in my life. It's no wonder you have no one if you force yourself on people like this."

"It's called being an extrovert. Introverts don't make a lot of friends."

"Not true, Sandy. They do. They just don't make them by shoving themselves down people's throats. Neither do actual extroverts, for that matter."

"Just give me one more chance," Sandy cried, tears now cascading down her face.

"What part of 'I'm not here to make friends' don't you get? If you don't leave me alone, I'll have to talk to Henry. And if you harass me, I'll call the police. I'm not playing, Sandy. I moved here for solitude. And peace. Bye-bye." Jayla closed the door and took a deep breath. She looked upward again. "Enough now?"

"I'm going to kill myself! Right now!" Sandy shouted through the door. "And it will be all your fault."

"Shit!" Jayla said softly as she heard Sandy's door slam shut. She looked upward again. "I do *not* need this. I really don't."

Running over to her desk, she opened the top drawer and grabbed a Swiss Army knife, then stuck it in her pocket. Furious, she hurried out the door and pounded on the door. "Open up! Now!"

"Oh, Jayla, I knew you wouldn't let me die," Sandy said dramatically, opening the door. "I was going to take a bottle of pills, but I only have four left and that's not enough. My prescription hasn't arrived from Canada yet. That was so nice of you to help me with that website. I don't know what's wrong with me; I just can't seem to do anything right. I'm so sorry I made you angry; I'm an idiot. I'm the most horrible person ever!"

"No, you're not," Jayla said softly. "But I meant what I said. I came here for solitude. I don't want to make friends with you or anyone else. And I'm getting kind of tired of repeating that."

"Please come in, Jayla. So I can really talk to you."

"No. I don't want to come in. Whatever you want to say can be said right where you are."

"But you're standing in the doorway."

"A good place for me to be." Jayla smiled.

"Now I'm all discombobulated and can't remember what I was saying."

"You were saying you're the most horrible person ever."

"I am!" Sandy sniffled. "I always dreamed of being an actress, or maybe a singer. I just wanted to be front and center with all eyes on *me*. My family always told me I was a drama queen, so I thought I'd be really good at acting. I just want people to look at me, to hear me, to find me fascinating and want to know more. I want to be so intriguing and have so much to teach the world that there isn't enough time in the day.

"But nobody wants to learn anything from me. Everyone always wants to teach *me* something, which is how to get lost! I tried out for so many community theaters, and not only did I never get any parts, they wouldn't even let me work behind the scenes. I'm never allowed to be a part of anyone's club. I don't understand that. How can you know *so* quickly that a person has nothing to offer you? And I've gotta tell you, Jayla, you're just like them."

"Yeah, fine. So how long were you married?"

"A year. I met him in Vegas. We were both drunk when we got married. But that didn't stop me from loving him when I was sober. Just like with my first husband, he was sorry right away. But he waited a year before he left me for my best friend. He was probably seeing her almost the whole time, though."

"Uh-huh," Jayla said.

"Can't you see what an open and wonderful person I am?"

"Well, it's good to know you don't really think you're the most horrible person ever." Jayla took a deep breath. "Sandy, I'm going to say this yet again. It's not for me to judge you. But I have a right to make my own choices for my life. I do not want to be your friend."

"Can you at least tell me your last name," Sandy said. "Mine is Imboden. Ugly, huh? It's German. I think it means 'in the floor.'"

A good place for you, Jayla thought.

"Please, tell me your last name."

"Barmy," Jayla said. "Jayla Barmy."

"Awesome," Sandy said. "That's exactly what I'll change my name to. I always thought that a new name would be just what the doctor ordered. It'll give me a new lease on life."

The doctor should order you a padded cell. "All right, Sandy, I'm leaving. Do not pound on my door again, okay? And hear me on this again: taking another person's name is downright as disturbing as it gets! No more games. No more fake suicide attempts. Fool me once, shame on me. You know the rest. I'm outta here."

☠☠☠

"I know, Derek. I was an idiot to chase after her. But I didn't want her death on my conscience."

"She played you, Jaybird. But that doesn't mean you didn't do the right thing by going over there. That time. She's left you alone for three days so far, right?"

"Right."

"You did good, kiddo."

"Thanks. I needed to hear that." Jayla walked over to the window and looked down. "That scrap-goods guy is back with his truck."

"Oh, yeah, tell me, what wares is he toting today?"

"Looks like three mattresses piled up. That's weird. What would anyone want with old mattresses? Can you recycle them?"

"Sure," Derek told her. "Most all of a mattress can be recycled, actually. The metal springs, foam, wood … oh, and the cotton … all of that has the potential to come back into the world in one form or the other."

"Ah, I see. You're so smart. Thanks for the education. And Der, thanks for calling to check on me. I just couldn't bear to call you again. I didn't want to be the same kind of pain to you that Sandy's been to me."

"Rubbish!" Derek said. "We've known one another for fourteen years … in good times and bad. I know your heart and your soul. And you're nothing like her … Jayla Barmy!"

Jayla let out a laugh. "Can you believe she said she'd change her name to that? However, now that I think about it, going around and introducing herself as Ms. Barmy—"

"… would be highly appropriate," Derek said, laughing. "Hey, I hope she leaves you alone. Just know I'm here for you, okay? Now, I've got to get to the florist. Abby thinks I've forgotten our anniversary, but I haven't. I also have a beautiful pair of pearl drop earrings in my pocket to prove it."

"Happy Anniversary, Derek. Wish Abby the best from me too."

"Will do, my friend! Talk soon. Cheerio."

Jayla smiled as she ended the call and put the phone in her pocket. "I really am happy for you, Derek. I hope you know that. Abby got a wonderful husband and I have a lifelong friend. We're both lucky."

Although he couldn't hear her, she felt good saying the words aloud. Jayla walked over to the upholstered chair and sat down. She looked up. "Hey, ceiling, don't be dropping your bits on me again. I've got a kickass paint roller, and you're getting a new coat. Two new coats for that matter. But first, I've got to sand you." Jayla laughed. "Hey, I said 'sand,' not 'Sandy,' no worries."

Feeling good, Jayla put her head back on the chair and drifted off to sleep. A half hour later, a familiar pounding on the door awakened her. Unnerved, Jayla got up slowly and walked to the door but didn't open it.

"Sandy?"

"Open the door, Jayla. I just want to thank you for being so honest with me. Other people talk behind my back and laugh at me, but you tell me the truth. And I know you are hard on me because you care. How can I ever thank you? We just have to be friends. You're so special, and I need you to know that I understand why you said such mean things."

"You're delusional, Sandy. Go away."

"I love you, Jayla. I'm standing here until you open the door."

Jayla smacked the palm of her hand against her forehead. "You don't love me; you don't know me."

"No, Jayla. I do know you and I do love you!"

"I don't love you back, Sandy. I don't even like you. I don't want to know you either. In fact, fair warning: I'm getting ready to call the police and report you for harassment. So you might want to get away from my door."

"My psychologist said you were showing me tough love."

"Then tell your shrink that he or she needs therapy too."

"I don't really know her. I just met her once through an app on my phone. We had a video chat. I told her you were my best friend, and you yelled at me and said really harsh things."

"I'm neither your best friend nor even a casual one. I met you about a week ago, and that's a week too long. Get out of my life, Sandy. I'm serious. I'm not fucking around!"

"You don't mean that, Jayla."

"I so do! Now leave me alone. Do you hear me?"

"I hear you and you need to hear me. I'm going to kill myself … and this time for real. Not with pills. I'm gonna jump right onto that junk truck and tear my head open on those pointed metal thingies he collects. Go to your window and watch if you don't believe me. Good-bye, forever, Jayla!"

When she heard Sandy open and shut her door, Jayla exhaled. "How convenient for her that the guy's got a load of mattresses today. Well, I'm up for a show." She strolled over to the open window and stared down at the truck. Jayla could hear Sandy raising the window next door.

"I hope you're watching, Jayla. I'm getting ready to plunge to my death now."

Surprised, but silent, Jayla listened as she heard the screen being detached from the window. Holy shit, that barmy bitch is really going to jump. Well, she'll bounce like a rubber ball, but she'll survive.

Jayla watched as an attractive blond woman stepped out of the diner and waved to the truck. "See you tonight, baby doll!"

In a split second, the truck was gone, and Sandy's body landed face up on the street with a thud that almost made the building rattle.

The blond woman let out a blood-curdling scream, and a rush of people came flooding out of the diner as well as from both directions on the sidewalk. Jayla watched the chaos ensue as blood poured out of Sandy's head and trickled down her face. People jumped over the flowing streams of deep-red liquid as they stained the sidewalk with Sandy's special brand of unbridled, barmy extroversion.

Her jaw lowered, Jayla stood and stared in exquisite disbelief. Within minutes, sirens blared, and residents from the Obscure had joined the looky-loos on the street. Cells phones were out, and Sandy had been photographed and video recorded from every angle until the police got there, pushed the people back, and had their own people take more photos. Minutes later, two local TV station vans arrived on the scene.

Mesmerized, Jayla kept watching. "You're a star, Sandy. Just like you wanted. All eyes are on you. Even mine."

ELLMORE J. BADGET, JR'S VERY UNUSUAL DAY

Ellmore straightened his tie in the mirror. Every day of his adult life, he had worn one. Watching his reflection as he finished perfecting the Windsor knot was all part of the routine. To adjust his tie in the middle of the room, or perhaps while looking out the window, was unthinkable. The thought of it made him queasy.

Parted on the left, his chocolate-brown hair looked exactly the same as it always had except for the increasing gifts of gray left with each passing year. A small dab of gel kept it neatly in place, except in inclement weather. His dark round glasses were nearly identical to every pair he had ever worn.

Ellmore owned eight ties; seven of them were assigned to a day of the week. Saturday's tie had sky blue and gray diagonal stripes, and it was his favorite.

"Oh, no," Ellmore said, looking in the mirror. "Drat!"

To his horror, a little bit more than halfway down, he noticed a grease stain that had to be a week old. He couldn't even blot it out. The stain had set. He had no choice but to have it dry cleaned and that meant tweaking his budget. But much worse, it meant wearing his eighth tie, the burgundy and yellow emergency option, the one not assigned to a particular day. That meant he would look different than he had for all the previous Saturdays he could remember. It was very rare that this happened, but every time circumstances changed in his routine, events beyond his control always followed, multiplied, and drove Ellmore a bit mad.

"To think bad things is to will bad things," Ellmore said to his reflection. He held the bottom half of the tie to his eyes for closer inspection. "Must have been the spaghetti sauce from last Saturday's dinner. And I was so careful too." He shot himself a punishing look. "Not careful enough!" He made a mental note to check the lapel of the suit he wore every Saturday. (He had four suits: each one also assigned a day of the week. Some, of course, did double duty.)

Ellmore owned only two colors of dress shirts: white and pale blue. Once, while on business in a better part of town, he caught himself admiring lavender and pale apricot shirts in the window of an upscale men's clothing store. When his self-awareness caught up to him, he strode quickly away.

The Obscure had been Ellmore's home for the past five years, but he had lived in the neighborhood for thirty-seven years, since he was twenty-one and a new graduate of Putney Smith Business College. Hired as a management trainee at the Bentley Home Goods Warehouse, Ellmore worked his way up to Assistant Director of Human Resources, and for the last ten years that the facility remained open, he held the top spot. His life was always lonely. While he was reclusive by nature, there had been, in the early years, one woman in the secretarial pool he had considered asking for a date, but having done so would have been awkward, unacceptable, and unprofessional.

Every day, Ellmore strove to carry himself with respect, but his father, Ellmore (Morey) J. Badget, Sr., a judge, was ashamed and angry that the strict regimen he had imposed on his son had failed to give Ellmore a reason to aim higher in life. Morey never missed an opportunity to let Ellmore know what a disappointment he was to the family name. But when Morey was disbarred and sent to prison in a statewide bribery scandal, Ellmore never so much as uttered a word to him, shooing away the unpleasant thoughts that tried to claim his consciousness while he dutifully attended to his mother as best he could.

Three years later, despite her son's efforts, she could no longer handle the disgrace, lack of money, social prestige, and loneliness. Suffering a complete break from reality, she lived for the next five years in a psychiatric hospital, until she died.

Ten years later, Morey died in prison: a pauper. There was nothing at all left to pass on to Ellmore except shame and disappointment. But there was a part of Ellmore, one he barely acknowledged, that felt triumphant and strong in having chosen a different path in life. Perhaps he had always suspected his father's imperious facade was fallacious, but he hesitated to give himself too much credit for anything.

Every Saturday, Ellmore had lunch at the diner, then treated himself to an afternoon matinee at the Blue Palace Cinema. Self-conscious about wearing his least-favorite tie, he walked down one flight of stairs to the lobby, where a greater number of the residents than usual were gathered, talking to one another in oddly animated tones. When he saw a police officer talking to Henry, the front desk clerk, he hurried out of the Obscure and around the corner to the diner.

A chill ran through him as he approached his favorite eating establishment. On the street he saw two police cars, a TV station van, and the scrap dealer's truck that was often there twice a day. Several of the neighborhood's homeless population were talking amongst themselves, two peering in the large window to see what was going on. Ellmore only knew that he'd never seen so many people in the diner at once in all of the years he'd been going there.

He picked up the tip of his burgundy and yellow tie and gave it a dirty look. Just as he had imagined, if one thing changed, everything would change. Perhaps the tie was jinxed … really jinxed.

No, I don't believe that for a minute, he thought. But he knew that a part of him did.

Ellmore stood across the street and stared at the diner and the commotion inside and outside. The change frightened him, but there was no other comfortable place to go. The deli was six blocks away, and having his lunch there would be akin to eating on another planet.

Gingerly, he opened the door of the diner. The cacophony of voices hurt his ears. Scanning the counter, then the room, he saw a disparate number of people: police officers, regulars, and a whole lot of people he didn't recognize. But what upset him most was the sight of strangers sitting in his regular booth.

"Ellmore!" a familiar voice called.

He turned to see Addie, one of the regular servers, motioning for him to come to the end of the counter. He hurried over to her. "What's going on here?"

"You didn't hear?" Addie asked incredulously.

"Hear what?"

"You know, what happened yesterday … late afternoon. It's all anyone is talking about."

Ellmore's blank face stared at her. "I didn't hear a thing. On Fridays, I listen to classical music with my earphones on, and I read great literature until I go to bed."

"Does your room look out over the diner?"

"No, I overlook the bodega, the laundry, the locksmith, and the thrift store. Other side of the building."

"Well," Addie said, drawing nearer to him. "One of your brand-new neighbors, who had just moved onto the fifth floor, jumped out of her window and went splat right here on the street. Blood gushing all over like a ruby red tsunami. I heard a chunk of her scalp … with bright red hair … just floated away."

Ellmore's cheeks inflated, and he put his hand over his mouth.

"Oh, sorry," Addie said. "Am I making you sick?"

"You're certainly not helping to whet my appetite. What you just described, aside from making me nauseated, sounds quite improbable at best."

"No, she jumped! She really did."

"That much … I believe," Ellmore told her. "I can see from the influx of strangers that something has happened. No, it was what you said about …"

"Her scalp floating away?"

Ellmore put his hand over his mouth again.

"Well," Addie said. "That's what I heard. But forget about that. You didn't hear the best part!"

"I find it dubious that such a thing exists … considering the circumstances."

"Valerie and I were interviewed by TV reporters. I was on the news last night, but she got to be on five different stations! The one reporter who spoke to me, Ken Roberts, is the hottest man on Earth. I know I'm too old to ever get a chunk of a hunk like him, but you can't fault an old gal for her fantasies, can you? I nearly melted when he spoke to me, asking me how I felt and all. I just love a good-looking man."

"Yes, over the many years, I have noticed your appreciation for them. But what about the woman who jumped to her death?"

"Well, the police think it was supposed to be a stunt for attention. But as timing would have it, Valerie's boyfriend, Nick, who owns the truck, pulled away only seconds before she jumped. Otherwise, she would have landed on some old mattresses."

Ellmore placed a palm on either side of his face. "Oh, dear."

"That's why Valerie got interviewed more than I did, lucky duck. She had come outside to wave good-bye to Nick and saw the whole thing happen. Splat! Smash! Whack! Crack! And who knows, maybe float, too."

"Very insensitive," Ellmore mumbled. "Extraordinarily so."

An attractive blond server sidled up next to the duo. "Hello, Ellmore. I see you've been displaced today."

Ellmore sighed with obvious relief. "Hello, Valerie. Addie

was just telling me—"

"Oh, I'm sure she was," Valerie said, giving Addie the side eye. "Hey, I've got one booth in my station free." She pointed. "It's a bit far from your usual spot, but it's yours if—"

"I'll take it!" Ellmore said, walking toward the empty booth in the back.

About three minutes later, Valerie stood by his side. "I'm sorry, Ellmore. I didn't hear what Addie said to you, but I've heard what she's been saying to other people, and I could see by the look on your face—"

"That she was making me quite ill."

"Yes. I'm so sorry. She didn't even see the poor woman fall. I did. Yet she's acting as if this is the best thing that's ever happened to her. I barely slept last night, and when I did, I had nightmares. The last thing I want to do is to foist those horrific images onto other people!"

"You and Addie are night and day," Ellmore assured her. "Always have been. Why are the police and the media here now?"

"Because nobody knows anything about the woman who was killed. They keep hoping to find someone who knows what happened. They don't suspect any foul play, but it seems to me that a lot of people, Addie among them, would be happier than a pig in—well, you know—to find out there was. I just want to go back to my life." Valerie pushed a tendril of hair over her ear. "I look a wreck today. Having your usual?"

"No. No I'm not. Nothing is usual about today. My appetite included. No Cobb salad and sourdough bread for me. I'll have a bowl of tomato bisque soup and a BLT. Whole wheat toast, please."

"Coffee and a glass of water?"

Ellmore sighed. "That much will remain the same. Yes. Thank you, Valerie. And I'm very sorry for the ordeal you're going through. I hope the memories don't haunt you for long."

Valerie smiled appreciatively and left. Ellmore looked around the room. The sound of laughter unsettled him. "Inappropriate people," he mumbled to himself. "The world is rife with their ilk."

Two minutes later, Valerie returned with a glass of iced water and a pot of hot coffee. As she poured it into the cup already on the table, she noticed the discontent on Ellmore's face. "This is a bad situation. It is. My boyfriend just left. Before he got into his truck, I saw him look up at the Obscure. Then, he looked around at the sky. Who checks the sky before getting into their vehicle? Well, Nicky did. And I'm afraid he always will now, fearful that someone is about to crash land from another building, or the heavens or something. He feels guilty that he didn't have an extra cup of coffee or remain another minute to tell me he loved me again. That woman's death is certainly not his fault. I keep telling him that."

Ellmore watched the steam rise from the hot coffee. "I'm afraid time is the best healer, Valerie. It was very traumatic for both of you. I am sorry."

"Thank you. Of course, it's the biggest shame for the woman who died."

"Absolutely," Ellmore said with conviction.

"I wish it wasn't so hectic in here. I'll be back with your lunch soon," Valerie said, turning to leave. "There isn't even time to ask you what movie you're seeing today."

Ellmore blinked and she was gone. He watched the steam dissipate from his coffee cup. When it had done so, he took a sip. Startled, he looked up to see a forty-something brunette in a blue-flowered dress, standing by his table.

"Mr. Badget," she said. "Don't you recognize me?"

Ellmore studied her face. "Indeed I do. Marilyn Haw..."

"Hawkley. But I go by Marilyn Dellamor now."

"I remember," Ellmore told her. "You worked in the secretarial pool a year or so after I first came to Bentley. You were there maybe six years when you got married. And you left two years after that, to have a baby."

Her face radiated happiness. "Oh, you do remember me. Very well, I might add. May I sit?"

Ellmore edged out of the booth and stood. "Please. Where are my manners? Have a seat, Marilyn. And please, call me Ellmore."

Smiling graciously, Marilyn sat across from him as he resumed his seat.

"Would you like something?"

"Oh, no thank you. I just finished lunch with a friend. She's already gone. I stayed behind to use the ladies' room, and on my way out, I saw you sitting here. I recognized you right away. It's been a very long time, but I just had to say hello. I take it you're working somewhere else."

"Why do you think … oh, because of the way I'm dressed. No, I'm not. I retired when the warehouse closed. I looked for a new position, but Lady Luck was unkind to me. So, I make do with my pension and savings." He took a sip of coffee. "Your child must be grown by now, yes? Do you have more than one?"

"I do. My daughter, Ellen, is twenty-one and my son, Blake, is nineteen."

"And your husband? What does he do?"

"I'd guess he's still gambling away his paycheck," Marilyn said. "If he even has a job. I divorced him years ago and haven't seen him since. My kids have very little to do with him. He was a terrible father and a dreadful husband. I shouldn't have married him. But I was getting close to thirty, and while that seems insanely young to me now, back then, I felt like an old maid."

"You're still young and beautiful," Ellmore said. "Do you live in the neighborhood?"

"I work for a lawyer about seven blocks from here. Not a very ritzy office, as you can imagine, but it pays the bills and I'm treated well. I don't usually work on Saturdays, but my boss has a big case to prepare for, and I offered to come in today." She laughed. "For pay, of course. So, when my friend, who lives about ten minutes away, heard I was working today, she insisted I meet her at the diner on my lunch break. I never eat out. I've been brown-bagging it for years, so I can't even remember the last time I was here. As for my friend, we never seem to get together. We just email. But today, she was adamant about seeing me. Struck me as kind of weird, being out of the blue and all. It wasn't until we walked through the door that I realized she wanted to find out what happened yesterday, with that lady falling to her death and all." Marilyn sighed. "My friend used to work at the warehouse too, but not in human resources. You probably wouldn't know her."

"What's her name?"

"Snoopy!" Marilyn said.

Ellmore laughed. "Her given name?"

"Nosy Parker," Marilyn said, laughing. "Just kidding. It's Janet, but everyone has always called her 'Snoopy,' and as you can see, the name fits."

Valerie smiled as she saw Marilyn and Ellmore laughing. She placed Ellmore's lunch in front of him, then turned to Marilyn. "Well, heck, I didn't know you two knew one another."

"We worked at the warehouse together ... many moons ago."

"Oh, I see," Valerie said. "A lot of our regulars used to work there. Quite the employer in its heyday." Valerie looked behind her to see if anyone was motioning to get her attention. "I know you've just had lunch, but would you like anything else?"

"No, thank you," Marilyn said. "I just stopped by to say hello to Mr. ... to Ellmore."

"Okay then. Let me know if you change your mind," Valerie said, then hurried away.

An awkward silence sat between them.

"Ellmore," Marilyn began after a long pause. "I embarrass readily, so this isn't easy, but I'll never forgive myself if I don't say something, given this serendipitous reunion we're having."

"Yes," Ellmore said, picking up the soup spoon. "What is it?"

"Well … um …"

Ellmore tasted the tomato bisque approvingly, then carefully placed the spoon on an unused bread plate. "A bit too hot. I need to let it cool some."

Nervous, Marilyn reached for an eight-sided glass saltshaker in the center of the table, and without realizing it, began to fondle it. "Back in the day, I always thought … well, I sort of half expected you to ask me out."

"Oh," Ellmore said. He paused to let the past pull him back in time. "Observant. I must admit, I did consider it. But it would have been highly inappropriate. Even as a naïve young man in my early twenties, I knew that much."

Marilyn looked into his eyes. "I really liked you. I did. Very much. I would have agreed to date you in a heartbeat."

Ellmore fiddled with his soup spoon. "Well, no doubt it's for the best things happened as they did. Despite your ex-husband's unfortunate behavior, you do have two beautiful children now, yes?"

"I do. They are my world. Do you remember what my daughter's name is?"

"Ellen. Right?"

"Yes, I named her after someone who was still dear to my heart."

"Looks like the soup has cooled," Ellmore said, taking the spoon from the plate and dipping it in the bowl. "Perfect."

Marilyn's face turned alabaster white as her cheeks burned a deep dusty rose. "Forgive me, Ellmore. I'm sorry; I should never have told you that. I didn't mean to make you uncomfortable. I just thought that—oh, are you married?"

"No, I've never married," he told her. "I'm rather set in my ways. I'm quite the bore, actually. Being duller than ditchwater, a term my dear grandmother used, was never my plan. But it kept me safe when the world scared me. Then, as the years went by, I just became more attached to patterns, routines, and the inescapable tedium that enveloped me. And now, I find myself in a prison of my own making."

"Oh, dear. I'm so sorry to hear that."

"Don't be. And don't fret on my account. Please."

"But …" Realizing what she was doing with the saltshaker, Marilyn slid it back into place. She gasped as it exceeded the tabletop's speed limit, then smacked into Ellmore's soup bowl before toppling over. "Oh, sorry! How embarrassing. I'm absolutely mortified!"

"Don't be," Ellmore told her, chuckling as he used his napkin to clean up the small bit of spilled salt. "I find it charming, actually."

"Oh, good. I'm so relieved. I have no idea why I was playing with the saltshaker." She smiled. "And I was so sure I had grabbed the pepper."

Ellmore paused, then laughed heartily, making a mental note that he hadn't laughed this way in a very long time. "That's very funny. I remember now: you had a wonderful sense of humor. And you never got flustered like the other ladies did, either."

"Thank you. That's nice to hear. And terribly sweet that you remember."

Another awkward pause sat stubbornly between them.

"I heard all about your father in the news," Marilyn finally said. "I'm so sorry."

Ellmore reddened. "One good thing came out of it: he never berated me again for not having had loftier aspirations. He was a very bad man. But the events during his arrest, trial, and subsequent incarceration were the most unpleasant of my life. It was quite hellish to hear my father's name in the news every day, especially as I was named after him. Everyone was talking. In whispered conversations, I'd hear their scurrilous speculations and idle chatter. There were many who wondered if I was anything like him, or worse, if I'd been a part of his criminal pursuits. So many times, I'd look at people and they'd quickly turn away. I knew they were gossiping. It was all so humiliating."

"Entirely your father's shame," Marilyn said matter-of-factly. "You did nothing wrong. I'm just wondering if his actions were what caused you to keep a low profile all of these years. Maybe too low?"

He tried to respond, but felt the answer catch in his throat. "Aside from being funny, you are also a very smart woman. Come to think of it, I always thought you were the smartest in the group."

Marilyn laughed uneasily. "Well, you wouldn't have thought that if you'd known the man I chose to marry."

"We all make mistakes. We all get confused."

"That's very kind of you to say." As she noticed something in her peripheral vision, Marilyn felt uneasy and turned to look, then returned her gaze to Ellmore.

"You look concerned about something … or some*one*."

"Oh, just that this older woman with poufy strawberry-blond hair, dressed all in purple, keeps looking in our direction. She doesn't look familiar to me at all."

"I come here twice a day," Ellmore said. "And I have for years. I don't know a soul who fits that description. She's probably one of the many that came here for the excitement. I can't imagine why this tragedy has drawn such a crowd. It's as if they have all found a soft, rotting log in which to congregate. The decay of the wood is a magnet for organisms, you know, just as the decay of our society is to some people."

"Quite possibly. But maybe," Marilyn began delicately. "Living in a rotting log is preferable to being a prisoner to one's own strict standards." She took a deep breath. "And I say that with the greatest respect and concern."

Ellmore laughed, again as he hadn't in years.

"What's so funny?" Marilyn asked, her eyes twinkling. "If anything, I was worried about offending you. But you're laughing."

"I live at the Obscure," Ellmore explained. "There is no greater rotting log I can think of."

"Oh," Marilyn said, trying to suppress a giggle. "I see."

"Go ahead," Ellmore told her. "Laugh. It's funny. It's time we both had a good howl."

"Time!" Marilyn exclaimed. "Goodness, I've lost all track of it!" She glanced at her watch. "I'm already twenty minutes late. My boss will be fine with that, but I do have to get back. Or I'll end up working late to finish everything."

"Oh, well, I wouldn't want to see that happen. But this has been a delightful surprise."

"For me too," Marilyn said. She reached into her purse, took a card from her wallet, and wrote on it. She handed it to Ellmore. "Your company is wonderful. If you'd ever like to do this again, please call."

Ellmore took the card, looked at it, then placed it in the inside pocket of his jacket. "This has been lovely."

He edged out of the booth again and stood. "Good-bye, Marilyn."

She looked at him, unable to read his face. "Good-bye, Ellmore."

He had no sooner started to sit down again, when a tall woman in a tight purple pantsuit appeared at his side.

"Hello," she said with a smile.

Ellmore angled his head and studied her face. "Hello."

"I would really like to talk to you. Now that your friend has left, might this be a convenient time?"

"Do I know you?"

"I'll explain everything; I promise. I do need to use the little girls' room first." She glanced at the table. "And I see you have a sandwich to eat. When I come back, may I keep you company?"

"I s'pose so," Ellmore said cautiously. "All right then."

As she walked toward the back, Valerie hurried over to him. "Is everything okay? You're quite popular today."

"It's a very unusual day," Ellmore told her.

"You've barely touched your soup. And you haven't taken a bite out of your sandwich yet."

"I'm afraid the soup has gone cold," he told her.

"No problem. I'll heat it up again. It'll only take but a minute."

"No, that's okay. You can take it away. I'll eat the sandwich. Oh, and please, seeing as it's so busy in here, why not leave the check now?"

"Okay. If you're sure." Valerie took the order pad out of her apron pocket, flipped through it, ripped off a sheet, and put it on the table. She picked up the soup bowl. "We'll talk soon; I'm sure." With a smile, she was gone.

Ellmore looked down at his tie. Confident no one was looking, he took it in his hand and spoke to it. "You really *are* upending my day, aren't you?"

"I hope you weren't standing waiting for me," the woman in purple said as she returned, her lips freshly glossed.

"Oh!" Ellmore said, letting go of the tie. I didn't expect you back so quickly. Have a seat." He gestured toward the side of the booth that Marilyn had vacated.

"Thank you," the stranger said as she sat down. "And please, call me Dee."

"Okay, Dee," Ellmore said as he sat. "I'm Ellmore. And I have no idea why you've been so eager to talk to me."

"So eager? How do you know—"

"My friend saw you looking over here. Frequently."

"Oh, yeah. So I was." She smiled awkwardly. "I'm not always as subtle as I should be. Old habits die hard, you know."

"Yes," Ellmore said. "I know that very well." He looked at the jeweled hair combs in her teased strawberry-blond hair. "I'm here every day. I've never seen you; I would remember." His tone darkened. "Are you here about that woman who jumped to her death? Might you be of the many who have congregated to learn more of the stranger's story?"

"I *am* here because of the woman who jumped. But it's not what you think. I'm not an idle curiosity seeker. Trust me, honey, not much curiosity left in me. I've seen way too much. Let me tell you: if I had to live the rest of my life under a rock, well, that'd suit me just fine. Damn fine."

Ellmore said nothing, calmly taking a bite out of his BLT.

"It's like this," she continued. "Can you imagine hearing something on the news, something terrible, and instead of hearing the name of a person involved, hearing your own name?"

"Actually, I can."

Dee thought for a moment. "Oh, hell. I forgot."

"You forgot? Forgot what?" Ellmore said, his eyes fixated on the stranger. "What exactly does that mean?"

"I'll get to that. I promise. Just let me address your first concern. You asked if I was here about the woman who jumped. I am. You see, when I saw the story on the news, you could have knocked me over with a fuckin' feather, excuse my French. They said her name was Sandy Imboden. Well, that's my name."

"You just said your name was Dee."

"I go by that name. It's the second syllable in Sandy. I prefer it. Also, my mom named me after the actress Sandra Dee. So the name works for me."

"I see," Ellmore said. "Well, go on. You were talking about hearing your own name on a news broadcast."

"Yes. And after the shock of hearing that dead woman had my name, the reporter said she had bright red curly hair. Well, all I can tell you is that every hair on my head—and everywhere else for that matter—stood on end."

Ellmore turned scarlet, looked down at his sandwich, and took another bite.

"Oh, hell. I'm sorry. I forgot how damn easily people shock. Not here for that." She took a calming breath. "Let me backtrack a bit. See, I live in apartment building, bit of a ways from here. One day, I'm coming home from getting a mani-pedi, when I hear this woman screaming bloody murder from inside one of the apartments. So, being the concerned citizen that I am, I knock on the door, askin' if she's okay and all. I figured if some goon was in there beating on her, I'd karate kick the testosterone outta him. Or give him a spritz of pepper spray."

Ellmore took a sip of his water and looked at her.

"That's when I met her. This crazy ginger named Renee Druffman. The bitch was going apeshit crazy. Tells me all about some Joe Blow she was gonna marry and move to Hawaii with. Well, turns out she'd just learned that he'd ripped her off for pretty much everything she had, save a thousand or two. He, or hell, maybe he was a she, was some scam artist she met on the Internet. You'd think women wouldn't fall for these cons, but oh boy, you'd be wrong. The lonelier they are, the more quickly they give it up." Dee leaned forward. "And I'm not just talking about money."

"Yes." Ellmore cleared his throat.

"I made a big mistake that day. Renee was one messed up lady. Had to tell me all about her marriages, which weren't really marriages at all. She chewed my damn ear off, ranting on and on about her miserable childhood, and about how nobody loved her.

After about forty-five minutes, and I'm not exaggerating here, I'm suddenly her best damn friend. Oh, boy. I knew she was a nut bag. I said good-bye and hightailed it outta her place fast as I could, never stopping to think that she was watching from her door to see where I lived. It's a big building, see, like twenty units on each floor, and she made damn sure she saw which was mine."

"Oh, dear," Ellmore said, then took another bite of his sandwich.

"Ten minutes later, she's pounding on my front door. Crazy bitch. I let her in and read her the riot act. She got all blubbery and fell to my floor like she'd just been shot. So, silly me, I thought maybe kindness would work. Helped her up, made some tea for us, and told her a little about my life story. I thought that changing the channel on her shipwreck of a life, and talking about mine instead, might inspire her to look forward. You know? I told her how I once used a different name for a different profession, then changed it back to my real name, accepted who I was, and became happy again." Dee motioned to Valerie, raising her voice to be heard. "A glass of water, please."

"Go on," Ellmore said, unfolding his napkin to wipe his mouth.

"Well, when I got to the part about my life getting better, after using my real name, Sandy Imboden, Renee tells me she's gonna change her name to mine." Dee smiled at Valerie, who had just placed a glass of water on the table. "Thanks, hon." She looked at Ellmore. "And I'm tellin' myself, knowing this chick is nuttier than fuck, that she's just spewing nonsense. But still, it ruffled my tail feathers hearing this stranger say she's gonna take my damn name. Instantly, I'm kicking myself for having been stupid enough to think that a little kindness and sharing might help the situation. I'm usually smarter than that, but I've got a heart. Gets me in trouble sometimes. I mean, hell, it wasn't like I didn't already know she was full-on bonkers. Just thought I could help." Dee paused. "Just grateful I never told her that people call me Dee."

"Did she continue to impose herself on you?"

"Honey, that crazy hellcat would've glued herself to my living room wall if she could have. She'd have let a steamroller flatten her like Wile E. Coyote so she could slip under my front door. The only thing that saved me was that it was that time of the month."

Ellmore turned scarlet again and stared at his half-eaten sandwich.

Dee burst out laughing. "Oh, sugar, not *that* time of the month. The *first* of the month. Rent time. Renee left two days later because she couldn't pay. The whole damn floor knew she'd been ripped off, and the landlord knew the cash wouldn't be forthcoming. She left kickin' and screamin', but she left. Told the landlord it was cruel to make her leave her best friend … me!

"I have no idea what happened to her in the two months before she moved into the Obscure. I can only confirm one thing: she legally changed her name to Sandy Imboden. Can you believe that? Let me tell you, my phone was ringing off the hook when the news broke. Everyone who knew me thought I'd kissed the pavement on my way to the happy hereafter."

"That's unbelievable," Ellmore said. "Of course, I believe you; I meant that only as an expression. What a very disturbed woman."

Dee took several sips of water. "Yes, and so, I came here to tell the police, and the media, what I know. I also need to make sure that she hasn't stolen my identity and that her antics won't bite me in the butt forever. You hear me?"

"Of course. I understand."

"I sure as hell didn't come down here for the sensationalism. I've just got to protect myself. There are still some loose ends I need to tie up before I feel completely secure. And I doubt Renee Druffman was her original name. Probably got that from her last 'best friend.'" Dee made air quotes as she spoke.

Ellmore took the last bite of his sandwich, then slid his plate to the left. "I apologize if I judged you. I must say, your story is quite intriguing." He straightened his glasses. "But nothing that you've just told me offers even the slightest explanation of why you were watching me or why you came over here to sit with me."

Dee sighed. "No, I suppose it doesn't. The only part of my story that has any relevance to you at all is the part about my having once worked under a different name."

Ellmore squeezed the fingers on his left hand with his right.

"You and I met over thirty years ago. Right here in this neighborhood. I went by the name Lola Winters."

As the color drained from his face, Ellmore dropped his head and stared at the table. Several moments later, he looked up at her, meeting her eyes with a cold stare. "Why would you bring this up to me now? I am a man who can understand many things; this is not one of them."

Dee's tone softened. "Ellmore, you were unlike any man I'd ever met in that business. I'd been plying my trade for less than a year when you came to me. I never forgot you. For thirty years, I wondered what happened to you. When I saw you today, I knew instantly it was you. Except for some gray hairs, you look exactly the same."

Ellmore swallowed the lump in his throat. "So it is my staid businesslike appearance that stuck with you for over thirty years. I know I'm unusual in some respects, but that seems quite preposterous."

"Oh, no, it wasn't your appearance at all. Please don't be embarrassed when I say this, but I'd never had a virgin before."

Ellmore put his hands over his face.

"Please, listen. It wasn't even *that*. Really," she said.

He took his hands away. "Then what? What was it? My

patience is wearing thin."

"Don't be angry, Ellmore. But you were the first man who I was unable to pleasure in any way. I know it sounds ridiculous, seeing what I did for a living, but I began to doubt my ability. That's when I confided in my friend. She went by the name Brandy Apple." Dee shook her head. "Sounds kind of silly now, those names we had."

Ellmore's eyes nearly rolled back in his head. He laid a hand on his stomach to calm the flutter.

"Of course," Dee continued, "we only knew you as Morey, until the news broke about your father and all. Then we figured out you had used his nickname."

Ellmore glanced down at his tie. "This more than exceeds my expectations for an unusual day."

"What?"

"Nothing."

"You see, Brandy was older than me and far more versed in the ways of the world. Despite selling my body for a living, I was still wet behind the ears. She told me that you'd been to see her twice, and each time, you had the same unpleasurable experience."

"Oh, my." Ellmore's head dropped into the palm of his hand.

"In my naiveté, clueless hooker that I was, I asked her why you bothered doling out the cash."

He sighed painfully.

"Because he *wants* to find women pleasurable," she told me. "He *needs* to. But he can't. His attraction lies elsewhere but he can't accept that. *Now* do you get it?"

With empty eyes, Ellmore looked at her.

"I got it all right. I never asked her or anyone else another dumb question again. And you never came back to either one of us. But we saw you in the neighborhood. You never deviated from your routine, and we never, ever, saw you with a soul." Dee reached across the table and put a comforting hand over Ellmore's. "There was something about you that stayed with me long after I had left the life. I couldn't stop wondering if you ever found peace and self-love, or if you'd finally accepted your true identify. I couldn't shake the image of a man trapped in fear, afraid that if he took one step out of line, his life would crumble. Because … as I have learned, life is much more likely to crumble when one hides from reality, not when one embraces it."

Ellmore squeezed the hand that held his. "Thank you."

Dee smiled brightly. "Well, I've overstayed my welcome and you've finished your lunch. I need to get back to my reconnaissance mission, and I'm sure you have your own plans. I wish you well, Ellmore."

He could only nod as she slid out of the booth, then walked away. He sat at the table for several minutes, silent and still. Finally, he reached into his pocket, took out money for his lunch, and laid it on top of the check. Once up from the table, he headed to the back of the diner and into the men's room.

"Good afternoon," said the policeman washing his hands.

"Good day," Ellmore said to him as he left. He looked around. He was alone. Once inside a stall, he closed the door, put the lid down on the toilet, and sat. Tears fell from his eyes. He watched as the droplets stained his tie. The entirety of his life choked him so hard he could barely breathe, like the time his father put his big hands on his twelve-year-old head and tried to "squeeze out the stupid." The tightness intensified, crushing him from either side. He was sure it would kill him. Right there, his life would end, sequestered in a stall, sitting on an old toilet. More memories flooded back to him as he imagined they do when a person is dying, and the whole of their life flashes before them. Ellmore was only nine, and his father was lecturing him on the evils of mediocrity. He was a teenager, and his father was angrier and more unyielding, cursing him for his "pedestrian" goals and mindset, calling him "Mr. Disappointment." He graduated with honors from Putney Smith. His mother had sneaked out to attend his graduation. She slipped him a one hundred-dollar bill after the ceremony, then admonished him to spend it wisely and never tell his father she had been there. He was hired on his very first interview. His new boss told him he was the most impressive candidate by a mile and could he start Monday. There was nobody to share his news with. Then the desires that he'd first acknowledged in his youth returned. Desires that were at odds with every fiber of his being. He had to hide them. He had to make them go away. He had to stuff them down ... down, down, down, until every vestige of desire disappeared.

With more and more force, the memories swept through him, more personal, more painful, and more debilitating. Every memory he had ever suppressed manifested itself as intense physical pain. He knew the weight of remembrance would kill him. His heart would stop, and he would cease to exist as a sentient being. He would slip to the floor below, only to be discovered as a well-dressed corpse by the next unfortunate soul to enter the room.

But even at the brink of death, humor did not escape him. Ha, he thought. First, a strange woman plunges from the Obscure to her death; the very next day, a five-year resident dies on a diner toilet, encapsulated in and extinguished by fear. They'll never understand. They'll wonder if the deaths are related. And Dee, a former prostitute with a passion for purple, will become an instant celebrity. With TV cameras in her face, she'll endeavor to explain the odd connection between the two ill-fated souls to the scandal-mongering society at large, frothing at its mouth for another piece of the salacious pie. And how apropos it will be to serve up such a feast in an aging diner, one that is hugged by the blight of a dying populace.

Ellmore burst out laughing. Like a lifting fog, his pain was nearly gone. His limbs that had stiffened in fear now felt as light as a rag doll's. It was almost as if he might float away. Oh, my! I can't have anyone come in and find me laughing inside a bathroom stall now, can I? Pushing open the door, he walked over to the urinal to relieve himself, washed and dried his hands, then stood in front of the mirror.

He had never seen himself smile, much less laugh. The pain began again, but this time it was limited to his stomach, an organ not used to hearty laughter. Quickly, he removed his tie. He held it in his hands. "I would flush you down the toilet, but it is not my intent to incur any plumbing problems for the diner. I would dip you in cold tomato bisque, but that has long been taken away." He laughed some more. "No, I'll just place you gently in the trash. I no longer need you, but nonetheless, I thank you for this most unusual day," he said as he pushed the swing top on the trash receptacle and let go of it. "Geronimo!"

Ellmore looked at himself in the mirror. "Oh, no, you, are not going to be seen looking like this. He turned on the spigot and gathered some water in his cupped hand. Transferring it to his hair, he tousled it until it looked nothing like it had before. "First chance we get, head of hair, you are going to be styled."

He took his glasses off and looked at them. "I'd toss you, too, but for now, I do need to see where I'm going. Although, ironically, for the first time, I can see better than ever."

Ellmore put his glasses back on, unbuttoned the top of shirt, and removed his suit jacket. Reaching inside, he pulled out a business card. "You are a delightful woman, Marilyn. I haven't had a real friend in many years. It was a blessing to see you today. I hope we will have many years of friendship ahead of us ... with abundant laughter and warm companionship," he said to himself. He reached into his pocket, opened his wallet, and tucked the card safely away.

As he started to step away, his smile briefly faded as he

looked at his image that reflected the somber man he had always been. "I know you haven't gone anywhere. I know you're still going to follow me around and try to envelop me in your woes, your misery, and your blasted routines. But I'm telling you here and now, I'm going to fight you with everything I have." Ellmore pointed to his image. "You have been warned, my friend. You'd be wise to retreat." He paused to let the affirmation take root. Draping his suit jacket over his arm, he smiled as he left the men's room.

As he crossed through the diner, there was a strange ethereal quality to the room. He felt weightless, imperceptible, and strangely renewed. He didn't feel the floor beneath him. Rather, as he walked, he felt he was being guided forward by a powerful force. It was not an external force, but one that had lain dormant within him for a lifetime. For the moment, he existed in an ephemeral new world while everyone else hurried about in the old one. He waved cheerfully to Addie and Valerie, and when their stunned faces looked back, he understood with certainty that his physical form was not obscured by the euphoria that cradled him, but more precisely, stood out. Yet still, the women seemed far away, mirage-like in form. He saw Valerie's mouth move as she said something to him, but he could not make out her words. Everyone and everything had been reduced to an impressionistic perception of a fading world, both in sound and sight.

Once at the front door, he pushed it open and walked outside, an action akin to passing through a portal to another realm. He laughed as he looked up at the robin's-egg blue sky. "Oh, life," he said, "where will you take me now?"

LISETTE BRODEY was born and raised in the Philadelphia area. She lived in New York City for ten years and now resides in Los Angeles.

She is a multi-genre author of seven novels and one collection of short stories: *Crooked Moon*; *Squalor, New Mexico*; *Molly Hacker Is Too Picky!*; The Desert Series: *(Mystical High, Desert Star, Drawn Apart)*; *Barrie Hill Reunion*; and *Hotel Obscure*.

Additionally, in January 2013, the author edited and published a book of her mother's poetry (written 50 years earlier) called *My Way to Anywhere* by Jean Lisette Brodey.

She has also published two short stories in an anthology called *Triptychs (Mind's Eye Series Book 3)*.

❅ ❅ ❅

Website & contact: lisettebrodey.com
Twitter: twitter.com/lisettebrodey
Facebook: Facebook.com/BrodeyAuthor
Instagram: @ca_lisette
Pinterest: pinterest.com/lisetteca/

Printed in Great Britain
by Amazon